Joan Thompson

MARBLEHEAD

G.K. HALL & CO.
Boston, Massachusetts
1979

Library of Congress Cataloging in Publication Data

Thompson, Joan, 1943-
  Marblehead.

  Large print ed.
  1. Large type books. I. Title.
  [PZ4.T47Mar 1979] [PS3570.H63] 813'.5'4
  ISBN 0-8161-6664-1   78-27139

Published in Large Print by arrangement with
St. Martin's Press.

Set in Compugraphic 18 pt English Times

To Stephen

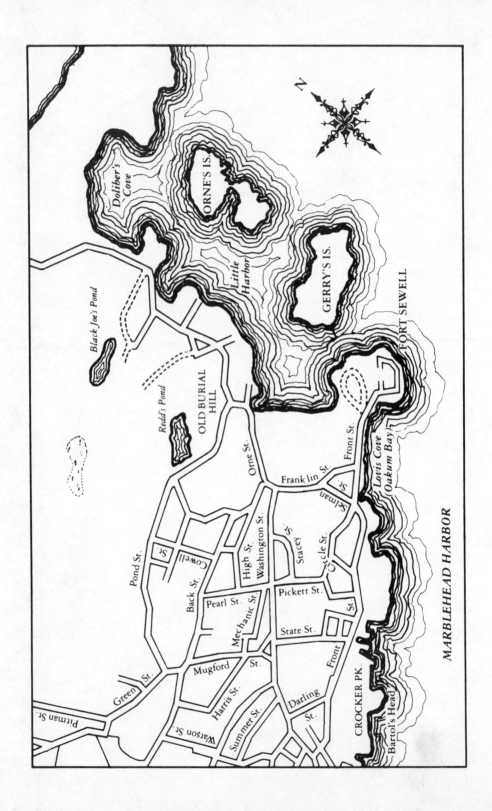

MARBLEHEAD HARBOR

CHAPTER 1

"But I don't want to wear the green dress. It makes me look like a frog!" Abby spun away from the mirror, stamped her small foot, and tossed her auburn curls in all directions as she swiftly pulled away the hated green frock.

"Why can't I wear the pink? It's much more becoming, and besides, if you force me to go to this party, the least you can do is let me wear what I want!"

"Now, Abigail, you know perfectly well that redheads can't wear pink."

"Then why did you let me have it made?"

"Because, if you recall, you made such a fuss about wanting it that your mother finally gave in to save the peace. If you were my child, there would never have been a pink dress to begin with!"

"Nevertheless, Mrs. B., there it is, and

remembering your maxim 'Waste not, want not,' I shall wear it on Saturday. Surely you don't imagine that our dear relatives from the sticks will have any idea of fashion anyway!''

''Marblehead is not the sticks!'' retorted an exasperated Mrs. Byors. ''Many fashionable Boston families spend their summers there. And,'' she continued sharply, ''your uncle and aunt are highly respected merchants in their area. Boston is not the only place in which civilized people live, you know!''

Mrs. Byors was not being entirely truthful. She had not only spent her entire mature life as governess to a Boston family but had adored every minute of it. She thrived on these confrontations with Miss Abigail Curtis, which had been taking place with astonishing regularity ever since young Mrs. Byors, a widow, had accepted the tiny redhead as her charge.

And Boston was her home. She understood its social intricacies and was eagerly awaiting the day when she would see Abby through the necessary corridors of custom which would establish her as a social force in her own right.

Abby's mother, Henrietta Curtis, was thoroughly entangled in her own matronly social web and had entrusted her only daughter almost entirely to the capable hands of the genteel but impoverished Mrs. Byors. Consequently, Abby had been alternately spoiled and controlled since childhood. The end result was pleasing if unpredictable.

Fortunately for all concerned, Abigail had inherited her father's sense of humor along with his red hair. Although his hair was now a startling shade of silver, his forceful laugh was undiminished. The house assumed an entirely different personality when he was in it. The lethargy of long, shallow days was put aside at the sound of his heavy footstep coming home from his club each afternoon. Engaged in business and banking, he kept short working hours in order to enjoy his middle years to the fullest. If he enjoyed them rather too fully in some respects, there was no one to complain in his own house.

It was the specific job of Mrs. Byors

to keep the diverse elements of this household from intruding upon each other in any manner which might provoke a confrontation. In this task she succeeded so well as to keep Mrs. Curtis if not unaware, then at least unconcerned, about her husband's occasional indiscretions, while at the same time she encouraged Mr. Curtis to pay gladly the respect due to one of Mrs. Curtis's not inconsiderable social accomplishments.

As to where this left Abigail, Mrs. Byors was not entirely certain. The girl possessed qualities which delighted her mentor. She was academically gifted and had a more than limited talent for painting and music, although she lacked the discipline to perfect herself in any of the arts. She was kind to a fault, yet capable of wounding unintentionally because of inattention and a generally unobservant nature. She was frighteningly acute at perceiving that which concerned her and was a ferret at discovering secrets, yet, at the same time, she could be totally unaware of what was beneath her nose if it did not concern her directly.

4

Self-centered, Mrs. Byors would think, but even as she thought it, Abby would surprise with an act of kindness which revealed great empathy for others.

Well, I've done the best I can for her, thought Mrs. Byors. But Heaven help her husband, if indeed she ever deigns to marry. She put away the green dress.

In the meantime, Abigail, having once again prevailed upon the doting governess, had retired to her sitting room on the second floor and resumed her waiting. Looking down at Louisburg Square, she mused on the private lives of those whose stately brick townhouses concealed their idiosyncrasies from prying eyes. It bothered her not at all that two of those eyes were her own. Certainly she was unconscious of the exclusiveness of her own neighborhood.

Directly below her was the oblong central courtyard around which were set, in a discreet rectangle, the compatible houses. Within the fenced-in area was an oval of grass marked by a statue at either end. This area belonged to everyone on the square. Perhaps it was this sense of common ownership which gave Abigail the notion that it was permissible to spy on her neighbors, the Madisons, who lived across the square.

Eleanor Madison and Abigail were contemporaries and friends, but Eleanor was not the object of Abigail's vigil. Each time a carriage passed, Abby would pull back and peek around the curtain, hoping it would stop in front of the Madison house and discharge its eagerly awaited cargo.

Burton Madison had left Boston two years before, rather hurriedly, it had been bruited. "Something to do with the wrong girl from the other side of town," his sister hinted darkly. Abigail had been but a schoolgirl then, but Burton had captured her already overactive imagination, and now she tenaciously awaited his return, which should occur momentarily.

When the dark carriage finally pulled up just before dusk, Abby's head was heavy with waiting and she had red marks on her elbows from leaning on the sill. As Burton Madison emerged, however, she felt her waiting had been worthwhile.

"Come quickly, Mrs. B!" she cried, and the two of them peered as discreetly as curiosity would allow, as a tall, slender young man of about age twenty-three stepped easily down and onto the brick path. He took a quick look around, thereby causing Abby and Mrs. Byors to duck most awkwardly below the sill, and then, evidently satisfied as to the unchanged demeanor of his former neighborhood, he strode gracefully up to the door. He was greeted by happy squeals from Eleanor, a swift kiss from Mrs. Madison, and a firm but serious handshake from his father. Then the door shut, and once again Abby was left to imagine all sorts of variations on the homecoming of the prodigal son.

"Did you see how tall he is? I don't recall his being that tall. And those eyes! They see right through you, don't they, even from across the way? He's very handsome, isn't he, Mrs. B? Well! Why don't you say something?!"

"Because it's quite bad enough to find myself a partner in your spying without commenting on the attributes of your

7

prey. Poor boy! Little does he know what consternation he's caused in your romantic head. I'd advise you not to get any notions about Mr. Burton Madison the third. From what I've heard, his father was quite correct in sending him away. I only hope it's done some good!"

"Oh tell me, tell me Mrs. B! I didn't know that you knew the story. Oh, how could you have kept it from me all this time when you know I've been dying to hear the whole disgusting thing?"

"Evil to them that think it, Abigail. You'll not hear one word from me or anyone else, and furthermore, you'll do no more asking — and that's an order. Eighteen is not so old that I can't still give you an order!"

"Well, I'll find out anyway, wait and see. There's no way Eleanor can keep it a secret now that he's home again. Of course, I don't believe she ever knew the whole story. She just likes to tease me by pretending she did! But now that he's around town we'll get to know him for ourselves. Oh, Mrs. B. — I know what! Let's invite him to the horrid old party on

Saturday. We could have Eleanor too. It would all be perfectly proper!"

"But the party on Saturday is just for your mother's Marblehead cousins. She'd never permit you to turn it into a circus," said Mrs. Byors disapprovingly.

"But if we don't include any outsiders, our dear provincial cousins will feel we're ashamed of them. And think what a kindness it would be to the Madisons if we could relaunch Burton into a group that knows nothing whatever of his past."

"All very well, miss, but I see right through your schemes. You want a close-hand look at that scalawag across the way, and you also wouldn't mind a whit if the Madison finery made your cousins feel uncomfortable!"

"Now, Mrs. B., you know I'm not so cruel as all that. Admit it! You'd like a closer look at young Burton too. After all, Eleanor is practically my best friend — after you, of course. What could be more natural than to invite them to dinner?" Abby's eyes danced with excitement as she watched the struggling countenance of Mrs. Byors.

"It's not my decision to make. Go ask your mother. I've no doubt she'll be more amenable to your tricks than this 'best old friend.' But I warn you, don't make the Marbleheaders uneasy. Your parents are genuinely fond of that branch, and you'll not get off lightly if you offend them. Not that they can't look after themselves. Heaven knows, they don't need protection from a willful chit of a girl."

At precisely four o'clock Henrietta Curtis stepped out of a hansom cab onto the far end of Louisburg Square. She had spent the afternoon making calls — calls on friends, acquaintances, even calls on ladies whom she did not remember ever having met but whose calling cards had found their way onto the silver dish in her front hall and demanded a similar card left in return. The entire procedure was tiring and seemingly pointless, but it was the backbone of Boston society. Out of these contacts would evolve the nucleus of an entire way of life. It mattered little to Boston society if one had money; there were countless families who survived their inability to entertain lavishly by keeping up to the mark in other ways.

Henrietta Curtis was fortunate to have come from one family of impeccable background and to have married into another. Occasionally her social obligations would annoy her, but usually she dismissed these moods as being the result of fatigue. After all, this was the only acceptable life she had ever known, and as no one who was intimate with her had ever expressed anything but the highest respect for her way of life, she continued on, carried by wings of tradition. With straight posture, which belied her fatigue, she walked toward her own door, unconsciously taking in every detail of her neighborhood, from the cat curled on the statue of Columbus to the old purple glass which adorned the windows of several houses.

She arrived exhausted at her front door, to be greeted by a bright-eyed Abigail. Dear Heavens! The child was overwhelming! Not only must Henrietta cope with an endless round of teas and charity committees, but invariably she must endure the seemingly boundless high spirits of her only child. Where the girl found her energy she would never understand. Surely not even her father had approached life with such gusto, even in his youth. A faraway look came into her eyes as she recalled the red-haired lad who had so dazzled her nineteen years ago.

And here he was again, personified in this determined figure making her way alongside her mother as outer cloak and hat were shed.

Ah well, I may as well face her now. Then, at least, there is a hope for peace at dinner, thought the unnerved Henrietta.

The proposal was made, refused, and restated in more persuasive terms.

"But the Darcy cousins will be offended if we hide them from our neighbors," stated Abby, sensing victory.

"But that would make too many at dinner. Let's see, there are the three of us and Mrs. Byors, plus Cousin Belle and Maurice and the three children."

"That will only make eleven if we invite the Madisons. You always said a dinner party should have at least ten, and Cook can manage perfectly well. I've already asked her."

"Really, Abigail, you are too presumptuous! Oh, very well, ask them if you must. Perhaps that will divert your attention from finding fault with my relatives. But don't ask the parents — that would make thirteen at the table!"

"Oh, thank you, Mummy! And I won't find fault, I promise. After all, I've never seen them all since that time we went out in the boat and you got sick. Don't you remember?"

"I'd rather forget, if you don't mind," responded her mother, amused despite the impertinence she always suspected whenever Abigail looked at her directly with that guileless stare.

"How old are they now? The children, I mean," asked Abigail, eager to change the subject before her mother could change her mind.

"They're hardly children anymore. Andrew must be twenty-two, Susan is just three weeks older than you, and young Tad must be at least twelve by now. Goodness, how time flies by! It seems only yesterday that Belle and I spent our summers at Doliber's Cove walking out to the islands at low tide. That was, naturally, without the permission of your grandmother. Your opinion to the contrary, Abby, I was not without spirit as a girl," said a nostalgic Henrietta.

Abigail had noticed how the small lines around her mother's eyes relaxed when she recalled her girlhood in Marblehead. How she could have enjoyed all those rocks and that water was beyond Abby. There had been dances, of course, but the life her mother described seemed boring to the point of nausea. Thank heavens she was to be spared such healthful bliss as was to be found along the coast of her mother's beloved Marblehead. Marblehead — even the name was ludicrous! Kissing her mother affectionately, she scampered off to deliver the news of her victory to Mrs. Byors.

Eighteen years old and still running off in all directions, worried her mother as she quietly ascended to her room to prepare for yet another onslaught — this one a regular occurrence — in the form of her husband, warm with late afternoon whiskey, coming in to kiss the nape of her neck and urge her down to the library where he would enjoy still another drink before presiding over his "harem" at dinner.

Not one to be daunted by the tepid embrace of his wife, he continued to court her endlessly, hoping for a rare glimpse of passion. Henrietta, recognizing his need, had in past years succumbed to his charm, but last year, after her weakness had led to the greatest fright of her married life, she had finally decided to put an end to that side of their relationship.

The very recollection of her panic when she had suspected another child might be on the way was enough to send chills down her straight New England spine. The thought of bearing a child at the age of thirty-eight was repugnant. She remembered, too, her prayers, full of solemn promises of abstinence should she escape her dilemma. And a false alarm it proved to be, whether through nature or divine intervention she was never to know.

Now, although her husband's touch on

her bare arms might awaken the old tremor in her loins, she was determined to remain in control. No matter if Thomas Curtis stayed at his club too often for her liking; anything was preferable to the pain and humiliation of another childbirth. So she continued her prayers and included a new request — that Abigail might not have inherited her father's physical needs. "And," she would conclude, "may we see her suitably married within a year, if possible." More than a year of this grown-up Abigail was unthinkable. Yet what properly reared young man would consider marriage to such a headstrong creature?

She must speak to Thomas. Perhaps he could do something with the girl. There must be no more bowing to her whims. That business tonight about inviting the Madison boy and girl . . .

Suddenly fear gripped her. The Madison boy! Surely he was the one involved a few years back in that scandal with the girl who claimed him as father to her unborn child. Oh, that Abigail! Imagining I would forget and invite him to dine with my own family! No, this time reason would prevail. Resolute, she pinched her cheeks as she heard familiar footsteps approaching her room. She never could contain a flush as two heavy hands were placed on her frail shoulders and the warm lips touched her neck.

"Thomas. You simply must inform Abigail that under no circumstances can I permit her to invite that scandalous Madison boy into this house!"

"So that's it, is it? She was looking rather smug when I greeted her downstairs. Don't tell me you agreed?" queried Thomas with a distinct twinkle in his eye.

"Naturally, as soon as I remembered all the talk, I changed my mind. You must tell her, Thomas. I simply cannot go through that again. Go along and do it now. I'll join you in the library momentarily."

Several minutes later Henrietta, refreshed, appeared at the library door. Her husband, rising, spoke rather loudly.

"I'm afraid there's no help for it. She had already invited them before I could speak to her."

"That's not possible. She hasn't left the house all afternoon," replied Henrietta somewhat sharply.

"She used the telephone, my dear," said Thomas sheepishly.

"Oh, why did I ever let you install that infernal contraption in this house? It terrifies me when it goes off with that frightful noise, and now look how Abby's using it to circumvent us!" cried Mrs. Curtis, fluttering a small hand.

"Now, Henrietta. She had no idea that you had changed your mind. She's not one to waste any time getting what she wants, is she?" said Thomas, pleased in spite of himself by his daughter's gumption. To tell the truth, he had not quite become accustomed to the telephone himself. He always felt somewhat of a fool shouting into the box on the wall.

"It's too late to back out now, Henny dear. The Madisons are decent people even if young Burt did get himself into a little scrape. We can't offend them by retracting the invitation now."

"A little scrape? Is that what you call

it? Why, he behaved very badly! It's only lucky for him that the girl had no standing, or he'd be a married man with no expectations right now. But I forget. You men always defend each other in such matters. And don't call me Henny. You know I detest it!''

''There's no need to be upset. A short dinner, and that's the end of it,'' replied Thomas firmly.

''You had just better hope that's the end of it. From all accounts, the young man is considered to be very attractive, and our Abigail is nothing if not impressionable. Besides, if my cousins found out, they'd think us quite mad to risk her reputation in such a fashion.''

''That's nonsense, Henrietta, and you know it. Your cousins are the most down-to-earth bunch I've ever met. I know you think Belle married beneath herself, but I happen to think Maurice Darcy is a capital fellow even if he did work with his hands a bit before he made his way up in the world. There's some, including our Abby, who could benefit from a little hard work. Why, she's about as spoiled as a girl could be. You wouldn't find that in the Darcy family. Hard workers, all of 'em. They'll not be concerned a mite about any past transgressions of Mr. Burton Madison the third. They take a man as they find him.''

''That may do very well in Marblehead, where standards are flexible, to put it mildly. But this is Boston, and it's here among her own kind that Abigail must make her way. And believe me, Thomas — having the Madison boy here is not going to help, not one bit.'' Having stated her case, Henrietta reached for the small glass of sherry being extended by her husband as a peace offering. The dinner bell put an end to further discussion.

In the large oak-panelled room, Abby looked from parent to parent trying to detect any sign of conflict on their faces But years of accommodation had provided them with a proper dinner countenance, and Abigail was unable to discern the slightest sign of dissension.

How they do stick together, she thought, not altogether critically, as she attacked her lamb with such vengeance as to elicit a sharp snort of disapproval from Mrs. Byors.

Mrs. Byors, aware that her charge had once again overstepped herself, felt it incumbent upon herself to make amends. She brought up several topics of conversation until one finally captured the interest of Mr. Curtis. Sarah Bernhardt was to appear in Boston the following week. The entire city was agog to see the French enchantress.

Since her first appearance in New York in 1880, just eight years before Abigail's birth, the theater world had talked of little else. Her performance in *The Lady of the Camelias* was eulogized endlessly by Mrs. Byors, who, never having seen Madame Bernhardt perform, had nevertheless heard firsthand reports on the clarity of her voice and the eloquence of each gesture.

Tonight the conversation revolved around a series of theater parties which were being organized in honor of the great visit. It was said that Madame Bernhardt was to perform in a tent because the theater owners were united in protecting their own talent from being overshadowed by her grandeur. It was fervently hoped

21

that the weather would permit the theatergoers to enjoy their muse in spite of her less than elegant surroundings.

Henrietta stated her disapproval of the theater in general, fearing it to be an overly stimulating force on impressionable minds. Abigail rushed to the defense of the divine Sarah, and soon everyone was happily debating the virtues of both ancient and modern theatrical productions. Once relieved of her burden of guilt, Mrs. Byors secretly admitted to herself that she was at fault for allowing Abigail to spy and plot in secret. The girl was entirely too romantic and naive to be allowed such imaginings. Abby's determination masked a vulnerability which alarmed her companion. She would be easy prey for some man-about-town who lacked scruples in such matters. Mrs. Byors would be relieved when the Saturday dinner was over. Then would follow a spring cotillion and a series of musicales at which, she hoped, Abigail would meet someone more suitable to a young lady in her position. With the innate snobbery of the near-rich, Mrs.

Byors aspired to ever greater heights for Abigail.

During the following week Abigail was circumspect in her spy mission. Fortunately Mrs. Curtis and Mrs. Byors were kept busy in preparation for the visit from the Darcys. Thus released from their observation, Abigail gave free reign to her thoughts. She tried to picture herself as the faceless girl who had succumbed to young Burton Madison. How must it feel to be seduced? Delicious, she was sure! But how did one go about it? One couldn't very well say to a girl, "How do you do? Please come into my bed." No, there must first be a series of innocent meetings, perhaps over tea, with jesting words followed by serious conversations. Then, and only then, would the first advances be made, at first lightly so as to gracefully elude possible rejection, then more and more insistent embraces until resistance melted and all reason fled. She fancied she felt an insinuating hand on her bosom. And after that? She found herself unable to accurately picture the remainder of the scene. Obviously, though, one would have to be quite carried away in order to go through with it. She stretched and yawned like a cat as she voluptuously fell dozing.

She awakened with one thought in mind. Somehow she must appear sophisticated on Saturday without risking her mother's disapproval. The pink dress would do nicely. The neckline was just low enough to reveal the rounded curves of her bosom when she bent over. Perhaps just before she went down to dinner she could manage to pull it an inch lower. And her hair — she must wear it piled on her head so as to show off her slender neck to advantage. Should she try to sit beside or across from him? If beside, she could be assured of his appreciating her new Paris scent, but if he sat across from her, she could turn the full force of her emerald eyes on him. Oh well, she must manage to seem alluring from all directions just in case.

CHAPTER 2

Saturday arrived much too swiftly for Henrietta Curtis. Still unnerved at her daughter's audacity, she dreaded yet another scene and so kept her silence. The evening was, after all, in honor of the rare visit from her Marblehead relatives. She decided to focus on their comfort and forget as much as possible the threat of young Mr. Madison. As good luck would have it, her cousins were the first to arrive, thus giving her the opportunity to sit happily by the fire reliving memories with Belle.

Belle Darcy had changed very little. Small but resilient-looking, she retained the outspoken charm of her childhood as she pushed a stray blond lock from a rosy cheek with the careless grace of one half her age. Maurice seemed more staid and controlled than she remembered him, but he became more extroverted after accepting a second glass of sherry from Thomas who was, as was customary, savoring the role of host.

"Well, Maurice, what do you think of our Roughrider president?" he asked. "Do you think he's earning the fifty thousand we taxpayers are paying him each year?"

How good to see him relaxing in his own home, thought Henrietta with a slight twinge of guilt. Their social evenings brought out his best. Once again he had the light step of youth. Bending over to whisper to Belle, he seemed to have stepped back in time to the days of their courtship.

"Goodness, Tom, you're just as saucy as ever!" pouted a delighted Belle. Thomas beamed with self-satisfaction that his sally had hit the mark.

"Now, you two had best behave!" said Henrietta with mock disapproval. "Here come our other guests now, if I'm not mistaken."

Thank heavens! said Abby to herself. I thought they'd never get here.

Talking to Cousin Susan had been pleasant enough. After all, the two girls were practically of an age. Young Tad was another matter. Full of repressed high spirits and altogether lacking in respect for his elder sister, he was the obvious darling of his family. Totally out of place was Cousin Andrew. Tall, muscular to the point of vulgarity, he looked through Abigail as though she were a piece of his beloved Marblehead rock. When his eyes did make contact with hers, there was in them a thinly veiled contempt.

Horrid boy — or man, she amended. Accustomed to receiving a certain deference on account of her charms, she had been taken aback by his haughty indifference. He seemed completely at ease in their ornate drawing room and also, Abigail thought, quite the superior of his redheaded cousin. Undoubtedly he found her frivolous. She understood from her mother's description that he was an extremely hardworking young man, intent on owning his own fleet of fishing boats before his twenty-fifth birthday.

Well, if he found her shallow, it was his

own fault. By his failure to contribute anything to the conversation, he had forced her to prattle on about all manner of trivia in order to camouflage his own social failings. She took secret glee in anticipating the contrast between her surly cousin and her dashing neighbor from across the square.

When Eleanor and Burton Madison entered the room, she felt her heart leap forward. Handsomely attired in palest blue, young Mr. Madison greeted her with what seemed to her eager ears an unusual warmth. As she had expected, his manner stiffened somewhat after he received the rough handshake of her cousin Andrew. Strange how Andrew dwarfed them all. Even Burton, who had seemed a good height from a distance, appeared smaller here in the drawing room next to her lumbering cousin.

"How delightful to meet you at last, my dear Miss Curtis!" Burton greeted her. "My sister has been singing your praises for such a long time that I swear I was most anxious to see this perfect creature for myself. And, if I may not be considered too bold for one of so recent an acquaintance, you certainly do live up to and surpass my expectations. How can it be that we have been neighbors all these many years and never before met?''

His blue gaze fastened on her face with a strange fire. For one brief moment she wished her neckline was not quite so low.

''Why, Mr. Madison, you have been away at school and then . . .'' Oh dear, she thought, how can I finish my sentence without reference to the scandal! She blushed painfully, loathing herself for her indiscretion. But Mr. Madison was as adept as she was blunt.

''Call me Burton, please. Surely that's permissible for the brother of your best friend. Speaking of which, my dear sister Eleanor seems to be enjoying the company of your cousin Andrew immensely. Strange! Oh, I beg your pardon. I didn't mean to sound insulting; it's just that he doesn't seem to be the sort of young man she usually admires.'' Now it was his turn to be rescued by Abigail.

''Do not, Burton,'' — she savored the name on her tongue — ''think to offend me by your observations. I confess to feeling a certain antipathy for the young man myself. So scowling! Not at all the sort one would enjoy conversing with on any subject of interest. Oh, that reminds me — are you planning to see the performance of Miss Bernhardt next week? I am so afraid that Mummy won't let me go. She has terribly old-fashioned notions about the modern theater!"

"Not let you go? How appalling! Surely you can get around her. Why, our whole set is planning to take box seats, if indeed they provide boxes in a tent. Amusing, don't you think, to envision the jewel of the French theater performing in a tent? Disgustingly American, I fear. Let's hope she won't hold it against us."

"Well, they call her 'The Divine Sarah.' I trust her angelic qualities extend to charity."

Dinner was announced. Abigail had finally decided to be seated to the left of Mr. Madison. This put her directly across from Andrew, but there was no help for it if she wanted to show her right profile to advantage. Besides, Andrew was conversing most seriously with Eleanor. Whatever did she find to say to him? And to think she once thought she understood her friend completely. Here was obviously an unexplored facet to her character. She resolved to question Eleanor at the first available opportunity.

In the meantime everyone was enjoying the dinner, and, bolstered by the ample supply of wine and the informality of the Marbleheaders, the conversation never flagged. Thomas was buoyant, and even Tad seemed to be having a grand time despite being the only young child present. Abigail soon discovered why. At every opportunity, Andrew was pouring a few drops of wine into young Tad's water glass. Tad, in return, was gazing at his brother with frank adoration. Once, when Andrew was about to abet the crime once more, she met his eyes boldly. He looked away abruptly, but she fancied she saw the ghost of a smile at the corners of his wide mouth. How brazen of him to make her a conspirator in his unsuitable behavior, she thought.

Turning back to her more agreeable

dinner partner, she returned to the subject of Madame Bernhardt. Not one to willingly appear at a disadvantage, she had carefully read and committed to memory every piece of exotica that she could glean about the French actress. She now put her homework into action with Burton Madison.

"Do you know, Mr. Madison — excuse me, Burton — that it is said that Madame Bernhardt actually sleeps in a coffin. Don't you think that's romantic?"

"Romantic?" interjected Andrew forcefully. "I'd call it downright demented. That is, if it's true at all. Young girls should be careful about believing all they read in the journals these days."

"Oh? And I suppose you find it unnecessary to read the papers, having little use for cultural matters in your line of work. What is it now? Fishing boats, I believe father said?" retorted Abigail, stung into a strong response by her cousin's condescension. Her look implied that the before-mentioned boats might possibly be within smelling distance at the very moment.

Unperturbed by this sudden flash of ill temper, Andrew contrarily seemed to be enjoying her bad spirits immensely.

Curse him! she thought. I'll not let him provoke me with another word. I shall be serenely above all his attempts to unsettle me.

"Why, Cousin Abigail, I assure you that we are not entirely savages in Marblehead. As a matter of fact you will probably be astounded to know that we actually have a public library with several thousand books. Perhaps that is why I have always preferred reading drama to seeing it performed, especially by a bizarre Frenchwoman who chooses to enjoy somewhat macabre sleeping arrangements."

His voice was resonant and had attracted Henrietta's attention. "Abigail dear, whatever have you been telling your Cousin Andrew? I fear you are not being as gracious to our cousins as you might be." She spoke lightly, but there was steel under the velvet of her voice.

Now I've done it! She'll be furious with

me for looking down on her precious cousins, thought Abigail.

But Burton Madison stepped smoothly in to save her from parental wrath. "Not at all, Mrs. Curtis. Why, these two cousins have merely been enjoying a lively discussion about Madame Bernhardt. Hardly an unpleasant topic, if I may say so. Speaking of which, Abigail informs me that you are unsure as to the suitability of her attending Madame Bernhardt's performance. It happens that my parents are forming a small group to attend her opening night. We would be most delighted if you would allow Miss Curtis to accompany us. The group will be most suitably chaperoned, but, of course, if you do not feel secure in the protection of my parents, then of course . . ."

Oh, well done, Burton! thought Abigail joyfully. Now mother must give in or insult your parents outright.

"Not at all, Mr. Madison," replied Thomas vigorously. "That sounds like a very sensible solution to a ticklish problem. Besides, Henrietta, now you won't have her pestering you about it for the next week! Our Abigail can be a most persistent adversary when she sets her mind on something."

"So I have noticed," said Andrew pointedly. "A most attractive one, however." And he smiled wickedly at her, causing a bite of veal to stick momentarily in her throat.

How dare he flatter her! Did he really think she was so vain as to like him for a single hard-won compliment?

She forced a smile. "Then it's all settled! Please inform your parents that I should be delighted to join your party if you are sure I won't intrude."

"Now, how could a charming creature like you ever be considered an intrusion? After all, my parents must get a bit tired of the same dull old son and daughter all the time."

Dull! thought Thomas. *That's about the last word I would apply to that young man!* Thomas was a bit disgruntled at having stepped so willingly into the charming snare that had been set for him by Burton Madison. The boy was no fool, that was obvious. Neither was he the escort

Thomas would have chosen for his beloved Abigail. He resolved to be more wary of his dealings with this fellow in the future. Things must not be allowed to get out of hand.

Glancing at his daughter, he was momentarily startled to observe the catlike glint in her eyes as they darted back and forth between the two young men. He did not enjoy this scene in which his daugher insisted upon playing the central role. Certainly her dress was too low in the bodice! A connoisseur of beautiful women, Thomas was nevertheless disconcerted to realize that Abigail was indeed under the scrutiny of young Madison. For an instant, the boy's eyes would fix on Abigail's green ones; then his gaze would drop to the fair expanse of throat and bosom below. When had Abby developed into such a voluptuous minx? It was most unnerving to see other men appraising his daughter as if she were a piece of horseflesh. Well, not exactly horseflesh, but flesh certainly.

Even as these thoughts crowded into his mind, he felt the guilt of one who has done his share of lusting. Why, hadn't he only minutes before savored the round curves of Belle's ample bosom as she gaily laughed at one of his own pleasantries? He guessed that his male appreciation of his wife's cousin was at least as improper as young Madison's frankly admiring glances. The difference was that Thomas knew how to handle his impulses. A certain discretion about one's sensual side was essential. He was sure that Abby had no notion whatever of the havoc she was causing in Burton Madison's young body.

He was only half-right. Abigail was only too well aware of the flush she had raised on her dinner companion's face. The implications of his high color might have escaped her, but not its cause. Aware also that she had perhaps overplayed her hand a bit, she retreated into a safer demeanor. She switched her attention to her mother's cousins.

Cousin Maurice was good-looking in a swarthy way. Perhaps he had some Portuguese or Spanish blood. After all, here he was, a prosperous import merchant with offices in both Salem and

Marblehead. The Spanish were famous for their seafaring ways. One of his ancestors could have passed on some interesting foreign blood in the old days when widespread trade was more common. But Maurice didn't act Spanish. He was quiet, introverted almost. No blazing passions here! It was difficult to imagine him married to Belle, who was different in every way. Small where he was tall, rounded where he was spare, laughing when he was somber, she verified the notion that opposites attract. Belle was more like Thomas Curtis. Fond of a funny story, quick to respond to a jibe, she looked younger than her Cousin Henrietta in spite of her forty-plus years.

Now it was Abigail's turn to notice the glow in her father's eyes as he conversed with Belle. Abby wondered if his appreciation of other women ever bothered her mother. Serene, seemingly untouched, her mother spoke quietly with Maurice as the laughter of their respective spouses rippled over the table. Sometimes Abby wished her mother would react more strongly to Thomas's flirtations. He was a very handsome man. Her mother seemed either to have forgotten that fact or else to have decided to ignore it. Abigail couldn't understand the cool exterior her mother presented to her husband. Couldn't Henrietta see the wonderful effect Belle was having on Thomas? Surely Thomas's own wife should be able to stimulate him at least as well.

Feeling instantly disloyal, Abigail turned her attention to young Tad, who was valiantly trying to stifle a yawn. Maurice followed her glance and, noting that his youngest child was almost asleep, signaled to Belle that they must be returning home. Over protests from Thomas and Henrietta, the Darcy clan called for a cab and bid their good-nights.

"Really, you should spend the night. The train ride to Marblehead will have you up until midnight," urged Thomas.

"No help for it," returned Maurice. "There's a ship at anchor awaiting unloading on Monday, and the cargo must be counted tomorrow afternoon at the latest, Sabbath or not. Next time we'll have a longer stay. Why don't you plan to spend a week or so with us sometime this spring? Belle would love that, wouldn't you, dear?''

"Indeed I would. In fact, I insist on it,'' responded Belle happily. ''The children could get to know each other so much better if they had more time together.''

The thought of "getting to know" Cousin Andrew repelled Abigail. She glanced at him. Once again he was looking at her with a deliberate disdain. Meeting his glance, she held his look, then dropped her gaze under the ice in his eyes. Terrible man! She bade them good-bye with her prettiest company manners and saw the approbation in her mother's eyes. The Madisons departed soon after.

CHAPTER 3

Ordinarily Abigail dreaded Sundays. The ritual of church services and afternoon calls was tiresome in the extreme. This Sunday, however, found her bounding from her canopied bed with uncharacteristic zeal.

"Now, don't disturb your parents, Abigail," chided Mrs. Byors. "They retired late last night and must need extra rest this morning. In fact, I asked Cook to bring them breakfast on a tray."

"Huh! That shows how well you know my father, Mrs. B. Why, he'd perish before he'd allow anyone to treat him in such sybaritic fashion. What do you wager he's in the breakfast room this very minute?" retorted Abigail. Gathering her wrapper around her, she scampered down the circular staircase two steps at a time, an undertaking which caused Mrs. Byors to catch her breath in alarm.

Sure enough, there stood her father gazing out onto the first buds of spring, a half-drunk cup of tea on the table beside him. At moments like this, Abigail sensed that her father was far away from her in some adult world where eighteen-year-old daughters were most unwelcome. Her instincts were partially correct.

After the departure of their guests the previous evening, Thomas had felt unwilling to end what to him had been a most enjoyable evening. Heedlessly putting his arm around Henrietta's still slender waist, he ushered her peremptorily into the library. One dark curl had escaped her usually severe chignon. The effect, against her white neck, was marvelously erotic. Thomas poured two fingers of brandy for each of them and gently pulled Henrietta down beside him on the gold settee. They sat silently for some moments until Henrietta broke the stillness with a soft sigh. The fire curled around a solitary remaining log on the grate. Outside, the last echoes of carriage wheels could be heard retreating slowly into the distance.

How good it was to be here with Henny beside him again. Usually she avoided intimate moments with her husband, but tonight she seemed vulnerable, receptive to his male presence. His fingers trailed lightly over her nape, just touching the wanton curl. She gave a little tremor as his hand passed down to her exposed shoulders. God! How beautiful she was, like some piece of statuary somehow alive here under his insistent touch. His fingers traced a pattern over her shoulder until they rested lightly on the exposed curve of her bosom. For one brief instant she yielded under his touch. Her body was the liquid velvet so longed for and remembered. Then, raising her eyes to his, she gave him a look of such pleading and desperation that his heart lurched. Stiffening, she stood and left the room, calling her goodnight behind her.

Damn it! thought Thomas, confused and angry. Pride kept him from following her up the stairs. No, he thought, I'll not plead for any woman. But inside there was pain and rejection. Why couldn't she be more like Belle? He guessed that Maurice never had to force himself upon the lively and physical Belle. If only he could stop wanting Henrietta. Other men found bedroom doors shut and managed to survive. But the women he occasionally possessed were mere receptacles for his frustrated passion. However much he needed them, he was always left afterwards with an even greater emptiness than that which had originally driven him to their artificial warmth.

For a full hour he brooded thus, torn by the demands of a healthy body and the wishes of his wife. Her untouched brandy filtered the glow from the fireplace. Staring at the distorted amber reflection, he remained convinced that there was fire still in Henrietta's heart. She betrayed her own longings each time he touched her. There would be a time for them, he was certain, but with each new rebuff his soul withdrew a bit further into its manly shell.

There was a time in April when he had made a foolish error in judgment. Throughout that winter, a Mrs. O'Connor had been working in his bank. Thomas had often admired her lithe form and her delicacy of movement as she worked diligently over the ledgers in the back room. This interest had been that of any man for an attractive and cheerful co-worker, and Thomas had taken much pleasure in this innocent camaraderie. Mrs. O'Connor (her first name was Edith, but Thomas didn't know that at the time) had become a part of each working day, and Thomas took her completely for granted until one day she failed to appear. This was no earth-shattering occurrence — many workers were out with winter colds — but when he heard through the bank grapevine that her husband had died, he felt genuine sympathy. After all, Mrs. O'Connor was only thirty years old at the time, and many hearts went out to her. She returned to work a week later dressed in black and efficiently went about her usual duties. Admittedly she smiled little and her movements were heavier, but this was all to be expected in one so recently bereaved. Thomas had expressed his condolences, and Mrs. O'Connor had accepted his obviously sincere sentiments with a sweet gratitude.

One morning in late March, Thomas went into the small supply room and found Mrs. O'Connor sitting on a tied-up stack of accounting tablets. Her blond head was on her hands, and she was sobbing. Thomas was greatly distressed by her misery, and Mrs. O'Connor was equally distraught at having been discovered behaving in such an unprofessional manner.

"Please don't cry," said Thomas. "I know this must have been dreadful for you, but surely you have friends who care, and certainly all of us here at the bank would be happy to do anything we can." He was not good at this, but she responded nevertheless.

"That's just it. You see, my husband had been ill for some time. That's why I went to work. This winter he had to stop working completely, and we were forced to move out of our apartment on Commonweath Avenue and move into Charlestown." She gazed up at him with brimming eyes. "Our friends are so far away now, it's as if we were on the other side of the moon. With Harry gone, it's

46

been so lonely.

Suddenly she sat upright. "Oh, please forgive me, I had no right to burden you with all this!" She blushed a furious red and wiped her eyes.

"Not at all, not at all!" replied Thomas, deeply touched. "Please let me buy you a nice lunch. It's almost noon. Honestly, I'd like to; it would make me very happy to feel I had done something to help."

"Oh, I couldn't, sir. It just wouldn't look right — you a married man, and me so recently widowed." But Thomas could see that she was tempted.

"Nonsense! Now you just get yourself all fixed up and go to the little restaurant across State Street on the corner. I'll be along presently, and no one need be the wiser." He felt oddly titillated by the idea of a clandestine meeting. She still seemed reluctant, but he said, "Run along now. I'll see you in a minute."

Up until that moment his intentions had been completely honorable; he felt no differently toward her than he had a month earlier, and surely Henrietta would want him to lend a sympathetic ear to anyone in Mrs. O'Connor's position. But over lunch he had begun to respond to the young widow in a new way. Picking at her lunch, she shyly unfolded her feelings in such a touching way that Thomas began to feel an attachment to her. Perhaps it was her grief that made her so vulnerable, but she confided many things about her privations during the long siege of her husband's terminal illness. She seemed a woman of good taste and her bearing and style were impeccable. Over coffee Thomas covered her hand with his for a brief instant and felt the response in her eyes. She quickly removed her hand from his, and soon they returned separately to the bank. That was how it had begun, but once started, they seemed to be very involved despite the outward propriety. Thomas took her to lunch again the next week, and slowly their relationship deepened. He never told her about his difficulties with Henrietta, but she sensed his need.

On that particular day in April he had stayed late at the office. Edith (he called her that now when they were unobserved) had left promptly at four o'clock, donning her small gray hat and white gloves. Some instinct led Thomas to the personnel file, where he quickly found her name — Edith O'Conner, nee Watson, born in Boston, 1876. 14B Wapping Street, Charlestown, Massachusetts. That evening he walked out to State Street and hailed a hansom cab. Leaving Boston proper, he ordered the cab to drive to Wapping Street. His heart raced with the foolhardiness of his act. Several times he leaned forward to tell the cabbie to reverse the direction, but each time he held back. They traveled out to the Charles River and then left across the bridge into Charlestown, passing the North Station as they rode. Arriving at Wapping Street, Thomas ordered the cabbie to stop, as he wanted to walk the rest of the way.

How different was Wapping Street from the sobriety of Beacon Hill! He had to jump aside as an S. S. Pierce wagon almost ran him down in its obvious haste to escape the neighborhood, and once again he felt the warning signals go off in his mind. He continued down the street passing tiny shops on the right and left, shops which seemed to sell everything from tobacco to raincoats, even several shops which sold food of all nationalities. Nearing the end of the street, he saw the Charlestown Navy Yard and suddenly felt as if he were in another world. He might as well have been in the other Wapping Street in London, for the contrast to his own neighborhood was complete.

The street was messy; one would have called it squalid were it not for the vitality which poured from the street peddlers and the noisy passersby. Despite the peeling paint and the shabbily dressed children who passed him, there was a charm here. The residents were obviously poor, but they seemed to have great spirit as they pulled down the shades in their shops and came out onto the streets. He located the house he was seeking, but before he went in the door he realized that he had come empty-handed. Impulsively he stopped, bought a hot carton of some oriental mixture from a passing food cart, and holding it under his arm, went to the door marked 14. On the street level was a tailor shop, and he had to climb two flights of unpainted and malodorous stairs before he came to a landing and found two doors, one marked 14 B and the other 14 C. Taking his courage in both hands, he knocked boldly. After a moment the door opened, and there stood Edith O'Conner. She seemed astonished to see him.

"Well," he said, "Will you ask me in or shall I stand out here with this ridiculous container of food all night?"

"You shouldn't have come!" said Edith, but she looked pleased.

The apartment was spotlessly clean, almost spartan in its simplicity, but there was a gas fire lit and the antimacassars which adorned the chairs were sparkling white. To Thomas the greatest surprise was Edith herself. At the office she was habitually dressed in the severest of clothing, her hair knotted neatly at the back of her head. Now she was wearing a soft green dressing gown, and her hair was long and silken gold as it hung down her back. She was nervous and looked around with worried eyes at the landing before she closed the door.

"Have you eaten?" he asked, holding up the carton.

"No. Well, yes, I had a boiled egg. It's not much fun cooking for one person."

"Well then, let's try some of this dreadful concoction." He walked purposefully to the small kitchen area which was part of the central room and helped himself to two plates.

"Let me do that," she insisted. She moved a small table into the center of the room, and soon they sat down together.

"God only knows what they put in this stuff, but at least we'll be poisoned together," Thomas laughed, and the ice was broken as Edith described the many unusual foods she had been introduced to on Wapping Street.

"I think I have some wine here somewhere," said Edith. "I hope it's still good — it's been there for months."

"Then it's undoubtedly aged to perfection," said Thomas, aware that he should have brought wine himself.

After a meal of some mixture of

vegetables and chicken that Thomas chose not to examine too closely, they both sat on a small divan near the fire. The furniture was good but bore witness to better days. They sat quietly for a few moments, and then Thomas took her in his arms. The rest seemed to follow naturally until Thomas lifted her onto the neatly made bed in the corner. For a few moments her body responded to his almost desperately. Their mutual need was obvious in their haste to come together, but as soon as it was over Thomas saw the tears gliding down her cheeks and felt a barrenness inside himself. Suddenly he was overwhelmingly sorry for having taken advantage of this gentle creature. He was in no position to offer her his protection.

"I'm sorry," he said. She said nothing. "That's not enough, I know. It was terribly selfish of me to come here tonight. You are not the sort of woman who deserves that. I'm afraid I've made a cruel mistake, but I suppose it's rather late to realize it." His words came haltingly. "Please don't misunderstand me, Edith. You are a lovely and desirable woman —

too good, in fact, for the likes of me. I have a wife and daughter and no chance whatever of abandoning them."

"Don't be sorry. I didn't have to let you in," said Edith, her eyes shining. "Do you have any idea how long it has been since I've been with a man? Eight months. A long time, too long. This was enough for now; I think I can pick up the pieces myself. It's a relief to feel a bit alive again at least."

Thomas stayed a while longer, anxious to be off, to put this whole incident behind him; but he knew that would be caddish. When he said good-bye, they shook hands like strangers, and he went out onto a darkened Wapping Street and mercifully found a cab. All the way home he felt ashamed.

The next month he arranged for Edith to receive a raise in salary which enabled her to move back into her old neighborhood. Gradually she stopped calling him Thomas in private and amazingly seemed neither to expect anything or bear him any grudge.

By the evening in May when the Darcys

came to dinner, it was as if nothing had ever happened.

On Sunday morning he was reflecting on his life of the last few months when Abigail burst in upon him. Thank God for this lovely creature, he thought, pushing away his sombre musings.

"Why all the energy, miss?" he asked playfully. "It must be the fascinating sermon that the minister is going to deliver this morning. Something about the necessity for decorum and virtue in young ladies, I believe. Perhaps he'll hold you up as a perfect example of modesty and submissiveness for all the congregation to emulate." Good spirits restored, he reached for his tea.

"Cold of course. Pour me another, would you, Abby? I must have had a bit of wine last night. My head's a bit cloudy."

"Not mine! Oh, Papa, wasn't it grand? And don't you think Mr. Madison just the handsomest thing you ever saw? And such a conversationalist. Why, I was laughing myself silly all evening at his wit. I do admire wit, don't you, Papa?"

"Of course, child, when it is tempered with good sense. Actually, a fellow like young Andrew Darcy would be more apt to inspire my trust."

"Andrew? That arrogant fisherman? Oh, Papa, surely you can see he's not in the same class as Burton."

"Yes, my dear, quite right," Thomas returned with an amused grin. His implication sailed unimpeded over his daughter's red curls.

"Speaking of the witty Mr. Madison, I feel I must warn you that he is, in all probability, much more sophisticated than you realize. Five years may not seem too great a span to you, my girl, but a great deal of living has undoubtedly gone on in his life during that time. You would be well advised to discourage the attention of young — Burton, did you say?" Affecting a look of mild alarm, Thomas scrutinized his daughter's face and found there all the telltale signs of a youthful infatuation.

"Seriously, Abby, go to the theater party, enjoy yourself madly, and then come home and forget all about Burton

Madison. I don't like to bring up mercenary matters, but you are due for a handsome inheritance someday, and Mr. Madison — excuse me, Burton — appears to be the kind of chap who would be very aware of that fact."

"Papa! Are you saying that Burton is a fortune hunter? Because that's rubbish and you know it! The Madisons are very well off, and I'm sure Burton has no need to marry for money." Abigail scowled and bit her lip.

"Nevertheless, after his antics of a few years ago, a good match would be greatly desirable in his family's eyes, not to mention society's. So be wary darling. There are many handsome men around. Don't be taken in by the first one you meet."

"But Papa dear, surely you are the first handsome man I ever met, and you haven't taken me in yet. Well, not often." Smiling engagingly, she hugged her amused papa.

"Just be careful, Abby, and for heaven's sake, control your enthusiasm for Madison when you're around your mother, or you might find yourself missing out on the divine Madame Bernhardt.''

''Oh, she wouldn't do that, would she?'' cried Abby in alarm.

''My dear, there is no predicting just what a mother might do if she felt her daughter was being threatened in any way. So be discreet, my girl.''

Sobered by this new threat, Abigail sat down to breakfast. Ravenous, she devoured toast, eggs, ham, jam, and a whole pot of tea.

Henrietta did not appear until it was time to go to services. Composed, the wanton curl disciplined and contained under a hat of palest rose, she met her family in the hallway, and wordlessly they stepped out into the spring sunlight.

''What a marvelous day. Mother! Let's go for a walk around the square after church.'' said Abby. Catching a warning glance from her father, she fell silent.

The carriage ride to Trinity Church was pleasant. Perhaps Burton would be there with his family. They usually occupied a pew not far from that of the Curtises.

Beacon Hill was more sedate than usual. The shops were closed on Sunday, and the resulting calm was refreshing. The clatter of hooves on the cobblestones was always unnerving, however, and they were all relieved to pull up in front of the church. Oh good. There was Eleanor, and just behind her, in dark green — was that Burton? She craned her neck in a most unladylike fashion until she ascertained that it was indeed he, then resumed her churchgoing attitude, her heart pounding all the while.

Throughout the service, she felt his eyes on the back of her head. At least she assumed they were his eyes, that much did she crave his admiration. She was glad she had dressed carefully. The pale yellow silk of her bonnet was flattering to her auburn hair, although Mrs. Byors always complained that even pale yellow was flamboyant on Abigail. The sermon was endless as usual, but for once Abby wanted it to go on and on. At its conclusion Abigail realized that she had not heard a single word although she had sat in feigned rapt attention for thirty minutes or more. She hoped her mother would not choose to discuss it at Sunday dinner.

Leaving the church, her family was joined by the Madisons. All four were impeccable in Sunday attire. The two families were not close friends although they enjoyed a pleasant acquaintanceship, as befitted neighbors on the square.

"Good morning, Curtis. Understand my Burt and Eleanor had a fine time at dinner last evening," spoke Mr. Madison, smiling jovially. "Mrs. Madison and I are delighted that you have agreed to let Abigail join our little theater party next Friday."

Oh dear, thought Henrietta, is it that soon? Next Friday, thought Abigail, oh, it's much too long to wait.

"Yes, it really should be quite amusing, don't you think? Madame Bernhardt has become quite the only topic of conversation at our house. Perhaps you two would like to join us. It would be our pleasure," added Mrs. Madison from under her gray voile bonnet.

Oh, no, thought Abby.

"Oh, no thank you," replied Henrietta quickly. "I think not. Actually I'm not terribly fond of the theater. It disturbs me to see all those people waving their arms about and emoting. Please forgive me. But, of course, Abigail can report back to us in detail about the merits of Sarah Bernhardt."

"Oh yes, Mummy. I'll tell you every little detail about her clothes and hair. I don't know how much I can tell you about the words, however, as I'm not sure my French is up to it," said Abby pertly. This caused a minor flurry of laughter, and on this pleasant note the two families went to their respective carriages. Not, however, before Burton Madison whispered in Abigail's ear, "I adore your hat! Madame Bernhardt will be green with envy when she sees you in the audience." He dashed to the carriage and effortlessly sprang into the rear seat beside his sister, who was beaming at Abigail in apparent approval.

All the way home Abby felt warm and excited. She had been nervous about this daylight meeting with Burton. Burt, that was

what his father called him. So should she
from now on. Relieved that he found her
pretty by sunlight as well as candlelight,
she settled back between her parents and
savored the memory of his compliments.
Whatever would she wear to the theater?
She should never have worn that pink
dress to the dinner party! Now she would
be stuck with the hated green for the
theater. No, she couldn't. It would ruin
her evening to wear it. Perhaps the yellow
with the eyelet panels!

Riding along, their daughter between
them, Henrietta and Thomas appeared to
be the perfect Boston couple. Elegantly
attired and carriaged, they rode toward
the square, seemingly without a care. Only
Thomas could see the clenching of
Henrietta's small hand on the rail, and
only Henrietta noticed the stiffness in
Thomas's posture as he stared straight
ahead through the parting of the
blossoming dogwood trees. Only Abigail
heard the robins' song and smelled the
springtime welling up around her and in
her young heart.

During the week Abigail almost

exhausted Mrs. Byors with her constant trying on and taking off of dresses.

"Definitely not the yellow. It's too fitted at the hips," counseled Mrs. Byors firmly. "It may be acceptable for a dinner where you are seated for most of the evening, but for a public gathering it's much too revealing." This, of course, decided Abigail that she must, at all costs, wear the yellow. As this had been Mrs. Byors's plan from the beginning, she merely feigned disapproval and the matter was settled. The only way to manage that young lady is to resort to her own tricks, thought Mrs. Byors proudly. Although I'll never be the master of ruse that she is!

The dress decided, next must come the jewels, the slippers, and the hair. "Up, of course," said Abigail. "Long hair is for schoolgirls, and I refuse to be a schoolgirl any longer!" If only mother would show her how to arrange her hair properly — but mother was so distant recently. Abigail had decided to avoid making demands on her until after the theater party.

CHAPTER 4

Friday was cold for spring. This fact disturbed Abigail not at all, as it gave her the opportunity to wear her fox cape. As seven o'clock approached, she examined and reexamined every detail of her toilette. With her hair piled on top of her head and her figure modestly displayed in the yellow dress, she was far lovelier than she could realize. The blush of her youthful skin and the deep clarity of her eyes could only be truly appreciated by one whose youth had passed its ripest moment. It was with such eyes that her parents saw her out the door into the awaiting Madison carriage. For one moment they looked at each other with perfect understanding. In their love of Abby, at least, they were united.

Grasping Abigail's small hand, young Burt effortlessly guided her into the seat between himself and Eleanor.

"I thought your parents were to chaperone us?" ventured Abby, noting the vacant place opposite the three young people.

"Oh, but of course, I forgot to tell your parents," cried Eleanor, "Mother was taken with a spell of indigestion at dinner and was forced to stay at home. But don't worry. Daddy has promised to join us at the theater tent a little later on."

"Yes, so for goodness' sake Abigail, wipe those furrows from that lovely brow. We'll not eat you up, I assure you. Everything is the soul of propriety," added Burt, laughing easily.

He was mocking her for her childish scruples, thought Abigail. Forcing a laugh, she tried to erase the premonition of Henrietta's almost certain disapproval. After all, if Mr. Madison caught up with them at the tent, it would come out all right in the end.

"But of course, that's fine!" she said, her voice a shade too loud in the echoing enclosure. Abruptly the carriage halted.

"Why are we stopping?" she asked.

"I thought we might as well pick up a few of my friends as long as we find ourselves with extra space," said Burt, alighting.

In what seemed like mere seconds the group had grown to six with the addition of three young and handsomely turned-out men.

"Abigail Curtis, may I present Jack, Harry, and Rupert, three of the finest friends a fellow could have. Don't bother with last names Abby — I'm hoping you will have forgotten all gentlemen save me by morning." He smiled most flirtatiously at her, and Abigail felt the flurries under her bodice multiply tenfold. All the young men were very gallant and complimentary during the remainder of the ride, but Abby was made uneasy by their easy familiarity and the lack of proper chaperonage.

Abigail was at this moment acutely aware that she was in a situation which would have been deemed irregular by even the modern standards of 1906. Scruple warred unsuccessfully with desire, however, and the carriage ambled merrily along Commonwealth Avenue, joining Beacon and on past the Fenway toward the Arnold Arboretum, on whose grounds the tent of Madame Bernhardt had been hastily erected earlier in the day. Abigail had wanted to come during the morning to see this remarkable edifice going up, but one look at Mrs. Byors's face when she suggested it was enough to convince her to hold her tongue. No matter. Here she was at last, and in the company of not one, but four, attractive gentlemen.

The grounds were already crowded, many spectators having arrived early in order to peruse the lush grounds and marvel at the display of trees which were individually marked with identification tags. Mr. Arnold had donated this park to the City of Boston so that his fellow Bostonians might see flora of each New England species.

Walking along next to Burt, Abigail felt worldly and more than a bit daring. Stealthily she glanced up at him and then at the many fashionable young men who surrounded them. She felt admirably escorted and eager to show off her companion. She perused the fashionable crowd for a glimpse of Mr. Madison. Despite her outward show of sophistication, she knew she would be happier when her chaperon arrived.

Burton seemed totally oblivous to her concern as he guided the girls past the vendors and gawkers and up to the tent itself. It resembled nothing so much as a circus tent, after which it had been patterned. The diameter was easily one hundred and fifty feet, and from the rush of people entering by several openings, it appeared to have a seating capacity of thousands.

The young men seemed to have acquaintances everywhere who caused numerous interruptions during the short trip to their seats.

"Oh, Abby, isn't it thrilling!" trilled Eleanor, pink with excitement.

Goodness, thought Abigail, I hope I don't looked as flushed as that. But indeed she did, and a pretty sight they both were, eyes glowing as they tried to absorb the scene around them.

Nearest the stage in a sort of corral

were the members of the demimonde, dandified men, and women who were obviously not ladies. Abigail peered forward to verify that these women were indeed painted and at least two had dyed their hair. Nature had never created such color, she was positive. She nudged Eleanor to make sure that she also had seen these ladies of the evening. Eleanor followed her gaze with horrified delight.

The Madison party was seated among the rest of Boston society in box sections just behind and clearly separated from the rabble in front. Behind them were the ordinary folk, respectable but lacking the wherewithal to secure the favored boxes. Ushers passed among them handing out playbills left and right.

Accepting one, Abigail was relieved to see a detailed synopsis of the action written in English. She had been fearful that she would be called upon to translate from the French, and her usual confidence failed her in this respect. The play to be presented was *Les Bouffons* by Miguel Zamacoïs. Again, Abby was pleased to read that it was a comedy. Tragedy was romantic but hardly suited her present mood. The plot concerned a young woman named Solange who lived in a castle and whose father desired a buffoon to entertain her. A neighbor lad who loves Solange disguises himself as the hunchback clown Jacasse and woos and wins her despite the presence of a rival, the handsome Narcisse. Presenting the moral that wit and character are more important than mere physical appearance, it was reminiscent of the Rostand work *Cyrano de Bergerac* to which it was compared in the playbill.

"Look here, Abigail," said Burt. "Madame is not to play the role of fair Solange. It says here in the cast of characters that she will be Jacasse the clown."

"Oh!" cried Abigail, aghast. "That means she won't have any pretty costumes. Why, she'll have to wear pants! Oh, Burt, they'd never allow a woman to wear pants in public, would they?" she continued, forgetting herself in her shock.

"Abigail, dear," rejoined Burt, "in the theater such things as gender are transcended. The divine Sarah has been playing male roles for decades. It's only in America that anyone would see anything shocking in her doing so."

Feeling foolish, Abigail held her tongue, afraid she had lost face by revealing her naïvete. Well, she would not do so again. She could be as worldly as anyone.

"Abby, look! Miss Bernhardt is going to play the role of a man!" said Eleanor from her other side.

"Of course, dear," replied Abby languidly. "She does it all the time. No need to be surprised.

"Oh," said Eleanor, abashed, and settled back as the customary three raps from behind the curtain signaled the beginning of the play.

When Miss Bernhardt appeared, a roar went up from the crowd. Scarcely acknowledging the applause, she remained poised until the din subsided enough for her to deliver her first lines.

But she's old, thought Abigail, dismayed. And she's limping!

"Why is she limping?" she whispered to Burt, forgetting her vow to be sophisticated.

"A fall on her knee a while back," he whispered. "She has trouble with it constantly." The warmth of his breath in her ear was delicious enough to revive her flagging spirits.

Concentrating on the play, she soon forgot her heroine's limp, her advanced age, and even the frizzy hair which crowned the aquiline features. It was the voice which won her over. It cajoled, seduced, and eventually captured every soul in the tent. What if the acting was a bit exaggerated? By sheer force of will, the actress won her audience. At the end of the act, Abigail was left breathless. As the lights went on, she struggled to come back to reality. Oh, good. Here was Mr. Madison. It seemed so trivial now to have worried about such a minor detail as a chaperon.

"Sorry to be late, children, but you seem to have made out just fine on your own." He spoke to Burt, who, Abigail noted, made no mention of their carriage companions.

"Hope you don't mind going home by

yourselves," continued Mr. Madison. "I had to get out the small brougham for myself. Better run back to my seat now. They're about to begin the second act. Have a good time, if I don't see you before you go."

How extraordinary, thought Abby. He's even less concerned than Burt about our situation. That settled it. If Mr. Madison was unconcerned, then she was certainly not going to waste one more moment worrying about what her parents would think.

The rest of the play went swiftly, too swiftly for the enthralled Abigail. When the last curtain fell, she felt transformed.

"Burt, I simply must get her autograph," gushed Eleanor. "Oh, please, won't you wait while I go to her dressing room?"

"Why not?" answered Burt. "Abigail and I will take a stroll around the grounds and meet you by the front gate in a half-hour. Jack, be a good boy and escort Eleanor, will you?

"My pleasure, old man," replied Jack happily as he linked his arm through Eleanor's.

Never having been alone with a young man, especially in the dark, Abigail knew for a certainty that it was wonderfully exciting. She also knew that if her parents ever found out about it, there would be an end to her evenings out. But Burt was so handsome with his fair hair and supple form, and their arms fitted so well together as they slowly walked away from the crowd. For several moments they were silent, until the noise of the exiting theatergoers was a distant murmur.

"Stop here a minute, Abby. There's something I want to tell you." He turned her until she faced him. As her hands flew selfconsciously to her burning face, he grasped her slender elbows.

"I didn't want to come back to Boston. I had just begun to establish myself in New York and didn't want to desert my new friends. But Abby, I'm glad I came back. And do you know why?" His eyes looked deep into hers. He was so close that she could see herself reflected in them.

"Why, Burt?" she murmured, already

knowing the answer.

But he didn't answer. Instead his mouth found hers. At first his kiss was soft on her lips, but he didn't move away. His lips became hard and hungry, and his mouth opened insistently. She felt herself responding but knew it was wrong. He was not behaving at all like a gentleman. She fought for control.

At the moment a husky voice spoke directly behind her. *"Sois sage, ma petite, celui ci va très vite, je crois!"* And with a brittle laugh the voice ceased.

Tearing herself from Burt's arms, Abigail strained her eyes in the darkness to see the figure retreating across the lawn. Leaning heavily on a cane, the old woman never looked back but stepped into a lamplit carriage.

"That was Madame Bernhardt!" cried Abigail, ecstatic. "Oh, Burt, did you see, that was really Madame Bernhardt, and she spoke to me — she actually spoke to me! Oh, the others will never believe it when I tell them!"

"And to think she is so famous for her timing," muttered Burt darkly. But

Abigail wasn't listening. She was cherishing the privilege of having been noticed by a legend.

She was aware that Burt's arms were around her again.

"No!" she cried, pushing away. But he held her fast, and for the first time she began to feel frightened. "Let me go!" she insisted as his mouth sought hers impatiently.

With all her strength she broke away and ran back through the darkness toward the lights of the tent. Behind her she could hear his laugh, excited but with an angry edge to it that made her realize what a fool she had been to come out here alone with someone she hardly knew. Why, he must think she was one of those fast girls like the one he was involved with three years ago! Rage at him and at herself caused her to trip in her haste, tearing the ruffle of her dress. He was beside her in an instant.

"Abby, I'm sorry. I didn't mean to rush you. But you know, you are so very beautiful, and I am afraid I forgot myself."

"Don't touch me! I can get up by myself." And she did, carefully rearranging herself as she approached the main gate. Spying Eleanor, she hastened to where the others were gathered.

"Oh, there you are, Abigail. You will never believe what a disappointment we have had! Abigail? Are you all right? Why, you're positively out of breath!" cried Eleanor, anxiously taking in the flushed face and dishevelment of her friend. "And look, you've torn your skirt. Oh, what a pity — and such a lovely dress!"

"Contrary to appearances," cut in Burt smoothly, "Abigail has not been set upon by a pack of hounds. Her excited state was caused by quite another creature. Shall I tell them, Abigail, or would you rather dazzle my dear sister with the story of our encounter?"

"Encounter? Oh, tell us, Abby. Whatever happened to make you look so strange?" cried Eleanor eagerly.

Clever fellow, thought Abigail. And how would he have explained my condition if we had not come upon

Madame Bernhardt? she wondered, not without a grudging admiration for his quick wits.

"Well," she drawled, tantalizing poor Eleanor until the poor girl almost writhed with anticipation, "we were walking along just talking, you know," — this with a condemnatory glance at the unruffled Burt — "when suddenly who should speak up from behind us but the great Bernhardt herself. And she spoke to me, Eleanor, to me!"

"Now hold on a minute, Abigail. How can you be sure she wasn't talking to me?" pouted Burt in mock envy.

"Oh shush, silly. You know perfectly well that you could never understand one word of French," retorted Eleanor.

"Touché," laughed Burt.

"After she spoke, she went straight across the lawn to her carriage and drove away," continued Abigail, regaining her confidence amidst all this attention.

"Oh, how exciting! Tell me, what did she say?" This from the awestruck Eleanor.

"She said, 'Sois sage.' That means be

wise. I know that because we once had a French maid, and that's what she used to say to me every day when I would go out for my walk with Mrs. Byors. It's something that mothers say to children in France. It's rather like our mothers telling us to be careful or to take good care of ourselves, I think." Pleased with herself, she preened a bit while looking at Burt to see if he was impressed with her knowledge of French idiom. Then she remembered his behavior on the lawn and looked away.

"She must have noticed what a careless little girl you are." mocked Burt, not without a good-humored smile.

"Burt! I shall tell mother if you say one more disrespectful thing to Abigail! Just see if I don't," said Eleanor, rather confused by the repartee.

"But surely Abigail has a sense of humor, Eleanor. She would never approve of tattling, I'm certain. Would you, Abigail?"

How could he know that she was planning at the first opportunity to tell Eleanor about her brother's disgraceful ways? thought Abigail.

"Of course not," she replied pleasantly enough, furious inside at his ability to remain calm while her heart was still racing.

"And was that all?" continued Eleanor, unsatiated.

"All what?" said Abigail, momentarily losing the train of conversation.

"All she said to you, of course."

"Oh, there was something else, but I'm afraid I didn't catch it." She refused to divulge the fact that it was Madame Bernhardt's opinion that Burt was "too fast."

Disappointed again, Eleanor continued to press. "But your dress, how did you tear it?"

"Really, Eleanor, you sound like a grand inquisitor!" said Burt. "Actually, in her haste to tell her dear friend about our meeting with Miss Bernhardt, our Abigail started running and tripped over something on the grass. So that's all there is to tell. Come along now, fellows. I must get these lovely ladies home or we shall be denied the pleasure of their company at a future occasion."

Entering the carriage, Abigail was careful not to sit next to Burt. In fact, she practically pushed Eleanor aside in order to get in first. If Eleanor noticed anything amiss, she didn't act it, so caught up was she in savoring the glorious performance. And if Abigail refused to address her own remarks to Burt, that too went unobserved by the stagestruck girl. Thus, buffered nicely by the contented Eleanor, the threesome continued home after dropping the three young men off at a nearby tavern. Thanking Eleanor most politely, Abigail allowed Burt to hold her arm as she descended onto her own front walk.

"Don't tell me you are angry, Abigail," said Burt. "I, myself, cannot remember when I enjoyed an evening more." And he laughed as her door opened and she stepped back into her sheltered little world, never once turning around to meet his fascinating eyes.

Luckily her mother had retired, and her father was hardly the sort to notice a torn ruffle or to worry about a too rosy cheek.

She told him about the performance in minute detail, omitting only those things which it would be nice to save for her mother at breakfast. But Thomas, for all his sophistication, was a father after all, and he took note of the torn ruffle and of the nervous exhilaration in his daughter's voice. Yes, he would be wary of any further involvement with the Madison boy. Monday morning he would do some checking on the fellow. He had never seen that peculiar expression on Abigail's face before, and he hoped never to see it again. A curious blend of sensualist and puritan, he was not yet ready to concede the pleasures of the adult world to his own daughter.

In her bedroom, Abigail removed her dress and petticoat. Taking the pins from her hair (she never allowed Mrs. Byors to undress her), she repeated the foreign words to herself. *"Celui ci va très vite, je crois."* Yes, "go very fast," he did, this Burton Madison, and Madame Bernhardt was not the only one who thought so. Imagine kissing her like that, and with his mouth open, too! Remembering the kiss, her blood ran very warm, and, raising her eyes to the mirror, she saw in them the same dark look of desire that had so frightened her on Burt's face. Perhaps she was a fast woman. After all, with her usual honesty, she had to admit that she had never felt so alive as at that moment. And if Madame had not intervened, what then? Would she have lost her senses?

For the first time that she could remember, Abigail was unsure of herself. What was this man-woman thing? She vowed to stay away from Burt in the future. Obviously, if he was going to have such a devastating effect on her, she had no choice but to avoid him. Passionate she might be, but no fool! But what if he were to attend the cotillion next week? Would she have the will to stay away from him? Oh, dear — and no one to consult. How she wished Madame Bernhardt were here with her now. She imagined the worldly wisdom of her idol and soon fell dreaming about an animated conversation, in French of course, about the relative merits of virtue and a life of free love. Abigail had heard of free love but wasn't entirely sure what it meant. But of course, Madame would explain.

CHAPTER 5

Breakfast the next morning was unusually friendly and pleasant for the Curtis family. As was to be expected, Abigail was the center of attention, a circumstance which pleased her no end. Blooming under the rapt attention of her mother, she was soon on her feet demonstrating each gesture of her idol, Madame Bernhardt.

"And she was old, Mummy! I mean, really old. Much older than you and Papa. Her hair was all frizzled and stood up all over her head even in the buffoon costume. It's sort of burnt toast color, her hair that is, and her nose is sharp and she's quite thin. Oh, and she has a limp. At first it's very strange to see her limping all over the stage, but after a while you don't even notice it, she's so magnficent."

"Were you able to make out much of the French dear?" asked Henrietta, anxious to prove to herself that the evening, so rapturously enjoyed by Abigail, had been of at least some educational value.

"Some of it. Of course, she spoke quite fast, and it took me almost the whole first act to adjust to it. Her gestures were so eloquent, though, that everyone understood what was going on. Oh, Mother! How I wish you could have seen her!"

How frustrated she felt at not being able to tell her parents about her encounter with Madame Bernhardt on the lawn. She had decided last evening that under no circumstances would she mention this episode to her parents. She knew she was too straightforward to withstand any questioning should her mother decide to pursue the subject of how she happened to be on the lawn away from all the others. It was odd the way her mother could sense when she was hiding something. Over the years she had become adept at fooling Mrs. Byors, and her father, although perceptive, tended to overlook much in his indulgence of his only child. But her mother was a different story.

Henrietta, satisfied on the subject of Madame Bernhardt, returned to her breakfast. But not before she offhandedly inquired, "How did Mr. and Mrs. Madison enjoy the performance?"

Abigail gulped, then plunged in. "Fine. That is, Mr. Madison liked it, at least I think so — he wasn't sitting with us — but Mrs. Madison didn't come. She got sick at dinnertime and stayed home."

"Whatever do you mean, Mr. Madison didn't sit with you?" asked Thomas pointedly.

Oh drat! thought Abigail. Oh well, there's no help for it but to tell them. "You see, Daddy, when Mrs. Madison became ill, she sent Eleanor and Burt on ahead in the carriage. Mr. Madison joined up with us at the tent, but his seat was a few boxes away, so I didn't have a chance to ask him if he enjoyed it."

"Are you saying that you young people were on your own coming and going?" demanded Thomas, reddening.

"Yes, Papa." Abigail tried to sound confident, as though she saw nothing unusual in this arrangement.

"Damned irregular! What do you say, Henrietta?" asked Thomas, clearly disturbed.

"Why, I'm sure I like it even less than you do, Thomas. But if Mrs. Madison was unwell, perhaps her husband simply managed as best he could. At least he was at the tent. You did say he joined you at the tent, didn't you Abigail?" added Henrietta.

"Oh yes, Mama," responded Abigail.

"An odd bunch if you ask me!" said Thomas vehemently. "There's no help for it now I suppose, but that's the last time you join one of their little outings, Abigail. If he doesn't care for his own daughter's reputation, he ought to at least have some thought for yours."

Wisely Abigail remained silent. Perhaps if she was very quiet, they would move on to something else. Her hope was soon answered. Henrietta moved briskly to the subject of next Saturday's spring cotillion. As it was Abigail's coming out season, she must attend certain functions, the most important of which was the cotillion. Her gown had been made months ago, and she dreaded the whole affair. Each girl must wear white and walk with her father to be presented to the gathering which constituted "society." In her own mind, Abigail was fairly sure that the whole business was rubbish, but as it was precisely the sort of thing she knew her mother adored, she had early bowed to its inevitability. How hateful to be on one's very best behavior for an entire evening while all those dowagers and stuffy old men inspected you as if you were a negotiable asset. She supposed that some daughters were exactly that, an asset through which the family fortunes might be enhanced.

In her case, however, she doubted the use of it all. After all, she would have her own fortune someday, so she hardly needed to marry one. She had vowed as a small child to marry for love, a notion which she was sure would distress Mrs. Byors no end. She wondered if her parents had been in love when they married. Looking at them now, one might doubt it, but there had been times when she was small when there had been picnics and drives in the Common and laughter, always laughter. Surely that had been love! And hadn't she caught her father looking intensely at her mother when he didn't know Abigail was watching? Whatever had gone wrong, she didn't think it was for lack of love, at least not on her father's side. Her mother was the mystery. How she could be married to such a handsome and entertaining man and not seem to know it was beyond Abigail.

"Mrs. Byors," she asked later in the day, "did you know Mummy and Daddy when they were first married?" This question was posed as she sat cross-legged in the window seat of her former nursery. In checked blue gingham she looked more the little girl than the emerging debutante. Struggling to master the dainty stitching of a pillow she was making for her mother's birthday, she was frustrated yet determined.

"You had already been born when I came, Abigail, but yes, I had met your parents once or twice before that at dances and such," answered Mrs. Byors, who, despite her somewhat pudgy fingers, was stitching away at twice the rate of her protégée.

"What were they like then? I mean, were they very much in love?" continued Abigail.

"In love? Why, I suppose so. You must remember, Abigail, that the notion of marrying for love was not the vogue at that time. But yes, I believe they got along better than most young couples. Why all the questions?" asked Mrs. Byors suspiciously. There were certain topics she knew she must avoid, and the condition of the Curtis marriage was one of them.

"Ouch! Oh drat, I've pricked my finger!" cried Abigail, thrusting the injured finger into her mouth.

"Don't do that! Put a plaster on it before you spoil the pillow," returned Mrs. Byors.

"The pillow? How about my finger? Perhaps I'll lose quarts of blood and be unable to go to the cotillion." She fell back against the rose cushions of the window seat in a mock swoon. When this failed to unnerve Mrs. Byors, she jumped to her feet and, disregarding her wound, grabbed Mrs. Byors by the hands. Pulling the bulky figure up so suddenly that her needlework hoop fell to the floor with a clatter, she whirled the exasperated Mrs. Byors around the room until she got the desired giggle from the panting governess.

"Honestly, Abigail!" said Mrs. Byors, collapsing once more into the overstuffed chair. "How are we ever going to turn you into a proper debutante?"

"Why, Mrs. Byors dear, I shall be the picture of decorum at the cotillion. I shall glide, not walk, mind you, but glide down the center of the floor on the arm of my handsome father, and when I am presented to the sponsors, I shall curtsey so low that I will scrape my nose, and all the eligible young bachelors will punch each other in the ribs and say, "Who is that redhead with the funny-looking nose?"

"I give up!" said Mrs. Byors, laughing in spite of herself.

"Tell me more about my parents. When I was little, did they kiss each other a lot?"

"Abigail! What a question. I'm sure it's not my place or yours, young lady, to be curious about your parents' personal feelings."

"I just thought you might have seen them kissing behind a rosebush or holding hands under the dining room table or something romantic like that," said Abigail matter-of-factly.

"It is not my custom to lurk in people's gardens, and furthermore, the dining room table is easily twelve feet long, and it has always been your parents' habit to sit at opposite ends. Unless they are orangutans, I doubt if their arms would reach the distance," replied Mrs. Byors.

"Why, Mrs. B., you've made a joke! What fun," cried Abigail delightedly.

Coloring and feeling outmaneuvered once again, Mrs. Byors continued her sewing.

And still later that afternoon, "Mother, why must I be the one to carry the daisies at the cotillion? Eleanor is going to have pink carnations. I shall be all in white," protested Abigail, who hated the idea of a sweet-looking Abby with her sweet little bouquet.

"It's because of your red hair, dear," answered her mother. "The sponsors felt that your coloring makes you stand out and that it would sort of equalize things if the others could carry colored flowers."

"But I can't help it if my hair is red. Why can't I just wear it up, and then there won't be so much of it?" asked Abigail hopefully.

"We've been all over that dear. Now don't be persistent. It isn't becoming. All the other girls will wear their hair down. That was decided months ago. After all, you'll have years to wear it up. I don't imagine that you appreciate what a bother it is to put up one's hair day after day," responded Henrietta.

"Then why do you?" asked Abigail. "I think you'd look ever so nice with your hair long. It's such a nice, shiny black still."

"Women my age don't wear their hair down. It's custom. You're going to have to learn to bow to custom, Abby, if you're going to get along." She gave Abigail an affectionate squeeze. There was so much this lively little girl would have to learn. She hoped it would not be too painful a process.

"Very well. I shall wear my hair down," acquiesced Abigail, charmed by her mother's intimate mood. "But the daisies — I shall never be happy with the daisies. They're so, so . . . insipid!"

"Everything in life can't be thrilling and exciting every minute, Abby," said her mother, smiling.

"I don't see why not," said Abby. "If one put one's mind to it, one could fill up the days with all sorts of exciting things. The trouble is, Mother, that we are women. The men get all the adventures and we only get to go to cotillions and be proper." She sighed and went up to dress for dinner.

Watching the gingham-clad figure going up the stairs two at a time, Henrietta shook her head in amusement, but in her heart she agreed with Abigail.

It was indeed a man's world.

CHAPTER 6

Saturday evening found Abigail seated between her mother and father as the carriage went off into the night toward the hotel downtown where the cotillion was to be held.

"Now, Abigail. Are you sure you know just what to do?" asked Henrietta.

"Yes, Mother," responded Abigail. "I meet Papa at the door, take his arm and walk . . ."

"Slowly," interjected Henrietta.

"Walk slowly," continued Abigail, "to the sponsors, where I curtsey and wait for the others. Then we all dance. Oh, Mother, I know it by heart," pouted Abigail.

"Yes, dear, we've all been over it a hundred times," added Thomas, smiling. "If we talk about it anymore, even I'm going to become nervous." He laughed.

"It's just that it's important to do it well," said Henrietta. "There will be other events, but this is the one that will make the first impression."

"I thought the season didn't open officially until the fall," said Thomas.

"It doesn't. This is like a rehearsal. But don't be misled for a moment. Everyone who counts will be watching." answered Henrietta.

"Does it really matter that much to you about the people who count and all this coming out business?" continued Thomas, his brow furrowing slightly under the thick gray hair.

"Are you saying it doesn't matter to you? Oh, Thomas. You've been planning for this season ever since Abigail was born, whether you realize it or not," answered Henrietta firmly.

"Well, certainly, if you mean seeing that she went to a decent school and arranging for her financial security; but all of a sudden it seems so contrived, cold-blooded — do you understand?"

"Honestly! Sometimes it's you I don't understand," replied the disconcerted

Henrietta. She did, however, give his hand a maternal pat, as if to say that she attributed his strange behavior solely to parental jitters.

As the carriage deposited its elegant cargo, the less attractive members of society might well have been envious. Not only was Thomas sleek and handsome, his broad shoulders fitting neatly into the required cutaway, but Henrietta, dressed in rose, her hair softly arranged in large raven loops on her finely chiseled head, was almost too lovely to be classified as that bland thing, a parent. To the knowledgeable eye of Thomas Curtis, the young girls who were gathering in the foyer were mere promises of beauty. His Henrietta was that promise fulfilled. The years had brought structure where before had been unformed prettiness. He smiled inwardly, recognizing that these same young girls probably pitied their parents for their advanced age. They'll learn, soon enough, he thought ruefully.

"Mother, may I go up to the dressing room alone, please?" begged Abigail, not wanting to feel like a little girl.

"Very well, dear, but don't even think of changing a thing, especially your hair." Her mother's voice was stern. Abigail started to scamper for the stairs leading up to the powder room but caught herself in time and tried to make a perfect ascent, feeling her parents' eyes on her back all the way.

"Oh, Abigail! I thought you'd never get here," cried Eleanor, rushing over to take her place in front of the large mirror beside Abigail.

"Well, of course I'm here. How are you, Eleanor? You look very pretty. I love your carnations."

"But you know that it will be you, Abigail, who will surely be the favorite."

"Nonsense, Eleanor! Why, just look around you. See that little Nora Simmons? Why she looks like a perfect Dresden doll — you know, the kind you see spinning around on music boxes. And I meant it when I said that you look wonderful. Why, I've never seen you prettier. So there!"

All this was said amidst a scene of mass confusion as twenty-odd girls primped and fussed during these last few moments. Abigail did not exaggerate. The scene was charming, with even the plainest faces transformed by excitement. But Eleanor also had not lied. She looked wistfully as Abigail casually arranged a curl that had strayed from the gleaming red gold mass which crowned her. Abigail had escaped the usual freckled complexion of redheads. Her skin was like fresh cream, and her eyelashes were dark and thick over her vivid green eyes.

Some girls have it all, mused Eleanor generously. Why, even Abigail's figure was perfection with that tiny waist and round bosom. From head to bodice, Abigail was one continuous expanse of porcelain. How she could be so unassuming about it all was beyond Eleanor. Why if I looked like that, she thought, I would never ask for another thing as long as I lived. I'd just sit there and be admired.

"Oh, Abby," she cried. "Why, I almost forgot to ask you. Whatever did you do to poor Burt? I think he's quite taken with you. He keeps bringing up your name all

100

the time. He thinks I don't notice, but honestly, when I start talking about museums and he asks if you like art, it's difficult not to notice!'' Giggling, she picked up her carnations and turned from the mirror. ''We'd better get down. It's almost time.''

At the mention of Burt's name, Abigail's composure flew away. She hoped Eleanor wouldn't see the sudden color staining her cheeks. She, too, quickly turned away toward where the others were starting to go down the stairs in twos and threes.

So he was here! Whatever would she say to him? They had parted so awkwardly after the theater party. Surely he would ask her to dance; then what could she do? The memory of his arms around her awoke the same sickening throb of passion in her chest. She had hoped to be calm this evening, to make her parents proud of her. There was Papa at the foot of the stairs. Dear, wonderful Papa! Thank heaven she would have him to lean on! She forced a smile to her lips as she took his offered arm.

"You look positively beautiful, my darling," whispered Thomas.

"So do you, Papa. I mean handsome. Oh, Papa, I'm nervous; all of a sudden I'm terrified."

"I'll hold you up. Come on now. Let's show 'em all who we are." Smiling, Thomas ushered his daughter into the ballroom, where they began the long walk down the floor.

Abigail felt asleep, as if she were somewhere else watching herself. She was aware that she was smiling and that people were smiling back, but the faces passed unregistered on her mind. Trancelike, she made the formidable walk, the only living part of her seemingly her arm where she made contact with the real strength of her father. Then she was curtseying low (not scraping her nose), and then, at last, it was over and she was joined by her mother who squeezed her arm proudly and whispered, "You were perfect dear, just perfect."

"I was?" she answered numbly. But she was beginning to rejoin the world, and here was Papa, arms outstretched for the traditional waltz. What a fine dancer he was! They had practiced in his study, dissolving in gales of laughter as he had cleverly maneuvered around end tables and lamps, but here, unobstructed, they whirled in finest Viennese form until she felt quite herself again. Returning to the group at her side, she felt a gentle tap on her arm. It was a pale young man looking frightened.

"May I sign your dance card, please, Miss Curtis?" he asked shyly.

"What? Oh, of course." She pulled the small dance card with its pink tassel from the small, white, beaded wrist purse her mother had given her. The young man seemed quite delighted, which raised her spirits. Soon her card was almost three-quarters filled, and still no sign of Burt. Suddenly she felt a light touch on her shoulder and, turning swiftly, came almost flat against a white boutonniere. Raising her eyes, she met those of Burton Madison.

"May I, Abigail?" he asked, not waiting for an answer. He took her card, wrote in it, returned it to her without another word, and, smiling, went off into the crowd toward the dainty Nora Simmons, who was obviously awaiting his company for the first dance.

Oh, how could he ask Nora for the first dance! Why, he didn't even know Nora — or perhaps he did. Suddenly she realized how little she knew about him. He had no right to go off like that without a word. She was jealous — maddeningly, painfully jealous. Realizing this, she was thrown into a state of confusion. The indifferent steps of her first few dance partners did little to distract her from her misery. Catching a warning look from her mother, however, she made some attempts at conversation which produced in her partners pleasure which was totally disproportionate to her efforts.

At one point she was caught next to Burt, who was dancing again with the blond Nora. Feigning a lack of awareness, she flirted outrageously with her current partner, a spotty boy named George something, who responded with an eagerness which made her realize that she was perhaps overdoing it a bit.

"Why, Miss Curtis, I had no idea you were such a wit,' said George, pink with happiness and bad complexion.

"Why, George, I'm just the cleverest little thing you ever saw. Why, I agreed to dance with you, didn't I?" she purred. Good Lord! What was she doing? Now this creature would think she was smitten and probably follow her around all night! An approving glance from her father caused her to laugh, which caused George further joy.

In a corner of the ballroom, Henrietta and Thomas kept an eye on Abigail as they sipped punch from little glass cups.

"You'd think they could have served something a bit more substantial," complained Thomas.

"Now, this is not your club," rejoined Henrietta gaily. "It would hardly do to have our debutantes becoming tipsy."

"Yes, but what about the fathers. That walk was hard work, you know," said Thomas in a mock bid for sympathy.

"Seriously, Thomas, I'm so pleased to see Abigail having a good time. Isn't that George Withers she's dancing with? Isn't he the one whose father has a seat on the New York exchange?''

''Yes. Sorry-looking lad, if you ask me.''

''Well, at least it's not that Madison boy!'' Henrietta shuddered almost imperceptibly. ''By the way, Thomas, did you find out anything about him?''

''Nothing good. I'm afraid you were right about the fellow. His credit's not good at our bank. Gambling, they say. He has a trust, but he can only use the income, which he supposedly does very fast. His father must know about the gambling, because he won't give him money. Young Burton's a registered stockbroker but seems to take it lightly. He was with a firm in New York and got let go because he never showed up. The president of the firm was a friend of his father, too, so he must have been more than a little negligent. Since he's been home, he's been halfheartedly looking for a job, but with the income from the trust he can afford to be fussy. The word is that he's a charmer but a bit of a rake. He's moving out of his father's house soon, going to live with some young friends. More freedom, I believe. Evidently the gambling's a real problem. I'd like to keep Abby away from him, but it'll be damned difficult if he's going to show up at these affairs."

After several more dances with several more pleasant but ordinary young men, Abigail was happy to sit out the intermission with her parents.

"Papa, would you please pass me that little tray of sandwiches? I'm famished. Honestly, Mum, I could eat a horse. Dancing makes you very hungry."

"Are you enjoying yourself, dear?" asked Henrietta.

"Oh, yes. At first it was rather strange, but once you get used to talking nonsense with them all, it gets easier. They're all remarkably alike!"

Henrietta smiled. Abigail had not been out in the world at all. Her sole exposure to mixed company had been at her parents' dinner parties, which she was encouraged to attend, and of course her theater outing. She had gone to a private day school on Beacon Hill where she had met Eleanor Madison.

As a small child she had been brought to birthday parties at the homes of her mother's friends, but the children involved were generally reserved with each other. She had often played with the little girl next door, a blond, chubby child who always let Abigail choose the games and be leader; but this girl had gone away to boarding school and had left last fall for a year abroad. The girls at school had been fun, and Abigail was popular, but looking around the room at their faces, she realized that only Eleanor had become a close friend, and now that they were out of school and launched into the social world, they would also probably drift apart.

Certainly there had been no male friends. The girls at school had talked, of course, so they were not ignorant of all things sexual, but firsthand experience was rare. Some had brothers, which meant brothers' friends, which was nice. But for Abby it had been a small if pleasant world. Had it not been for Mrs. Byors, there would have been very little intimacy. But Mrs. Byors had been fine company, with a good sense of humor and a genuine love for Abigail.

"Mummy?" Abigail had reverted to childhood usage in her excitement. "Have you and Daddy danced yet?"

"No, but we shall do so this very minute," stated Thomas, standing. "If I'm not mistaken, Abby, here comes a fellow to claim you."

Holding Henrietta in his arms, Thomas knew that he would always love this woman; but her nearness was becoming more of a misery than a joy. He missed the warmth of her bed and of her body. Something must be done, but damned if he knew what. They had discussed it, after a fashion, but she was terrified of another pregnancy and refused to believe that Thomas knew ways to prevent it. He had asked her to discuss it with their doctor, but she was too embarrassed. Once, he had forced his way into her bedroom. He had been drinking, and it had only been a few weeks after she had started locking her door at night. She had forgotten the latch, and he, convinced that once in his arms she would give in, had come in abruptly. She was already in bed, her black hair spread out over the eyelet pillow cover, her bosom exposed by the thin silk of her nightgown. Bending over her on the bed, he had held her wrists and kissed her hard on the mouth. But she had been frozen with some unknowable emotion, and he was not a beast. He had not slept at home that night, and when he returned the next evening a wall had gone up, more like a thin veil, but enough to keep them apart. He felt cheapened by what he had done. Before that night he had been faithful, but it had become easier and easier to stay away. Now, as they lightly stepped over the floor, he realized that the rift had become more than physical. Damn it! What was she thinking? What went on behind those blue eyes? It seemed impossible to the intense Thomas that his feelings could be one-sided.

At this moment, Abigail was surreptitiously sneaking her dance card out of her wrist purse in order to see how long she must endure the sweaty palms of her ardent but unsophisticated partners. She hoped her dance with Burton was coming soon.

Good heavens! She caught her breath. Instead of claiming one dance, Burton had written his name all over the last four dances.

This will not make Mamma very happy, she thought, but even as she recognized the impropriety of his act, she felt her heart begin to fly around under the tight white fabric which unsuccessfully tried to camouflage her bosom. When she saw Burton approaching, she vainly tried to conceal her pleasure.

"Why, Burt. I believe you've made a mistake in my card. You've accidentally written for four dances." His arm slipped easily around her narrow waist, and his palm was cool in her hand.

"Not at all. I fully intended to have you for the rest of the evening. Surely you've had enough of old Withers and the rest of that crew. Not at all your type, Abigail. Not up to your mark at all." He whirled her easily from the chaperones.

"But my parents are going to be very cross if we dance this long," she stated unconvincingly.

"Do be still, Abigail. I just want to hold you," ordered Burt.

Biting her lip, Abigail swallowed her protests. Burt said nothing for the entire dance. Instead he moved her closer and closer into his embrace until she grew lightheaded from the masculine scent of his clothes and the movement of his shoulder muscles under her hand. She could scarcely breathe. Her breath was coming in soft little gasps as he held her nearer still. Somehow they were at the balcony door. Never missing a step, he led her into the dark night outside the protective stares of the others.

Before she could protest, he was kissing her again, and only his arm around her waist prevented her knees from giving way. She wanted this — oh, how she wanted this — but she mustn't let him do this to her again. But this time it was Burt who pulled away, and before she could regain her senses, they were back inside as if nothing had happened. Even as anger returned, she felt him drawing her back into the center of the room. There was light applause as the dance ended. Speechless, she looked up at him. He was looking at her with amusement. Infuriated, she tried to pull away, but the music started again. He held her fast, almost painfully, and she knew she would have to make a scene to get away. Still not a word from Burt and — oh dear, there was Mama whispering something to Papa, and they were both looking at her with a distinctly disapproving stare.

"Abigail? Where are you? You seem miles away," said Burt in completely normal tones.

"Burt, this has got to stop. I will not be treated like some shopgirl. Why don't you just go back to Nora Simmons? I'm sure you'll do much better with her!" She could have kicked herself for her temper. Now he would know that she was jealous of his dancing with Nora.

"Do you mean you noticed my dancing with that pretty Simmons girl? Lovely little thing, isn't she? She speaks highly of you." He smiled wickedly.

The third dance was beginning, and it was hardly possible to ignore the stern faces of her parents.

"We *must* stop dancing. My parents are furious," she whispered.

"Surely they'd be more furious if I left you unescorted on the dance floor," he teased.

"That's not what I mean at all, and you know it!" she answered, trying to sound severe. "We could go over and talk to them."

"And miss the last dance! Why, I wouldn't hear of it."

Thus they continued, Abigail unable to break from the spell he had woven around her. The last dance came. By the time it was over, Abigail was so aroused by his nearness that she was powerless to protest further. When he lightly returned her to her parents' side, she found herself shaken but standing.

Worse still was the confrontation with her parents. Seated decorously at a small table, they presented a united front. Her father's face was gray with suppressed anger. Without a word they rose and escorted her from the room, not even pausing as they bid civil good-evenings to their friends and, of course, the sponsors.

"Abigail, how could you?" Her mother began the unpleasant dressing-down. "Everyone noticed your preoccupation with that boy. You've doubtless ruined your chance with George Withers."

"George Withers? Why, I wouldn't think anyone would want to be seen with that overweight bore!"

"He's not overweight, just full-figured. And don't change the subject. You know very well that George Withers has nothing to do with this," replied the exasperated Henrietta.

"Before we all lose our tempers," interjected Thomas, "there are a few things Abby should know about the charming Mr. Madison."

"Is this necessary?" asked Henrietta, unwilling to add to Burton's mysterious appeal. She was aware that the very faults which men may deplore in each other can be the most romantic aspects to a woman.

"Yes, dear, I believe it is," responded Thomas. "You see, Abigail, I have learned that young Madison, in addition to having a bad reputation with women, is also a gambler and a man whose word is not reliable. Now a few youthful indiscretions might be overlooked — Lord knows we've all acted foolishly in our youth . . .''

"Thomas!" This from Henrietta.

"But this fellow has been behaving badly right along. I'm sorry Abby, but that's it. There will be no further dances or dinners or theater parties for you and Burton Madison.''

"But Papa, surely I'm old enough to decide whom I like, and he is so very nice," pleaded Abigail uncharacteristically.

"No, Abigail. I agree completely with your father. The risks are too great," added Henrietta. Then, seeing a tear forming in the emerald eye, she put her arm around her daughter. "I know it's difficult for you now, Abby," she said tenderly, "but he could hurt you badly. Not just your reputation, although that's certainly important, but in other ways that you're not old enough to understand. He's not fine enough, not decent enough to be able to cherish you in the way you deserve. There are many Burton Madisons in the world, and you must avoid them like a sickness, Abby." As she spoke, she grew vehement.

Thomas, sensing some undecipherable message in her words, grew silent and reflective as the carriage drove through the Boston Common. By moonlight the Common took on an eerie glow. The shadow of the Statehouse loomed over them as they left the confines of the park and bumped over the cobblestones of Charles Street. Turning up the hill to Louisburg Square, the horses strained. The last leg of this journey was always an ordeal for the coachman, with the sharp inclines of Beacon Hill and the abrupt turns and narrow streets to conquer.

The gas lamps were lit along the way, throwing the three faces into sudden relief only to plunge them into darkness once again between the lampposts. Abigail sensed a deep resolution in her parents. Strange, she thought, there had been many disagreements in the past, but it had always been rather like a game to be won or lost with equal good sportsmanship.

Something else was happening here. In this contest she was not a child to be indulged or disciplined. The stakes were higher, and they involved independence and wisdom and courage and obedience in equal parts.

A part of her mind stretched and began to work for the first time. She was unsure of where her duty lay. With her parents certainly, but also with herself. This was going to be complicated. Her forehead ached with fatigue as she wearily went into the house. Her parents bade her a quick good-night, and she went to bed feeling as if she had let them down. Yet at the same time, she felt very much like herself. After hanging up her white dress, she crawled gingerly between the cold sheets. She had told Mrs. Byors not to prepare her bed, but now her toes regretted that decision. Her door opened and Henrietta entered. Sitting down on the edge of the bed, she took Abby's small hand in hers.

"Darling, you were beautiful tonight, and we were very proud of you. If we acted harsh in the carriage, it is just because we love you so much. Now go to sleep and dream of sweet things. Perhaps we can go to the Public Gardens tomorrow if it's a nice day." She pushed an auburn lock from Abigail's brow and gently kissed the spot it had covered. After she left Abigail, she walked slowly past her husband's door, half-hoping he would open it and take her in his arms. But his door was shut, and she returned to her own empty bed.

CHAPTER 7

Everyone was tired the next day, but good spirits had been restored by a night's sleep, and so it was decided that there should be a family walk that afternoon.

"May we have a picnic?" asked Abigail excitedly.

"It's not dry enough underfoot yet," replied Thomas. "But," he added, "I don't see why we couldn't buy some peanuts from the vendor."

"Well, all right," said Abigail, partially reconciled, "but you must promise that as soon as the ground dries we can have a grand picnic with jam and bread and cold chicken and champagne."

"Abigail, do stop! We've only just finished breakfast, and you're already thinking of food," said Henrietta.

"But I'm a growing girl!" protested Abigail.

"Almost through growing, I trust," said Henrietta. "You will have to be more careful of what you eat in the future, or you'll end up like that unfortunate Betty Robinson."

"Yes," replied Abigail, "the poor thing looked like a big bowl of mashed potatoes last night, didn't she?"

"Don't be unkind," chastened Thomas, who loathed cattiness of any sort.

"Oh, I'm sorry, Papa. I didn't mean to be cruel. I like Betty. It's only that I'm sorry for her. But she is sweet and has lovely penmanship," said Abigail and, as if this closed the subject, excused herself and went to prepare for her walk.

"Wear something dark, dear. The ground is muddy," called Henrietta.

Henrietta was correct: the ground was muddy. But by sticking carefully to the path, the three wanderers were able to enjoy the Public Gardens with a minimum of damage to their clothing. The coachman had left them off at the Common, and they had crossed to the gardens.

Like most young women of her era,

Abigail didn't get enough exercise, and outings like this were marvelously beneficial both to her health and disposition. The day was sunny, and the gardeners had already staged a modest springtime flower display. The swan boats were not yet in operation, much to Abigail's disappointment, as she loved to ride around the small lake and feed the mallards who lived on the tiny island in the middle.

There were many people in the gardens this day, most of them dressed sensibly for walking. It was easy to identify the outsiders because of their unsuitable clothing. No proper Bostonian would ever dream of wearing such frivolous pastels or flimsy shoes for an outdoor excursion.

"I wish you would let me dress up more for our walks," said Abigail.

"You know perfectly well that no one with an ounce of sense would ruin their good clothes by trailing them through the dirt," replied Henrietta. And that subject was closed.

It seemed to Abigail as she walked briskly between the carefully cultivated rows of pansies and baby geraniums that being a Bostonian subjected you to a strange and unique set of rules and regulations. You must always wear a hat, for example, and sensible shoes. How many lovely dresses had been ruined for her by sensible shoes! Detestable oxfords under pretty ginghams, and flat little boater hats squashed on top of carefully arranged curls. And the gloves, the ubiquitous white gloves! Abigail could scarcely recall a time when she hadn't worn neat little white gloves. Perhaps she had even worn them as a baby. She had always felt that sensible shoes and white gloves contradicted each other, but she knew it was pointless to resist.

Church was another Boston tradition. She was certain that her father was in no way pious, yet each Sunday morning their house ejected its churchgoing party. Had she suggested missing services, her mother would have been aghast. It was a peculiar habit, this churchgoing. Grace was never said before meals in the Curtis household, and Thomas certainly used the milder forms of profanity with regularity, yet to stop attending church would be a social error beyond repair. Abigail was sure that the minister knew this. He often looked over his affluent flock with a resignation that bordered on despair, but he nevertheless gave them the sermons they wanted, grammatical exhortations urging the moral life, never evangelical and tasteless admonitions on the evils of wealth.

That her Bostonian traditions represented a mixture of good common sense and pure hypocrisy never occurred to Abigail. Things were as they were, and no eighteen-year-old girl was likely to change them. Had change seemed possible she would have attempted it; but in fact she was never offered alternatives. That is, not until meeting Burton Madison. He was the first attractive person she had ever met who behaved contrarily to her family's rules of order. Her mother's disapproval didn't bother her overly — her mother seemed to disapprove of many harmless things — but Thomas's attitude dismayed her. She sensed his worldliness, although she was ignorant of his peccadilloes. If he found Burt so objectionable, then perhaps she should accept the fact that her new admirer was flawed. It was confusing to find duty and desire in head-to-head conflict.

Today, however, was too pleasant for the contemplation of such dilemmas. Here were acquaintances to greet, and there were flowers to admire, and all around was the May sun. Suddenly she spied Eleanor Madison walking with her father. Seeing Abigail, Eleanor waved, and, taking advantage of the fact that Mr. Madison was engrossed in conversation with three prosperous-looking older gentlemen, she scampered to see her friend. Abigail, who had gone ahead of her parents, was also temporarily unchaperoned.

"Hello, Abby. I was hoping I'd see you today. Wasn't it wonderful? I had the most lovely evening last night. Do you know I danced twice with George Withers?" said Eleanor happily. "Oh, I'm sorry. I forgot you danced with him too."

"That's quite all right, Eleanor," said Abigail kindly. "I hope you and Mr.

Withers got on very well. I understand he's quite the catch. Also, he's more your type than mine, I believe. I'm much too flighty for such a sensible man. He'd never care for me."

"Do you really think so? Then it's all right with you if I like him?" said Eleanor, clearly relieved to have Abigail remove herself from the competition. "Mother was pleased to see him dance with me. She was also delighted that you and Burt were getting along so well, although she did scold him this morning for monopolizing you. Poor Burt. He was out ever so late and came down late for breakfast. The last thing he wanted was a dressing-down from Mummy!"

"Well, I got more than a dressing-down from my parents," said Abigail, trying to be tactful. "They don't want me to see too much of any one man for awhile. It's nothing against Burt." She crossed her fingers behind her back. "They are just being too careful of me, as usual."

"Maybe Burt understands that, because he gave me this note for you. It's sealed," added Eleanor.

"Sssh. Be careful. My parents are right behind me," cried Abigail delightedly as she deftly slid the small note into the pocket of her navy blue coat. "Did they see?" she whispered anxiously to Eleanor, who from her vantage point could see behind Abigail to where the Curtises were advancing on their daughter.

"I don't think so. Oh, Abigail, I feel like one of those go-betweens in Shakespeare," cried Eleanor. "Hello, Mrs. Curtis, Mr. Curtis. Well, I must go back to Daddy now. See you soon, Abby." And she walked quickly away from the scrutiny of the Curtises.

For the remainder of the walk the note burned the small hand thrust possessively into the coat pocket. Where before she had wanted to stay out of doors forever, she now could scarcely wait to get home to the privacy of her own bedroom where she could read Burt's message. How romantic to receive a secret note from a man. And how angry her father would be if he knew. Once again that knot of confusion in her chest.

"Here, Abigail. Let's get some of those

peanuts. The fresh air has given me an appetite,'' said Thomas, striding athletically toward the wizened vendor who reappeared each spring like the robins, with his red and yellow cart and the funny flowered parasol he had tied to its handle.

"I'd rather not, thank you,'' said Henrietta as Thomas offered her the roasted treats. He smiled, knowing that she found the vendor to be hopelessly unclean. He and Abigail munched happily, occasionally tossing a shelled nut to one of the garden squirrels.

When the three came to the Arlington Street gate, they reversed themselves and started back up toward the Common where the carriage was waiting. The walking was so pleasant that Abigail momentarily forgot her note. It was just as well, because the air was turning cool and the sun was dropping in the sky by the time they reached the daydreaming coachman, who sucked indolently on a blade of new grass before jumping up to attention at the sight of the Curtises.

Once home, Abigail rushed to her

room. She ran to the window, and, seeing Mrs. Byors in the garden behind the house, she smiled. Taking the note from her pocket, she smoothed it flat where she had rumpled it with her nervous clutchings. She subdued a pinch of disappointment when she saw how short it was.

"Dear Abigail," she read. "Meet me tonight at ten in the garden behind your house. B."

The nerve of him! she thought. Why it was nothing more than a command! Did he honestly believe that she would sneak out to meet him in the dark? She was convinced now, more than ever, that he thought of her as just another conquest. Well, she would show him! No clandestine meetings for Miss Abigail Curtis. He could just cool his heels in the shrubbery until he took root, for all she cared!

CHAPTER 8

If she was unusually animated at dinner, nobody seemed to notice, or if they did, they attributed it to the fresh air she had inhaled in such quantities during the afternoon. Her vivacity contrasted with her lack of appetite, however, and when she refused the ice cream offered her for dessert, Mrs. Byors spoke up.

"Are you feeling well, Abigail? Your color seems high to me, and I swear I've never known you to refuse ice cream. Did you get a chill today?"

"Oh, Mrs. Byors, I'm just fine. Mother seems afraid that I might become atrociously fat, so I've decided to skip desserts for awhile."

"Now, Abigail, I'm sure I said no such thing," said Henrietta, smiling in spite of herself.

"Actually, I do have a tiny headache.

Perhaps I'll take a walk outside after dinner," said Abigail.

"There. I told you so," said Mrs. Byors. "All this exercise is not healthy. Why, in my day no young woman would think of walking the entire length of the Public Gardens! This modern view of women is going to make trouble, mark my words."

While Mrs. Byors continued to rail against all newfangled things, Abigail sat back in her chair stunned by her own duplicity. She had not had a headache in years. Why in the world had she made that up? It was almost as if she was planning to meet Burt after all, which she certainly would not do under any circumstances.

After dinner they all went into the sitting room and looked at some new stereopticon slides that Mrs. Byors had received from a friend in New York. The pictures were of all the European capitals. Holding the viewer in her right hand, Abigail tried very hard to concentrate, but as the clock inched past nine-thirty and then to nine forty-five, she developed an acute case of the jitters which crescendoed at ten o'clock. Within seconds of hearing the chimes, she heard a voice saying, "Looking at these slides has made my head worse. I think I'll take a few turns around the garden."

She stood up. Had she really said that? She must be insane. Now she would have to go out into the garden. But he might not even be there. Surely he would have realized the impossibility of his request.

Wrapping a shawl around her shoulders, she looked back into the room where the other three were innocently passing the views from hand to hand. She felt guilty, but the excitement of what she was about to do was too compelling, and finally, quelling her feelings of disloyalty, she slipped quietly into the garden.

There, she was right. He hadn't come. How could she have believed for one minute that he would sink to skulking in the bushes? The night was warm for May, and she decided not to waste her deception by going back into the house right away.

The garden was not large, approximately forty by fifty feet. Abigail's favorite part was the corner where her father had planted two apple trees and surprised even himself when they bore fruit. All around the garden, enclosing it completely except for where the house formed the fourth side, was a brick serpentine wall. In its curves Abigail had hidden and fantasized away a good portion of her childhood. She had not spent any time here since winter, so her walk was even more enjoyable as she made out in the dim light perennial friends who were sending up their shoots for the season. In the darkness she could just discern the shape of the apple trees. Their blossoming was imminent, and she went toward them hoping to catch a glimpse of the first few blooms.

"I knew you'd come. You are the sort who will never run away from an adventure." The low voice came from behind the larger apple tree. Startled, Abigail almost cried out, but seeing the supple form of Burt emerging from the gloom of the corner, she instead composed her face into the sternest look she could muster.

"I didn't think you would come," she said. "If I had imagined that you'd go through with this silly scheme, I'd have never come out."

"Is that so? Strange then, how you came out just at ten o'clock." His eyes shone blue in the dim moonlight, but she could see his victorious expression. "Come on, Abigail, admit it. You couldn't have stayed away. God, but you look lovely in the moonlight. Come closer." Indolently he leaned against the tree waiting for her to take the necessary steps toward him.

And she did. Outraged at herself and at him, she walked trancelike until, reaching him, she stood stock still.

Still bantering, Burt continued, "Could it be that our sweet little debutante is more grown up than she thought? It takes two to kiss, you know, Abigail. Why can't you stop playing little schoolgirl games with yourself? I knew the first time I laid eyes on you that you were years older than Eleanor, at least in ways any man would recognize. Come here. I want to kiss you again without any interruptions."

He drew her swiftly into his arms and

kissed her with a teasing lightness until her lips grew impatient and she felt herself returning his kiss with an abandon she was powerless to control. He continued to kiss her, his mouth opening into hers until she felt a melting away, a loss of one part of her consciousness. Her shawl slipped off her shoulders to the ground as his hands pushed the thin fabric of her spring dress down over her shoulders. Now his lips were burning a trail down her throat, and his hand had sought and found her breast. His hair was soft on her neck as his lips found her bosom. She clutched feverishly at his back as she felt the cool air mixed with his warm breath on her naked breast. Her body had a will of its own, and its demands thrilled and terrified her.

"Good God, Abigail! What's the meaning of this?" The voice of her father rang across the garden.

Struggling to rearrange her dress, Abigail clutched for her scarf and, failing to find it, tugged awkwardly at the front of her dress.

"And you, you damn scoundrel, get out of here. Now!"

Thomas's voice thundered like an angry god. Scarlet with shame, Abigail watched numbly as Burt climbed over the wall by means of a trellis. How cowardly of him, she thought. Just like a boy caught stealing apples. Any romance that might have lingered in the air was dispelled by his ignominious retreat.

"Into the house this minute, young lady!" said Thomas, beside himself with rage.

Rushing past him, Abigail was as miserable as she had ever been in her life. She ran past Mrs. Byors, who stood bewildered by the garden door. Henrietta and Mrs. Byors, alarmed by Thomas's voice, had both rushed toward the garden; but Henrietta, sensing the nature of the problem, had drawn back as the disheveled Abigail ran up to her room.

Once inside her own room, Abigail locked the door and flung herself down on the white coverlet of her bed. She could never face them again. To think that her father had caught her in such a position was unbearable. Shame overwhelmed her, and great pounding sobs shook her body.

She expected a knock on her door, but none came. Thus she remained shut off from the rest of the household until she fell into a merciful sleep.

Thomas had gone out into the garden at the request of Mrs. Byors and Henrietta, who were both concerned about Abigail's headache. It was odd, come to think of it. Abigail had never been prone to headaches, and she had seemed the picture of health this afternoon. He suspected that she was merely feeling the effects of last night's cotillion, but he knew better than to resist the united demands of his wife and Mrs. Byors. He had enjoyed the idea of some time alone with Abigail.

Having only one child had been a disappointment to Thomas when he was younger, but when Abby had turned out to be such an enchanting little thing, he had become content with his lot. How proud he had been of his little girl when they would go out in the carriage or for a walk. Even at the age of five she had carried herself proudly erect, and that mannerism of tossing her curls had been firmly established by the time she was three. How bright she had always been, and how affectionate. During the last few months when Henrietta had turned away, it was the joy of his only child that had attracted him home, and when he became too lonely and found himself visiting Edith O'Connor in her room, it was the face of Abigail that triggered a large part of his remorse. He knew she was not going to be his much longer. Seeing her last night at the cotillion, he had faced the inevitability of her womanhood. Oh, but she was not there yet; he would still have this year to call her his own little girl.

It was in the middle of these fond paternal musings that he came upon the two young people in the garden. Seeing the extent of Abigail's disarray, he was shocked quite speechless. His mind went white at the sight of that idiot boy mauling his daughter. It was seconds before he found his voice, and he startled himself with the emotion in his words. He felt a blind hatred which was alien to him. He could have easily killed the boy without a trace of conscience. When he saw young Madison climbing the wall he was relieved, as he knew he would have done the boy harm in a moment if he had not left. He avoided Abigail's eyes as she raced by him.

After she went into the house, he shouted back to Henrietta and Mrs. Byors, "Leave her alone. I'll be in shortly."

Alone in the darkness he found some measure of self-control. Striding aimlessly around the small garden, he tried to decide what to do. He scarcely knew what to say to Abigail. Had she been a boy, he could have sat her down and told her a thing or two, but he was totally ignorant of how to handle this sexual side of Abigail. He realized that he had never really had this out with Henrietta. When Abigail was younger, her mother had had some sort of talk with her — he remembered Henrietta's embarrassment at the time — but he was sure that anyone as naive as Henrietta could scarcely have done justice to the subject.

Good God, though! The girl had certainly looked knowledgeable enough there in the moonlight, half-undressed. The remembrance made him queasy, and for the first time in his forty-three years he felt old, old and suddenly bereft of his little girl.

Taking a few more minutes to compose himself, he went back to the sitting room where the curious and alarmed women were silently awaiting him.

"Thomas, whatever happened? You look as white as a sheet," cried Henrietta.

"It was the Madison boy. He must have snuck into the garden to meet her."

"Why, I never! Oh, the nerve of him," cried Mrs. Byors. "Imagine, such a sneaky thing to do!" She was justifiably outraged.

"But what happened? Surely that's not all," said Henrietta.

"You're damned right that's not all!" said Thomas. "He had half her clothes off — that's all!"

"Dear Lord!" said Henrietta, paling. Mrs. Byors, horror-struck, fell back onto the divan and looked as if about to faint.

Thomas regretted his outburst. Surely this was not a thing to discuss in front of

Mrs. Byors, but damn it, she loved Abby too and had some say in the matter.

"Shall I go up to her?" said Henrietta.

"No," replied Thomas firmly. "Let's talk about this for awhile. It will do her no harm to think about what's happened. Please go up, Mrs. Byors, and tell her that we'll discuss it in the morning. Mrs. Curtis and I would like to be alone now. You understand."

"Very well, but if I may say so, I wouldn't let that horrible boy get away with this. I'd tell his parents, and then he'd get what for!" And on this vengeful note Mrs. Byors left the room. Knocking on Abigail's door, she received no answer and, rightly deciding that Abby had gone to bed, went on down the corridor to her own room muttering, "Scalawag! Trying to seduce my girl!" Naturally, she found Abigail entirely blameless in the matter.

Meanwhile, downstairs, Thomas, having poured himself three fingers of cognac, was struggling to come to grips with the situation.

"I think Mrs. Byors is right. We should tell his parents about this," said

Henrietta, who had two high spots of color on her cheeks.

"Yes, yes, you're quite right. But what if we get no satisfaction? After all, the man's been absolutely powerless to control the boy up to this point. There's no reason to think he'll be able to discipline him now."

"But we'll just forbid him to have any contact with Abigail again! Oh dear, I've just had a horrible thought. Supposing he talks — I mean, what if he tells his father about what happened? Think of her reputation?"

"Little chance of that after the way he left," said Thomas, the trace of a smile on his face as he recalled the ungainly exit of Mr. Madison. "He ran away like a rabbit. Poorest excuse for a man I've seen in my life. Wouldn't even face the music. He left Abby there all on her own. Damned coward!" Now he was angry again. There was something else eating away at him, and he began to realize that this was the crux of their problem.

"I'll certainly speak to his father, and by heaven, I'll make it hot for him if he doesn't take some action against the boy. But that's not our biggest problem, Henny. Abigail deliberately disobeyed us. They must have planned this somehow. All that business about a headache! The girl lied to us plain and simple. We made it clear we didn't want her to see the fellow again. There's no way she could have misunderstood that. But that's not the worst of it. She was very willing out there in the garden. God knows what would have happened if I hadn't come along. She'll have to be punished," he finished sadly.

"Oh, Thomas. Think how upset she must be. Couldn't we just forget it?" said Henrietta, who could not bring herself to face the implications of what Thomas had seen.

"Forget about it? No, Henny, we can't. That Madison fellow is going to be around her all summer, and we're asking for trouble if we don't do something."

"Couldn't we all go away? Take a trip? Surely that would put him out of her mind," suggested Henrietta.

"I'm afraid not. I'm going to have a lot

of business dealings on the North Shore this summer. Our bank is financing some commercial fishing interests in Salem. As a matter of fact, young Andrew Darcy's involved in one deal, so I'll have to be shuttling back and forth a great deal this summer. There'll be no time for trips until at least September. As a matter of fact, I had hoped you'd want to spend a little time with the Darcys yourself this summer. It would give me a chance to stay there awhile and know you weren't alone."

"Thomas! Why don't we ask Belle to take Abigail for the summer? I know she'd love to have her, and you could visit whenever you went up the coast. I could come for a few weeks in August, and we could be together. It sounds perfect." Henrietta was enthusiastic. The scheme suited her perfectly. She little realized that banishment to her beloved Marblehead was the worst possible punishment she could have devised for Abigail.

"It sounds fine to me," replied Thomas, surprised that he hadn't thought of it first. "But do you suppose Abby will be willing?'' He remembered her attitude toward Marblehead when the Darcys had come for dinner.

"Of course she won't want to go, but that's just why she should. She's been too limited here. Eleanor Madison is her only close friend, and in Marblehead she could have Susan for companionship. The fresh air and ocean would be wonderful for her. Summers are beautiful in Marblehead. There's sailing and picnics and the beach. She'll love it. I did, and look at what a city girl I am.''

"Now perhaps. But don't forget, Marblehead is part of your youth. You could be a bit nostalgic.''

"Maybe so, but Thomas, I don't want to watch over her like a hawk all summer. She'd hate it and so would I. In Marblehead she would have more freedom with no danger from Burton Madison the third. Oh, how I have come to hate that name! If only I had never allowed him to come to dinner!'' Henrietta looked as angry as Thomas had ever seen her.

"Very well. We'll tell her at breakfast. But promise me one thing. There will be no backing down on this. She's always been able to talk you in circles, so be prepared." Thomas finished his brandy in one gulp and, turning to the desk, picked up his pen. "Shall I telephone Belle or shall you?"

"You do it. The sooner we settle things with Belle, the better. She should really go at once; if I'm not mistaken, that boy will be in touch soon."

In bed Henrietta's emotions pulled every way except toward peace. She had never been parted from Abigail, and now she faced this unexpected rift. She knew they were doing the correct thing, but her heart ached at the thought of the big empty house. From what Thomas had said, he would be away off and on all summer. Now the summer loomed ahead like a threatening cloud over her happiness. The strain of her relationship with Thomas was taking its toll. She knew he believed her to be avoiding his bed because of her fear of pregnancy. What he didn't know was that her fears of childbirth were a mere screen for the emotional turmoil which lay beneath.

When she had first told him of her decision to sleep alone she had expected him to talk away her fears, reassure her, but he had instead withdrawn. After that night when he had forced his way into her room and she had rebuffed him, she had cried herself to sleep. When she awoke the next morning, she had run to his room to beg his forgiveness. She had decided to go to the doctor after all, to discuss her problem. She was intelligent enough to know that there were ways of preventing children, but as she had never before needed them, she was abysmally ignorant on the subject. After all, they had wanted more children, but after five years of trying they had accepted their Abigail as an only child. Only recently had the possibility of pregnancy presented itself again, and she had reacted dreadfully, she knew. Well, there would be no more nonsense! She would find out what she needed to know, and then they could be lovers again.

She tiptoed to his door that morning, and, finding it open and the bed made, she slowly realized that Thomas had not been home that night. Only too well aware of what this meant, she was heartbroken. How could this be? They had been too close for Thomas to seek satisfaction elsewhere. Perhaps he hadn't. Perhaps he had spent the night at his club thinking, and tonight they could talk. But apprehension gripped her, and when Thomas had come home that evening, she had only to look at his face to read the truth. And so she had slept alone again, hurt beyond belief, her self-esteem in tatters.

She had spent the next months involving herself in social affairs, and Thomas's absences caused her more and more pain until it was like a dull ache which she carried wearily from place to place. But pride would not give way to love, and now they were like strangers. Faced, however, with Abigail's absence and even less of Thomas's company, her will failed her, and finally she fell into troubled sleep.

Meanwhile, Thomas lay abed amidst his own thoughts and speculations. How easily, he thought, Henrietta had adjusted to the idea of a summer alone. Could he have been deceived all these years in his opinion of her? This cool figurine that she was now was in such contrast to the beloved Henny of his youth. How well he remembered that day last fall when she had tearily confided that she believed herself to be pregnant. He had laughed, thinking it a delightful surprise, but Henny had flown angrily from the room and cried for hours. Nothing he could say or do consoled her. When, a week later, she announced that she was not pregnant, he had been disappointed, having hoped that she would come around to the idea in time. She had taken to her bed for a few days, and Thomas, fearing a miscarriage had occurred, wanted to send for the doctor; but Henrietta was adamant in her refusal, and as she seemed completely normal within a week, he had acquiesced to her decision. What an idiot he had been. He should have brought the doctor anyway. At least a doctor could have established whether she had indeed been pregnant at all and provided some information about the prevention of pregnancy. Boston doctors were quite broad-minded on this subject, and the right one would confide his limited knowledge on birth control if he respected your discretion.

As things stood now, Thomas felt that the whole situation had been bungled. Henrietta had never been an overly passionate lover, but he knew she had enjoyed the intimacy of their marriage bed. The current situation was unbearable. Perhaps a summer apart would do them all good. He only hoped that Abigail would agree.

CHAPTER 9

"Marblehead! Oh no, Mama. Surely you'd never send me to Marblehead."

Abigail, puffy-eyed from last night's crying, sat upright in her bed and looked beseechingly from one parent to another. She had forgotten her shame in the light of this new disaster.

"I know I was bad, and I promise to never let another boy — well, you know," she faltered as the memory flooded her face with crimson. "Please don't send me away. I'd die in Marblehead. Why, I don't even know the Darcys. It'd be too horrible to be dumped on their doorstep like an orphan."

This overstatement restored her parents' sense of proportion. An instant earlier, Henrietta had been on the verge of relenting, but as usual Abigail, with her histrionics, had quite unintentionally introduced a note of humor and sealed her fate.

"It's been decided, Abigail," said Thomas firmly. "We telephoned Belle this morning. She's happy to have you."

Big tears plopped down onto Abigail's nightdress, but she was bright enough to know that this particular battle was not going her way. Besides, she had never felt so ashamed in her life, and her conscience demanded its own price.

How sad, thought Thomas, that her first real mistake had to be of a sexual nature. He hoped it would not scar her.

"Does Mrs. Byors know? She'll absolutely die!"

"We told her this morning, and although she is unhappy, I can assure you that she's quite alive," responded Thomas, fully prepared to hold his ground. "As a matter of fact, she's decided to use this summer to visit her friends in New York. She's never had a real vacation, you know."

"You mean I am to go all alone?" wailed Abigail, sinking back into the pillows of her bed in a way that would have surely aroused the envy of Madame Bernhardt.

"Your father will come at least one day a week to see you, and I have asked Belle if I might come for a few weeks at the end of August. Don't forget, there's Susan and Andrew and even young Tad to keep you company. Why, it should be like having real brothers and sisters of your own," said Henrietta.

"But I never wanted brothers and sisters. Never once have I asked for anyone else but you," pleaded Abigail vainly.

Seeing the pointlessness of further discussion, Thomas and Henrietta kissed Abby and left her to her breakfast, which they had brought on a tray.

Grabbing a piece of toast from a warm plate, Abigail munched in total fury. Sand and rocks and seaweed. Ugh! She would never tolerate it. Probably the children went barefoot and ate horrid slimy things from seashells. Nobody in Marblehead would appreciate her clothes, and she had heard that they talked differently and had strange names for things. She would probably not have a room of her own, and, good God, she would have to live in the same house as that horrible Andrew Darcy. Of all the grim realities of Marblehead, surely Andrew Darcy was the grimmest. She could just picture him, the insufferable oaf, coming in to dinner stinking of fish and looking at her as if she were a useless bit of fluff. Oh, how could her parents do this to her! If only they hadn't already called Belle. Now it was too late. She hoped they hadn't told the Darcys of the circumstances surrounding her banishment. That would be too humiliating.

Strangely enough, throughout this internal tirade the thought of Burton Madison had been conspicuously absent. He had ceased to exist for her from the last glimpse of his foot disappearing over the serpentine wall.

If Abigail could have seen what an attractive picture she made, she might have been mollified. Surrounded by ruffled pillows, her red, tangled curls framing her heart-shaped face, and her form chastely revealed by the white eyelet of her nightgown, she resembled nothing so much as an angel, despite her hellish thoughts. She felt cornered. Years of experience had taught her that while her parents might be individually vulnerable to her wheedling, united they were immovable. Shame, anger, and self-pity raged through the frustrated girl leaving her quite weak with despair. Listlessly she put up her hair, carelessly choosing any old dress to wear.

Avoiding both Mrs. Byors, whom she considered a traitor, and her parents, she wandered from room to room like some ancient queen condemned to exile. Falling quite easily into her role, she let huge sighs escape her as she fingered childhood mementoes as if for the last time. Catching a glance of herself in the upstairs hall mirror, she noted with satisfaction that she was pale and wan-looking, the picture of martyrdom. She tried as much as possible to avoid consideration of the reasons behind her banishment. To recognize that her parents were justified in their decision would have spoiled the self-image she was projecting. Surely when they discovered that she was losing weight and growing weaker by the day, they would retrieve her from Marblehead. A new picture sprang into her mind of a white-faced invalid being carefully aided from the Darcy doorstep into her parents' waiting carriage. How wretched they would be to see how frail she had become, and how lacking in spirit.

The thought of her guilt-ridden parents and of her emaciated self-to-be brought tears of remorse and pity to the green eyes. Poor Thomas and Henrietta! But once back in Boston, she would bloom again, and once restored to health, she would gently forgive them for her ordeal. Smiling for the first time that day, she began to lay her plans for the duration of her stay in Marblehead. She must be on her best behavior; there must be no cause for complaint from the Darcys. She would be compliant but aloof, allowing them to notice her lack of appetite by themselves. Above all, she must retain her dignity and not allow herself to be drawn into young Tad's mischief or to be piqued into ill temper by Andrew. Susan would help by providing the necessary companionship. Abby imagined that a small-town girl like Susan would be suitably impressed with city ways and would provide the necessary foil for her dramatic decline. The visit began to present possibilities to the vivid imagination of Abigail Curtis. Perhaps it would be bearable after all. If she stuck with her determination to suffer at all costs, she should be there two weeks at most. Running back to her room, she began to pack her things, much to the astonishment of the sad-eyed Mrs. Byors, who had come to commiserate with her poor little girl.

"It's quite all right, Mrs. Byors, you needn't look so miserable. I know I deserve my punishment, but I would have thought that you, at least, would stick by me."

"Oh, Abigail, I was just as surprised as you at the news. Who would ever have thought they'd send you away?" Mrs. Byors was literally wringing her hands. "But don't worry. I'll be here at summer's end. At first I was afraid that this would mean my dismissal — after all, you're in no need of a governess now — but your mother wants me to stay on as her companion for as long as I choose, so we'll be together soon. And your mother will bring me with her when she goes to Marblehead, so it's not so bad, is it?" Abigail could not resist the loving pain on Mrs. Byors's face. She embraced the stout dear friend and held her very tight before answering.

"Oh, I expect I'll live through it somehow." Once again a great sigh escaped, but she stifled the next one when she saw the tragic look returning to Mrs. Byors's face.

"Now, let's be practical. I shall need a bathing costume and a parasol and I suppose some sensible shoes. The streets are probably disgraceful! And bonnets. I shall not let the sun ruin my skin. We might as well leave my best dresses at home. No sense wasting them on Marblehead."

When the Curtis family met for lunch on Monday, Thomas and Henrietta were astounded by the change in Abigail's attitude. All morning Henrietta had been fighting down a large lump which had lodged at some indefinite point between her chest and her throat; but Abigail's resignation made her feel childish for reacting so strongly to what had been, after all, her own decision.

"Now that Belle has agreed to have you, there's no reason why we can't start out in the morning," said Thomas.

"So soon?" asked Henrietta.

"It's pointless to put it off. It won't be any easier to say good-bye in a week."

"He's right mother," said Abigail. "If I'm going, I'd rather do it quickly."

At this declaration her parents fell into silence.

In her plain muslin frock, Abigail was the picture of tranquil innocence. Any resemblance to the wanton of last night had vanished. Although there were traces of misery in the mauve circles under the green eyes, her complexion was unmarred. Picking at her fruit salad she gazed around the room.

"What do they eat in Marblehead?" she suddenly asked.

Startled by Abigail's conversational tone, Henrietta replied, "Why, I don't know. The same things we eat here, I imagine, although I do remember that my aunt made wonderful blueberry cobblers and, of course, there were chowders and, oh yes, there was a kind of cookie made of molasses and rum. They called it a frog or frogger. No, wait, it was a Joe Frogger. Each one was as large as a saucer, but even so, we always ate at least two. I can't remember how they got that odd name. Perhaps you can ask Belle; she knows everything about the town. There are so many legends and customs! My head could never hold them all." Henrietta smiled for the first time that morning. With her memories of Marblehead came reassurance. There was such a rich experience in wait for Abigail, if only she would relax and enjoy it!

Despite her vow to starve slowly while in exile, Abigail's appetite was piqued by any enthusiastic description of food; eighteen is not the best age at which to fast.

Her plate emptied as if by magic as her

mother rambled on about the haunts and habits of her own youthful summers. "But Mama, you were only a little girl then. Perhaps it'll be different for someone my age," said Abigail.

"The ocean never goes away," said Thomas. "And as long as there is the sea, there will be good walks and beautiful views and, mark my words, good food."

It sounded dull to Abigail but she kept her opinion to herself. If she were to be the elegant martyr, she mustn't whine.

CHAPTER 10

Dreaded moments come quickly. Less than twenty-four hours later Abigail and Thomas went out the door to the waiting carriage. Henrietta held Abby close for a heartbreaking moment and then released her while she still could. Abby's eyes filled, and she was unable to speak for fear that they would overflow onto her gray voile traveling dress.

Thomas had decided to drive the pair of matched chestnuts himself, and as the day was warm and sunny, he allowed Abigail to ride up front beside him. Passing through familiar streets, Abigail felt the same premature nostalgia that had pervaded her last day at home, but by the time they had reached Chelsea she was once again looking ahead.

"Papa, did you tell Belle why you sent me away?"

"We are not sending you away. We merely feel that we'd be more comfortable with twenty miles between you and that fellow!" He found that he could discuss the situation more calmly now that the immediate danger was over.

"Look out!" cried Abby as a motorcar came coughing toward them, charging like a bucking bronco.

"Damned contraptions! Scares the horses out of their wits. That fool has no more idea of how to drive a motorcar than I do!"

"Oh, Papa. I think they're so exciting. Why can't we get one? Then you could come and see me all the time."

"There is no way I'd give up these fine fellows for some filthy piece of machinery that makes too much noise and runs honest travelers off the road."

"Oh, don't be stuffy. Why, I'll bet that in ten years everyone will have one," said Abigail.

"Then everyone will be sorry! And furthermore, young lady, I'm not stuffy. Just because a person doesn't like every crazy contraption doesn't mean he's a fogey."

"When will we get there?" asked Abigail awhile later when they had pulled onto the Lynn Marsh Road.

"Not for another hour and a half, I imagine. Why? Are you getting hungry?"

"Famished. Actually I'd be all right if I didn't know that Mrs. Byors packed us a special picnic. I've been thinking about it since Chelsea."

"We'll stop up here. There's a pretty stretch along the marsh where we can picnic."

As soon as they stopped, Abigail scrambled down from the seat and stretched her legs. The two travelers disappeared in opposite directions into the bushes for a few moments, then rejoined each other at the carriage.

"Oh, look, chicken salad and cherry tarts, and here are pickles and — what's in there? Oh, wine for you and apple juice for me. Papa, may I have some wine? Just this once?"

She looked so pretty sitting on the blanket he had spread out that Thomas acquiesced.

"Why not? You're eighteen and about to be on your own for awhile. Why not a toast?"

Abigail accepted the small glass of rosé wine and held it up to the light as she had often seen her father do. Sipping gingerly, she made a face. "It's sour! Not at all like Mrs. Byors's blackberry wine."

"And just how do you know about Mrs. Byors's blackberry wine?" he asked teasingly.

"I used to sneak a few drops when I was younger. She never noticed. Anyway, it was nasty, but at least it was sweet."

"So I've been harboring a secret guzzler all these years, is that it?" asked Thomas, refilling his own glass.

"Oh, Papa. I only did it twice, and it was a long time ago!" she answered.

"I hope Belle knows what she's letting herself in for," said Thomas, settling back on his elbows.

"What's she like? Belle, I mean?" asked Abigail.

"Well, let's see; she and your mother are first cousins. She's always lived in Marblehead. Her father was in shipping.

So was Maurice, but Salem doesn't do the trade it used to do, so he runs a retail business now. Not that he's done badly, but Belle's father was wealthier.''

''But I want to know about what she's like!'' persisted Abigail.

''You've met her. Judge for yourself. She always seems good-natured, and certainly she's devoted to the children. Now that the family's growing up, she'll be happy to have another chick in her brood.''

''She's very pretty. Not as pretty as Mama, of course, but different.''

''No one is as pretty as Mama,'' agreed Thomas. ''But Belle is certainly good-looking. Maurice was lucky to get her. She's been a good wife from all accounts. Your mother and I used to see quite a bit of them when we were younger, but when all the children came along, we stopped traveling back and forth so much.''

''Mama misses Marblehead sometimes. Perhaps it isn't so bad once you get used to it,'' said Abby as they cleared up the picnic debris and climbed back aboard the carriage.

The wine had gone to her head, and this, combined with the noonday sun shining down on her bonnet, gave her a lightheaded sensation that quickly turned into drowsiness.

She dozed off, and when she opened her eyes, they had turned onto the shore road at Lynn Beach and were approaching Swampscott. The ocean on their right stretched in a curving line along the road, and for several moments the two said nothing as they enjoyed the smell of the sea and the warm glow of the early afternoon sun. Eventually leaving the ocean on their right, they traveled a bit inland as they approached Marblehead. Once inside the town limits, Abigail sat bolt upright so as to take it all in. On the outskirts of town were modest houses and shops, but once they made the climb up Washington Street past Abbot Hall, Abigail felt as if she had entered another world. Each house seemed older than the next. The big bank building downstreet from Abbot Hall on the left rivaled and surpassed the stately homes of Beacon Hill. And there was another and another.

Soon she saw more tiny houses and many shops. There was a grocery store and there, on the corner, a fruit store. She spied two other churches before they came to the Old North Church. She recognized it right away from her mother's description. Even the fish on the weather vane above the cupola was familiar. She began to get butterflies in her stomach as they turned right onto Franklin Street. But here was another surprise! She had expected a narrow village lane, but here was a wide street with big old houses on either side. Graceful elms and chestnuts scattered mottled shading on the sidewalks.

They pulled in at a large gray house about midway down the street on the left. The doorway had a curved arch over it, and even Abigail's inexperienced eye could recognize the skill of the woodworker who had carved its decorative moldings. Like rows of gapped teeth the dentils adorned the underside of the roof and the doorway. Great white quoins marched down the corners of the house like staggered steps.

What had she expected? Certainly not this. A rambling house on the water or perhaps a rustic farm, but not a formal house which sat plunk on the sidewalk on a broad street, a street urban enough to boast a firehouse and trolley tracks.

When the door opened, she was still off-balance as Belle swept her into her arms.

"Bless your heart, dear. You must be exhausted. Come right in now and have a cool drink. It's hot for May. Come in here; it's cooler in the kitchen. Thomas, let Tad carry the bags; you look tired too."

She bustled them through a large entrance hall, past an ornately carved stairway, and into the large country kitchen. Taking Abigail aside, she whispered, "Run upstairs if you need to, dear. There's a bathroom at the top of the stairs — indoor plumbing, you'll be happy to know. I worked on Maurice for a year to get it, but I notice he doesn't complain, especially when it's ten above zero!" She laughed gaily and Abigail suddenly relaxed.

"I'm fine, Aunt Belle, really, but I would love a cold drink," she said.

"It's root beer. We'll have raspberry shrub later in the summer. Now, tell me all about yourselves. I was so surprised to get your call, Thomas. Delighted, of course, but surprised. Is anything wrong?"

Thomas looked at Abigail before carefully answering her question. "No, not wrong exactly. Perhaps Abby better explain."

Well, that's done it! thought Abigail. No use pretending around Aunt Belle. I can see that she doesn't miss much. "I was seeing too much of a certain young man, and Mama and Papa wanted me away from him," she said bravely.

"Say no more. I should have guessed a pretty girl like you would be bothered with young men. And I'll bet I know who it was! That Madison fellow I met at dinner, right? I told Andrew that that one had big eyes for Abby. Never mind. There I go on where it's none of my business. We'll just tell the others that you needed a vacation. They'll be along soon. Susan and Tad

170

have gone clamming. They wanted you to have chowder on your first night."

"Wasn't that nice of them," said Thomas, pleased. "Don't you think so, Abby?"

"Oh yes, very nice! I've never had clams before," said Abigail, not at all sure whether she wanted them even now.

"Never had clams? Why, you're in for a treat. In a chowder with plenty of cream and butter, there's nothing better. You'll stay for supper, won't you Thomas?" She turned warm eyes on him.

"I'm afraid not, Belle, though I'd really like to. It's been a long time since I had your clam chowder. Maybe next week, if you have room, I could stay over one night. I'll be in Salem on business Thursday and Friday."

"Wonderful. Just come along whenever you can, and we'll keep you overnight. Then you can make sure Abigail is happy here. Here come your cousins. I just heard the back gate slam."

"Well? How'd you make out?" Belle smiled at the mud-streaked faces of Tad and Susan as they started in the kitchen door carrying a tin pail which, from its wet, sandy exterior, appeared to contain the awaited cargo.

"Whoa!" cried Belle. "Why don't you just leave the pail outside? Look, here's your cousin. Wash your hands and come say hello."

Seconds later, Susan and Tad reappeared and, coming over to Abigail, pumped her hand with unfeigned pleasure.

"We're so glad you've come," said Susan, pretty in her summer dress. The hem of her plain blue skirt was mud-soaked, and her dirty boots contained feet little cleaner, but her face was shining as she took Abigail's small hand in her own firm grasp.

"Just wait'll you taste those clams!" said Tad, grinning, "Why there's some as big as quahogs, I swear!"

"What's a quahog?" asked Abigail.

"Now Tad, don't be overwhelming the girl with your new words. She's only just arrived," chastened Susan.

"A quahog's a deep-sea clam. It's bigger, but I don't think it eats as tender as the ones we get close to shore," replied

Tad, ignoring his older sister's reprimand.

"May I go see them?" asked Abigail. She suddenly felt a great need to be accepted by these two friendly cousins of hers.

"Sure!" said Susan. "They're right outside. First we have to soak and scrub them. Then we leave them in cold water for awhile to clean out their insides . . ."

"Some people put corn meal in the water so they'll eat it and fill their stomachs up with clean meal, but we don't bother with that here. I think it makes them mushy. Besides, the stomach has all the taste," added Tad.

". . . then we steam them and eat them hot with butter, or we use the broth to make a chowder. That's what Mum is doing tonight. Some people don't like to eat them whole at first," said Susan.

"Now just hold on a minute. Abigail hasn't even seen her room yet. Tad, bring Abigail's bags up, and Susan, you show her where everything is," said Belle.

Disappointed but obedient, Tad lifted the two large bags with a strength surprising in a twelve-year-old. Abigail was struck by the vigor and energy of this family.

Abigail followed Susan back into the entrance hall. The hall neatly bisected the eighteenth-century house. From the heavy front door to the door which led into the kitchen, the distance was more than thirty feet. The width of ten or eleven feet was open until, leaving the front door behind, you reached the broad central staircase. This staircase was clearly the focus of the house. It led to an upstairs hall from which extended four bedrooms, plus one small one over the front door. This was Tad's room.

Downstairs the rooms were arranged similarly, with two front and two rear rooms. Behind the symmetry of four over four rooms was an addition which on the first floor contained the large kitchen and on the second floor held an additional bedroom and two baths. Over all were attics, a mysterious series of chambers and storage areas which alternately attracted or frightened Tad, depending on whether it was day or night.

"Will you mind being in with me?"

asked Susan. "Mum thought you'd feel better if we shared a room, but if you'd rather not we can arrange it. My room's in the front on the left. I love it because I can see the whole street from my windows. You'd be surprised how much there is to see and hear on a summer night, what with the trolley and the firehouse so near."

"It sounds like Beacon Hill," replied Abigail. "I used to love to look out of the windows at night when no one knew I was watching." This remark suddenly reminded her of Burt, and she fell silent.

Entering the room which would be her home for the summer, she was again surprised. The woodwork was painted a soft gray green, and the walls were solid white, as were the walls in most of the rooms. Beneath her feet were wide pine floorboards in a mellow shade of amber gold. In opposite corners were two beds, each one covered in sprigged flowered muslin which combined the soft green of the woodwork with blue and yellow in gentle harmony. A braided rug lay in front of the fireplace, and the total effect was one of warmth and homespun beauty.

"Do you ever use the fireplace?" asked Abigail.

"Oh, yes. It gets cold at night right up until June, and Daddy hates to turn on the central heat after April. It's one of his economies. Would you like a fire later on tonight?" asked Susan, happy to oblige.

"Not necessarily tonight, but some night I would. The fireplaces seem to fit in more here than in Boston. It's a lovely room; I'd be happy if you'd share it with me," she said.

"Good." She looked shyly at Abigail. "I was afraid you wouldn't like it here. It's so different from what you're used to. Marblehead's not much for formal ways. Just look at my boots if you doubt it," she laughed.

"Andrew will be home soon," said Susan, helping Abigail put her things away in the deep-drawered chest next to her appointed bed.

"Oh," replied Abigail without expression as she carefully took her dresses from the trunk. At the last moment she had been unable to resist packing a few of her prettiest clothes.

"He was the most surprised of all of us when we heard you were coming. Sometimes he doesn't get home in time for supper but he promised specially to be here tonight. He said he wouldn't miss it for the world," said Susan, unaware of the flush which was gradually overtaking her cousin's neck.

I'll just bet he wouldn't! thought Abigail. "How nice of him to put himself out for me," she said aloud.

"Actually he never misses supper when Mum makes chowder," continued Susan. "No one makes clam chowder like Mum. What pretty dresses you have, Abigail — though I don't know when you'll get to wear them. We don't dress up much here."

"I packed some daytime things too, but perhaps you can show me where to buy some plain skirts for walking."

"All right, but now let's get down to those clams. Tad's probably bursting to show off all he knows about seafood. What a fit he would have if we didn't let him have his chance to impress you," said Susan.

The two eighteen-year-olds went down to the kitchen and out into the yard where Tad was carefully washing a four-quart pail of clams.

"Hiya, Abigail," he called. "Just get a look at these. Sue said we should go to Fort Beach for 'em, but I've got a special place out by Gerry Island where there's hundreds at low tide."

"Where's Gerry Island?" asked Abigail.

"Why, I think Tad should take our dear cousin on a guided tour of all his haunts tomorrow." The voice was deep and full, and coming unexpectedly as it did from directly behind Abigail, it made her start and turn around, almost falling over backwards as she came face to chest with the tall form of Andrew Darcy.

The twosome were further jumbled when Tad, running to his brother's side, grabbed him in an idolatrous hug.

"Please forgive me, cousin," said Andrew. "I'm afraid I've startled you."

Yes, and didn't you just love it, fumed Abigail to herself. "Not at all, Cousin Andrew," she replied. "As a matter of fact, I would love to have Tad take me around tomorrow. I can see there's a lot to learn about Marblehead.'' She forced her prettiest smile at the tanned countenance of Andrew.

''There! You see!'' cried Tad. ''And you said she'd be too persnickety to go 'round with me. Well, there's one for you, Andrew!'' He was clearly delighted at the prospect of displaying his city cousin.

Andrew had, at least, the good manners to look embarrassed at his brother's blunder. Abigail said nothing but turned the full force of her eyes onto Andrew's face. For one awkward moment she held his stare, then unaccountably turned away, unable to sustain the contest.

''Well then, it's a date. First thing tomorrow you shall show me your island and all the places I'll need to know about. And,'' she continued, ''I shall try not to be too persnickety.'' Smiling in victory, she returned her attention to the scrubbing of the clams. Andrew laughed suddenly and went into the kitchen.

Supper was an experience. Abigail had not only to adjust to the boisterous company of the entire Darcy family, but she also had to eat clams.

At first, sitting around the large oval table in the kitchen, she found that the informality and cheerful conversation buoyed her spirits. Even the presence of Andrew was less threatening. How could he, after all, offend her in the presence of his own parents. She caught his eye, however, as the steaming bowls of chowder were passed around from hand to hand. Belle had a general kitchen and laundry girl, but did her own cooking whenever possible. Everyone had participated in the preparation of tonight's meal, even Maurice coming home with bottles of chilled beer in honor of the occasion. Andrew had built a fire in the kitchen fireplace — Susan was right, May nights were chilly — and even Abigail had helped by stirring up the johnnycake.

But when Belle lifted her spoon to signal the start of supper, Abigail's nerve failed her. Having seen the slimy clams uncooked, she felt her throat constrict. She was about to begin the first phase of her decline when she caught the critical eyes of Andrew upon her. Naturally he expected her to turn up her nose at the chowder. Well, she would not oblige him. She would eat every mouthful if it choked her. Scooping up a spoonful of the buttery broth, she delicately ladled it onto her tongue, where it sat, obstinately refusing to go down. Once she swallowed, then again. Finally the odd lumps of clam and potato stayed down. Smiling, she said, "Delicious!" The second spoonful was easier, the third almost pleasant, and the fourth delicious. Forsaking her fast, she devoured johnnycake and an additional bowl of chowder. Was that a grudging look of admiration on Andrew's face? Never mind — she had conquered clams; she could certainly handle him!

"Susan," said Belle, "after supper why don't you bring some chowder over to Aunt Gracie. It's been awhile since she's had any." Seeing the question in Abigail's eyes, she explained. "Aunt Gracie lives next door. She's not really our aunt, but all the folks on Franklin Street look after her. She lost her husband about five years ago; up 'til then she was as lively a soul as you've ever seen. Her tongue's still lively, but her legs gave out last year. She has a wheelchair, but we take turns doing her shopping and all."

"If you ask me, Belle," said Maurice, who had been quiet throughout most of the meal, "her tongue's a bit too lively. The things she tells Susan are hardly the same as she'd learn in church."

"Why, Maurice, I'm surprised at you! The Bible is every bit as racy as Aunt Gracie," replied Belle.

"Racy as Gracie! That's a good one, Ma," chimed in Tad. "Racy as Gracie," he repeated.

"Abigail, you may as well learn right now that it's impossible to have a serious discussion in this family," announced Andrew. "Actually," he continued, "if Abigail wants to learn about Marblehead, there's not a better place to begin than with Aunt Gracie. Be prepared for some salty language, of course."

Helping Susan with the dishes at her own insistence, Abigail was amazed at the things she had encountered in the short hours since she had kissed her father good-bye. It had been painful to see him go, but she kept repeating to herself that it was only four days until his return. She gathered that he would come by train next time. The carriage, she realized now, had been a tactful attempt to gradually bridge the gap between her old and new life. She wished he could see her now, doing dishes and eating clams. It was all very new and, yes, exciting.

After the cleanup Susan put the remaining chowder in a lidded dish, and the two girls went out the front door. Turning right, they tapped on the door of the Georgian house next door. Behind the door the squeak of wheels signaled the emergence of Aunt Gracie.

Aunt Gracie was that rarest of souls, a person who thought clearly.

Despite her deep affection for her many friends, she was able to cast sentiment aside and see through to the marrow of a problem. Her often sought advice was usually delivered in the baldest terms, but despite her frankness she had never offended anyone, because her advice was invariably right. So right, in fact, that receiving it, her friends were stunned by the simplicity of it and by the fact that it had been there under their noses all along; it just took Gracie to see it.

Unconventional, she relied on no dogma and mistrusted anyone with a ready-made set of rules and regulations. She was wise enough to realize that each problem was unique to its possessor just as each love is unique to those who share it.

"Ask Gracie" was a Marblehead byword. How she had acquired her wisdom was anyone's guess. She had been married to a Marblehead policeman, and she had two sons who were now almost elderly themselves. The sons lived in Chicago but came back faithfully twice a year, drawn as much by friendship as by maternal love. No, the basic stuff of her life was ordinary, but somehow she had observed more, learned more about human nature along the way than had other people. She could read more into a sidelong glance or a raised eyebrow than most people could find in a book, and she always managed to see things from a new angle.

If you went to her house angry at someone, you might find yourself coming home feeling sympathetic again, but always free of guilt. Gracie didn't believe in guilt. She believed in solutions and actions and sometimes keeping still and waiting. If Gracie thought you were exaggerating your dilemma, or if she knew you were better off on your own, she would likely as not shoo you off. She was, after all, old and had no time to waste on nonessentials.

Fortunately, she considered the happiness of other people essential.

To the unaware, the frowsy figure who opened the door resembled a barely civilized crone. But underneath the frazzled gray hair were bright eyes so dark as to seem almost black, and the grin, if resembling a picket fence, was kindly and sincere. And the heart beneath the gray fisherman's sweater — the heart belonged to dozens of people in Marblehead, people whose lives had crossed this path and been the better for it.

As for Abigail, this apparition was unlike anything she had ever seen before.

"Hello, darling. Step right in. Damned if she's not every whit as pretty as you said! The hair too. Same color as mine used to be before all the trouble. What's that you've got? Don't tell me! Chowder! Smelled it the minute I opened the door. Well, come in, don't stand out there on the street." Wheeling around, she led them into the house.

Abigail had never heard a woman say "damn" before. She was enchanted.

The house was simply furnished but was remarkably clean considering the physical limitations of its owner. After putting the chowder in the kitchen icebox, Susan sat down on a sofa near to Aunt Gracie. Abigail followed suit.

"Well, Miss Cityfolks, what do you think of us?" asked Gracie point-blank. The dark eyes fixed on the green ones.

"I've only been here a few hours, but so far I like it fine." Goodness, these people were direct. Rude they would call it in Boston, but somehow here it seemed right.

Her answer, however, seemed to please Aunt Gracie, who reached over and patted the white hand with her gnarled one.

"Good girl. Just go on liking us and we're bound to like you back. Now you two run along home. I'm ready for bed, and Abigail here looks tired out too; but come back soon and I'll bore you with all the old tales."

"Aunt Gracie, you've never bored anyone in your whole life and you know it, so stop fishing for compliments!" said Susan. She kissed the gray head, and Abigail shook the proffered hand.

The two girls rejoined the Darcys in the right front room. This room, which was one of two front chambers, was obviously where the Darcy family felt comfortable. The other room across the hall was more formal, but this room and the kitchen were the heart and soul of the house.

A fire burned brightly on the hearth. The flames lent a warm glow to the shelves of leatherbound books beside the fireplace. Entering this room, Abigail felt clumsy and snobbish for having thought her cousins uncivilized. Those books had been used time and time again, as the worn edges testified.

The family looked up as the girls came in.

"Sit down for while. I know you're tired, Abigail, but just relax for a bit before bedtime. You'll need a good night's sleep if Tad gets his way," said Belle. "Why, he's planning to walk your feet off tomorrow. I hope you have some good sensible shoes."

Abby burst out laughing. Startled, Maurice looked at her, concern in his voice. "Did we say something wrong?" he asked.

"Heavens, no. It's just that I hoped to leave sensible shoes behind me. Bostonians are in love with ugly, sensible shoes," said Abigail.

"Well, I promise not to tell if you take 'em off soon as we reach the beach," offered Tad.

"Thank you, sir. I can see that you and I are going to get along just fine," she said. She smiled at Tad so brightly that he turned quite pink and had to turn quickly toward the fire to hide his happiness.

"Will you be coming along, Susan?" she asked.

"I'd like to, really I would, but there's this meeting about the band concert, and I have to go."

"Sue's got a fella," said Tad. "He's the new choirmaster at the Old North, and she's got religion all of a sudden."

"Don't be impertinent, young man," said Maurice. "By the way, I believe it's bedtime, so hop upstairs now and don't forget to bring in the flag."

"My window's right over the front door, so I'm in charge of the flag," said Tad proudly. He kissed his mother and Susan good-night and gave his father a hug.

Andrew, who had been silent, rose to his feet and said, "I'll go up with you. Perhaps we can think up a few more things to show Abigail on her walk. C'mon now."

Abigail noticed how Tad slipped his hand into Andrew's as they left the room. All the edges of Andrew's face softened when he spoke to his brother, and as for Tad, he was delighted with Andrew's attention.

The fire made Abigail drowsy. Saying

their own good-nights, Susan and Abby mounted the stairs. Andrew was coming down at the same time, and despite the width of the staircase there was an instant when the three were abreast and Abigail felt his muscular arm against the sleeve of her thin dress. A shudder passed through her for an instant, and then she heard him say, "Good night, cousin; sleep well."

The girls undressed, and Abigail, who had never before shared such intimacies, was relieved to discover how easy it was once you got over the initial self-consciousness.

"Mum says you're to tell us if you need anything personal, like when your courses come," said Susan.

"My courses?" asked Abigail.

"You know — your monthlies. She doesn't want you to be embarrassed to ask for anything at all."

"Tell me about your beau," asked Abigail, who was a bit unnerved at Susan's frank discussion of what had always been to Abigail an unspeakable subject.

"Oh, he's not really my beau, but he's

very nice, and I think he likes me a little. His name is Josiah Hoffman.''

''Why wouldn't he like you?'' asked Abigail, slipping her feet between the cool muslin sheets. ''I should imagine you could have anyone you want,'' she added sincerely.

''Thank you, Abby. You're very nice. Good night,'' said the sleepy Susan.

Abigail had planned to think of many things — clams, homesickness, Aunt Gracie, and why the touch of Andrew's arm had so unnerved her; but she found she could not keep her mind clear. Sleep overtook her before she even had time to notice the full moon sailing outside her window.

CHAPTER 11

She was awakened by a sharp rapping on her door.

"Who is it?" she called, noticing as she spoke that Susan's bed was already made. She got out of bed and started to put on her wrapper.

"It's me, Tad. Just wondered when you were planning on coming down. We already ate." He sounded anxious.

"I'll be right there. Give me five minutes." She hurriedly put on her plainest dress and the omnipresent sturdy shoes and went downstairs.

"I'm sorry I overslept; I hope I haven't inconvenienced you."

"Nonsense!" said Belle, smiling at her rosy niece. "We had every intention of having you sleep in late today. Tad didn't wake you up, did he? He promised to let you wake up by yourself."

"Oh, no. I woke up by myself. It's such a lovely day. The sky looks so much bluer here. I wonder why?" She spoke quickly to divert attention from Tad.

"It's the reflection off the water," said Belle. "Or maybe the water reflects the sky — I never can remember how it goes. In any case, it certainly is blue today. Have some breakfast now and you can pack a picnic for later."

"Oh, good. I love picnics. Haven't had one since last summer."

"Where'd you picnic in Boston?" asked Tad, skeptically. "There's not even any beach," he added.

"But there's the Common and the Public Gardens," said Abigail.

"Don't go thinking that Marblehead is the only place in the world," chided Belle as she laid out hot biscuits and thick slices of bacon cooked through but still chewy, just the way Abby liked it. It occurred to Abigail that her fast was perhaps in a state of indefinite postponement.

She felt like a child as they left by the back door, and surprisingly the feeling was pleasant. The yard was not large;

rather long and narrow, it emptied into a boatyard which in turn edged the sea. Tad, however, bypassed the backyard and led her back out to Franklin Street, where they headed left down the street to the water.

Abigail was not prepared for the scope of the harbor. She discovered that her eye had trouble fixing on one spot, there was so much to see. Rocks, gently lapping waves, and pebbled beach dominated the foreground, while beyond lay the ultramarine blue of the Atlantic. Raising her eyes still higher, she saw a large spit of land directly across from where she stood.

"What's that?" she asked, pointing and shielding her eyes from the sun.

"Marblehead Neck. Used to be no one out there 'cept the Indians. Of course, that was a long time ago. Now there's fancy summer houses and yacht clubs and all. Mum and Dad go visiting there a lot, but me and Andrew don't like it much." He picked up a stone and skipped it neatly across the water.

"Why not? Why don't you like it? The houses seem beautiful from here."

"Andrew says those people don't know

anything about the sea. He says they come traipsing around on their expensive boats wearing their little white trousers, and half the time they don't know their fore from their aft.'' He skipped another stone.

"Will you teach me how to do that?'' she asked.

"Sure. Just take a flat stone; it only has to be flat on one side. Then hold it between your thumb and pointer, like this. That's right. Now just sort of flick it with your wrist so it lands flat side down. That's what makes it skip. I can do 'em so they skip four or five times.'' He demonstrated several times, and finally Abigail knew that glorious moment when she first saw her own stone skip in one bounding hop and then disappear under the waves.

"Good throw, Abby!'' Tad had used her nickname without even being aware of it.

"They call this Oakum Bay now, but it used to be called Lovis Cove. There was a woman murdered here once. She still screeches sometimes,'' he stated, hoping for a good reaction from Abby.

"Who killed her?" asked Abigail in rapt attention.

"I forget. Why don't you ask Aunt Gracie. She knows everything," replied Tad.

"What's the point of land on the left that goes up the hill and sticks out?" asked Abigail.

"That's Fort Sewall."

"Can we go up there?" asked Abby. Goodness, she was asking so many questions! But Tad didn't seem to mind.

They went back up to the street, which Tad identified as Front Street, and started the gradual climb to Fort Sewall. The fort was not visible until they reached the plateau at the top. In the center of this two-tiered flat expanse was a pitlike recess. Tad ran down the slope into this basin and then scampered up the other side. It was like going down into a large, shallow sink. When Abigail, having followed Tad's lead, had gone down one side and up the other, she came face to face with a spectacular panorama. In all directions from left to right was the sea. Ahead to her right lay the harbor, a horseshoe clearly defined by the neck, the downtown, and a narrow strip of land connecting the two. To her left the jagged coast stretched northward until the last land masses dissolved into lavender mist.

"That's Gloucester and Cape Ann," said Tad pointing to the left. "And you can see all the way to Boston on your right."

Sitting down on a jutting rock, Abby tried to take it all in. Below her, fishing boats dotted the harbor along with a few sailboats at mooring. Straining her eyes, she tried to identify the Boston coast. How remote it looked, like some distant land! Had she really come so far away? Surf crashed on the rocks below, sending currents of salt air onto her face. Overhead the gulls made looping circles as they soared in apparent suspension through the cloudless sky. She and Tad were alone on the hill.

"By next week, the harbor will be full. This first weekend in June is when most people get their pleasure boats in. 'Course the fishing boats are in all winter. See those three red ones over there? Those're

Andrew's. He's got more, but they're in Little Harbor 'round the corner. C'mon, I'll show you."

He pulled her to her feet and took her up another incline until they stood at the northernmost point of the park. Below them was a cove in which were two islands.

"That bigger one's Orne and the little one's Gerry. You can walk over to Orne at low tide in the summer if you don't mind getting wet. Gerry's not really an island except at high tide. Over there are Andrew's other boats. He's got six. One's in dock for repairs. They're all red. He says he likes to spot 'em easy." Abigail knew that there must be a sensible reason for the flamboyant color; Andrew did not strike her as a person who cared much for appearances.

"Let's go down in the pit again so you can see the old barracks where the troops stayed underground. It's not safe to go in, but we can get a look. They were in the pit so's the British couldn't see 'em."

"You're an excellent tour guide, Tad," said Abigail. "I had no idea there was so much to see."

"Nobody does. Most folks you could knock over with a feather first time I bring 'em up here. They've never seen anything like it." He was justifiably proud.

After admiring the underground barracks (which Abigail found dank and frightening) they descended from the fort. Abigail was reluctant to leave but Tad insisted. "It's only a hop from the house. You can come here twenty times a day if you like but there's more I want to show you before we finish, and Mum said to be back by three. That's when Susan gets back from her meeting. Just wait'll you see her Josiah. He plays the organ in church, and they've put him in charge of the band concert next week. Poor fella. When he hears Susan sing, he's gonna realize he made a pretty bad mistake. Why, she sings so bad that once when I was little, I was feeding the chickadees some sunflower seeds, and out she comes, just humming mind you, and they all flew off so fast it'd make your head spin! I told her that she better keep her trap shut around Josiah if she aims to land him."

"I'm sure Josiah has noticed all the other nice things about her," said Abigail, trying to keep a straight face.

"Oh, sure. She's a pretty good kid when she's not singing." And, having reached Front Street again, he led her between two fisherman's cottages into a large boatyard, the same one which abutted the Darcy's backyard. At scattered intervals were stacked lobster pots and boats standing up on wooden frames. "Those are called cradles," said Tad when Abigail questioned him. He went on describing the important points that she must learn about sailboats.

Abigail was enjoying this tutelage, even though it was peculiar to be learning so much from someone six years her junior. She wondered what it must be like to grow up in this town. Tad seemed so experienced, so sure of himself. If he lived in Boston he would probably be miserable. Cobblestones are no place for bare feet, and one could hardly skip stones in the Public Garden. She thought of her beloved mallards and had to admit that compared to the winged grace of the gulls they were earthbound and restricted. And how small her pond seemed when one thought of the huge Atlantic. Her confidence in her sophistication was slipping, but somehow, running through the boatyard down to the shores of the Little Harbor, she didn't seem to mind. That she had been ripe for a taste of freedom never occurred to her. She was more than willing to credit the sunshine for her good humor.

"This here's Little Harbor," said Tad indicating a smaller version of the harbor she had seen from Fort Sewall. "And that building on the beach is the gashouse."

It was a cove but not as enclosed as Abigail had expected a cove to be. Except for the docks by the boatyard and the gashouse, the Little Harbor was semicircled with a graduated rocky beach. Already, small children under the scrutiny of their guardians were digging in the patches of sand which dappled the expanse. During the hour since their excursion began, the tide had been steadily ebbing, and now it could be seen that Gerry Island was joined to the beach by a narrow umbilicus of rocks and shells.

"C'mon!" cried Tad as his feet hit the flattened beach. "Let's take off our shoes."

Seeing the incredible amount of crushed shell and pebbles which was stretched out before her, Abigail was reluctant to expose her city feet to the elements; but hating to disappoint Tad, she bent over and removed her already damp shoes. Gingerly placing her small foot on a sandy patch, she felt the cool water seeping under her toes as the weight of her foot turned the apparently solid sand into a gelatinous and shifting mass. Looking back at her footprints, she saw each one fill up with water and begin to dissolve.

They walked the entire length of the little harbor beach, stopping every few steps so that Tad might identify the dozens of marine specimens that lay scattered underfoot. Periwinkles, mussels, clams, crabs, and all manner of seaweed lay in fascinating profusion.

"Look! Out there about a hundred yards off Gerry — see that red boat? That's Andrew. He said he'd be around at noontime to have lunch with us. C'mon. Let's wave him in!''

Tad dropped the picnic basket and took off at a run down to the water's edge, where he waved his arms frantically until he saw the bow of the red boat turn beachward. Only then did he run back to where Abigail had retrieved the basket. Following his lead, Abigail went toward the water. Within minutes the red boat had stopped, and a white rowboat was being rowed strongly to where they stood.

''Little Harbor's too shallow to bring in the big boat,'' explained Tad.

Taken aback by this sudden turn of events, Abigail was confused and then angry to have her delightful walk spoiled by the disquieting company of Andrew Darcy.

Pulling the rowboat on shore, Andrew deftly alighted and strode through the shallow water to Tad. He lifted him high in the air and swung him into the boat. Turning to Abigail, he put two strong arms under hers and lifted her up as easily as if she were a cloud. As his hands touched her, she made a resisting movement with her foot and felt a stab of pain biting her toe. Controlling her urge to cry out in protest, she was suddenly beside Tad, and soon the three were headed toward Orne Island.

Andrew's sleeves were rolled up to reveal a massive strength of sinew and muscle which was constantly in motion as he rowed with clean, rhythmic strokes. Tad was chattering away merrily, describing what they had done on the walk and Andrew was supplying the necessary response to each of his brother's happily garbled sentences. Still, not one word had he said to Abigail until he finally caught her evasive eye and boldly stated, "You've cut yourself."

Looking down at her foot, Abby was horrified to see red blood seeping from her toe, making a pink pool of the water which had collected in the bottom of the rowboat.

"Oh, I'm sorry! There's blood all over your boat," she cried.

"Not so much. It just looks that way when it's mixed with water. Like when a baby cuts his lip," said Andrew, allowing his eye to rest comfortably on the expanse of calf and ankle which was so prettily exposed by the hitching up of her skirts earlier on the beach.

They were at the sandy shore of Orne Island now. Once again Andrew lifted them out to safety. This time Abigail stiffened visibly as he swept her in his arms and carried her to a log, where he deposited her.

"Now, let's have a look at that foot. See? It's just a slice, maybe from a razor clam."

"What's a razor clam?" she asked, finding her tongue now that he had released her foot from his calloused hand.

"Go fetch a razor shell for the lady!" he ordered Tad, who scampered off to the lapping shore of the island.

This was the first time that Abigail had been left alone with Andrew. She was suddenly aware of her tangled hair, her bare legs, and the drabness of her dress. Looking up, she met his eyes. He was looking at her with a puzzled stare.

"Tad's a good boy," he said.

"I know," she replied.

"He's very proud of Marblehead," said Andrew with the barest trace of a defensive edge in his voice.

"He ought to be. It's very beautiful," she said. Was this really the witty Abigail Curtis spouting these hideous banalities? Somehow, her wit failed her in the presence of this strange man.

"That cut will be practically healed by tomorrow. The salt water mends things fast."

"You love the ocean, don't you?" she said.

"Yes, I do. Maybe someday I'll tell you why."

He seemed oddly shy, and they were both relieved when Tad returned brandishing a long white shell that looked exactly like a man's razor.

"No need to ask what that is. It looks just like my father's own razor. Do you think that's what I stepped on? If so, I'm lucky to have my toe at all. May I see it?" she asked.

"Sure," said Tad. "But be careful. Andrew says the Indians really used to use 'em for razors."

"Is that so?" she asked Andrew, doubtful.

"So I'm told," he answered. "Say! I'm hungry. What's in the basket?"

They picnicked on the previous night's johnnycake and jam. Also there was soft pot cheese and pink slices of ham. As usual Abigail ate her share.

"I've never eaten so much in my life as I have here in Marblehead," she exclaimed.

"It's the sea air. But you won't get fat," said Tad, "because the salt air gives you lots of pep. The one takes care of the other. Say, can we go on the boat?"

"If I remember correctly," said Andrew, "your cousin has very little use for fishing boats."

Damn him! thought Abigail. Just when I was beginning to think he was human. "Not at all!" she said strongly. "I'd love to see your boat."

"We'd better get going then, because I've got work to do. I'm expecting Johnny Doliber in later on with a good catch, and there's the three yacht clubs all hungry for flounder, as well as the shore dinner crowd at Adams's to feed."

"That's the restaurant near the beach on Front Street," explained Tad. "They serve up a great shore dinner. Mum and Dad take us there sometimes."

This time, after Andrew had hoisted Tad aboard the rowboat and reached for Abigail, she protested.

"I can wade in, thank you. After all, you said salt water was good for my cut." She felt smug.

Getting into the rowboat while carrying a picnic basket and shoes was not easy. But even when Abigail had attempted to jump over the side three times, Andrew made no move to help her. Finally, tossing the shoes inside and swinging the basket onto the seat, she managed to get in the boat, not without a considerable loss of dignity. Andrew, in the meantime, had assumed that look of supercilious amusement that she always found so maddening.

The fishing boat was cleaner than she had expected. The deck had been washed down, and even the bait containers were relatively inoffensive, perhaps because the threesome was standing upwind. Nets were neatly wound, and altogether the boat gave credence to the term "shipshape."

Without ceremony Andrew gave them a quick tour of the vessel and then rowed Abigail and Tad to Gerry Island. The connecting sandbar was clearly visible now, so they would be able to walk back home without danger. He gave a mock salute and rowed away.

"Let's walk out to the point. There's a place where all the seagulls come to lay eggs and die," said Tad.

"Do you mean they die when they lay eggs?" asked Abigail. Tad looked at her critically.

"Of course not!" he said. "I mean they come here to lay eggs, and then later, when it's time, they come back to die."

"How do they know it's time?"

"They just do. Wait and see. You'll see old and wounded birds out here just waiting around to die."

They walked the breadth and length of the small island, seeing the wildflowers and tall grass as well as an abandoned shack and the seagulls' home. The last sight impressed Abigail in a new way. Here, surrounded by the sea and its creations, she was beginning to sense the order and strength of the world she was in. It was a world of vast space and tiny organisms. It was a world where birth and death were as inevitable as the changing of the tide.

"Now I'm gonna show you someplace I've never shown anybody, but you've got to promise not to tell!" said Tad, his dark eyes bright under the afternoon sun. He led her to the eastern cliff of the island; then, scrambling over the edge, he disappeared from view.

Minutes later when he had not reappeared, Abigail became alarmed, but just as she cried out "Tad!" his head suddenly popped up beside her.

"Where were you?" she cried. "I was frightened!"

"C'mere," he laughed. He helped her down the cliff until they saw a dark hole in the rock which was almost completely concealed by an overhanging growth of grass.

"See? You go in here and then you can

take the tunnel up again. It's a big crack in the rock, but I can fit through it. Great, huh?''

Abigail peered into the recess which had been created eons ago by the massive overturning of rock into coastal cliffs and ledge. Tad slid in carefully through an opening barely wide enough for his shoulders. He had to inch along almost on his back for the distance of a few feet, and then the crevice widened. Once inside, there was a flat place where a twelve-year-old boy could sit, knees drawn up, in relative comfort. From outside he was almost invisible, especially since several low-growing sumac trees hung swaying across the opening.

"It doesn't seem too safe, if you ask me," replied Abigail, peering into the recess.

"Sure it is! I sit there for hours when I don't want to be with anybody. But you've got to promise you won't tell!"

"I promise," said Abigail, flattered that Tad had shared this secret with her. Andrew was right. For once they were in accord. Tad was a nice boy.

"Guess we'd better get back. It's coming on to three. Mum'll skin me if I wear you all out," he said.

"I'm fresh as a daisy, sir," she insisted, but by the time they had gone through the boatyard and rejoined Franklin Street at the opposite end from where they had started, she was feeling heavy-legged and drowsy. She was so tired that she didn't even notice the admiring glances of the firemen who sat tipped back on their chairs in front of the firehouse.

Thomas Curtis looked, unseeing, out of the train window which was carrying him again to Marblehead. He was filled with a strange excitement at the prospect of rejoining the Darcy household. He knew that Maurice would be out of town on a buying trip. Ever since he had made the transition from importer to merchant, Maurice had traveled frequently.

Thomas wondered if Belle ever got lonely. The thought was provocative. He had sensed a vulnerability in his wife's cousin on the evening when he had said good-bye to Abigail. Even the cousinly embrace between Belle and Thomas had seemed more intimate than those shared previously in Boston.

Oh, damn. There he was letting his imagination run away with him again. Just because his needs were getting away from him was no excuse for projecting them onto Belle. But she was a fine woman to be with, and he refused to feel guilty for the pleasant anticipation inside him when he imagined the long summer evening ahead.

And in her kitchen, Belle brought out the best china and put new bayberry candles in the chandelier. Maurice would scoff at the waste, but she found herself defiant. What he didn't know wouldn't hurt him. She had been a happy woman until her dinner visit with Henrietta and Thomas. Seeing Henrietta perfect and serene in her pristine surroundings made Belle realize how much her own life had changed. Cooking and sewing had roughened the once white hands, and there were streaks of gray in the blond hair. Her waist was a good three inches bigger around than when she was a girl, and although Maurice seemed to like her full figure, she was sure Henrietta disapproved of her ten extra pounds. She felt an unreasonable desire to be young and beautiful for Thomas Curtis, and she was deeply ashamed of her feelings. Even as she arranged the flowers on the table, she felt foolish and old.

CHAPTER 12

It was the third of July, and the Darcy family was in an uproar. In the kitchen, Belle was preparing an elaborate picnic supper to be brought to the band concert that evening. Every few minutes she would ask Susan to kindly move her papers so that she could place a new bowl or container on the golden pine table.

"Mother!" cried Susan. "How will I ever get these songbooks in order if I have to keep moving my papers?"

"Why don't you work in the dining room, dear?" asked Belle a shade testily.

"It's too dark. Oh, Mama, do you think everyone will like my song? I've never led a singing group before."

"Now, Susan, Josiah wouldn't have asked you to write the song in the first place if he didn't trust you to do it right."

"But he's never heard us rehearse. He

keeps saying he wants to be surprised."

Out in the backyard Tad, hearing his sister's voice through the open window, said to Abigail, "He'll be surprised all right. As soon as she opens her mouth to sing, Crocker Park will clear out as fast as in a nor'easter!" He guffawed merrily.

"Shush now! She'll hear you. Besides, I've heard the words to her song, and they are perfectly lovely!" responded Abigail, who sat beside Tad on a rough woolen blanket which they had stretched on the grass. The two cousins were working industriously, cutting and stitching something out of bright red sailcloth.

"How are you going to do the feelers?" she asked.

"With wire," answered Tad. "My head will come out between the two big claws. Do ya think we should make all the little legs? It seems like a lotta work to me!"

"Of course we must! Your lobster is going to be the best costume in the Horribles Parade if it takes us all day," said Abigail, who had at last found an outlet worthy of her fancy sewing lessons. Mrs. Byors would have been proud of the neat little stitches.

Independence Day was the highlight of any year in Marblehead. On this night before the Fourth there would be a band concert at Crocker Park featuring a young ladies' chorale which would, as a finale before the intermission, sing a song honoring Marblehead with words by Miss Susan Darcy and music by Mr. Josiah Hoffman. The same Mr. Hoffman had not yet heard the words but had rehearsed the band well with regard to the music. Miss Susan Darcy had also held rehearsals of her small group of musical maidens, Abigail included, but was concerned about the final performance. Andrew had made her a fine baton from the slat of a lobster pot, and Belle had starched her daughter's prettiest blue dress until it stood up by itself in the bedroom upstairs.

"Y'know, Abby," continued Tad, "I'm not just kidding. Old Josiah really loves music. Haven't you noticed at church how he sorta rolls his eyes up when the choir sings? Sorta like he expected to see angels coming down or something. When he hears Susan sing, it's gonna be the end! I know he likes her a lot — I mean he's around often enough — but so far she's never had to sing before, I guess 'cause she's always playing the piano for him." He looked serious. "It'd be different if she just didn't sing so hot, but she really murders music. She even whistles out of tune! I dunno what's going to happen, but I'm gonna make myself scarce during her song."

"But surely if she knows her singing's bad she'll just sing quietly?" said Abigail.

"That's just it! She doesn't know her singing's bad. She sings at the top of her lungs once she gets going."

"Well, at rehearsals she hasn't been too bad. She does have trouble staying on key, but with everyone else singing we'll carry her along."

"I sure hope so, but it's a mystery to me that somebody who looks so good can sing so bad!"

The costume was taking shape. Each Fourth of July morning found the children of the town gathered together for a costume parade. The idea was to be unique or clever or patriotic. Winners were chosen in many categories, and the participants competed vigorously. Tad, when queried, was unsure as to the origin of the Horribles Parade, but in 1906 it was already a tradition.

Maurice was in charge of the dispensation of liquor, and even Andrew had agreed to lead a fleet of brightly lighted fishing boats around the harbor during the intermission of the band concert.

What delighted Abigail most, however, was that her father and mother were expected on the afternoon train. Henrietta had not left Beacon Hill since her daughter's departure. Abigail was happy to have her mother come for many reasons. During the month that she had been in Marblehead, many things had changed. At first she had been ecstatic whenever her father arrived, but recently she felt he was coming more and more frequently. This fact had meant nothing to her, but last week she had suddenly realized that her father was most often here when Maurice was away overnight on business. This puzzled her further because she knew that the two men got along well together. It was only when she had caught a certain look between Belle and Thomas that the situation became clear. She was sure that nothing amiss had occurred yet, but the thought of the two months ahead and the repeated exposure of Thomas to Belle alarmed her. She adored Cousin Belle, but her loyalty to her mother was infinitely greater. She trusted Belle to keep things under control, but she sensed a recklessness, a loosening of the moral collar, whenever her father appeared. All in all, it was high time Henrietta came to claim what was hers.

By the time Maurice rode to the Pleasant Street Depot, the household had assumed a veneer of normalcy. Abigail and Susan had washed their hair and were drying it in the sun. The lobster was completed and hung majestically in the large front hall where Tad had insisted it should be displayed until morning. The arrival of the Curtises was celebrated with hugs and kisses. Abigail was so full of things to tell her mother that she was almost incoherent.

"Goodness, but you look healthy. Perhaps a bit too much sun — you must watch out for freckles, dear," said Henrietta, but her joy on seeing Abigail erased any note of disapproval. She and Abigail went to the guest room, where Abigail talked about the concert, Josiah Hoffman, chowder, lobsters, Fort Sewall, Little Harbor and Stanford White.

Abigail had read an absolutely fascinating headline in the Salem paper which Maurice brought home each evening. The famous architect Stanford White had been shot dead as a doornail by the wealthy eccentric Harry K. Thaw. It was the circumstances which Abigail found so exciting. Poor Mr. White had been done in while standing in the elegance of the roof garden of Madison Square Garden in New York, an interesting aside because Stanford White had designed his place of death.

"What a pity about Mr. White!" exclaimed Abigail cheerfully. "And just because he had Mr. Thaw's wife as a mistress once!"

"Abigail!" cried Henrietta, horrified.

"Well, he did! It's all right there in the paper," continued Abigail. "Did you ever meet the Thaws? They say here her maiden name was Evelyn Nesbit and that she's ever so beautiful. That must be why he shot him three times. And he was all dressed up in a straw hat, too!"

"Who? Mr. White?" asked Henrietta despite herself.

"No, Mr. Thaw," said Abigail. "Evelyn — I mean Mrs. Thaw — fainted. It says he was known to be cruel to her. I wonder if he beat her?"

"That will be quite enough, Abigail," said Henrietta. "Such tales are hardly fit for young ears." Her look affirmed her attitude.

"Oh, all right, Mummy," sighed Abigail, and she wisely changed the subject to Aunt Gracie.

The distance between herself and her mother baffled her. She adored her mother and was secure in the conviction that her mother returned her love, but there had always been a constraint which interfered like a folding screen whenever they were alone. She often felt as if she were mentally peering around corners for a glimpse of the real Henrietta.

Henrietta, on the other hand, was a bit in awe of her daughter. The poise which Abigail seemed to have been born with had been a learned and practiced commodity for her mother. Henrietta had early resolved to frustrate as little as possible her daughter's natural enthusiasm, but there were times when caution made her fear for her daughter's happiness.

Above all, she loved Abigail with that intensity shared only by opposites. It was in the occasional moment when the two temperaments stood reaching out to each other from opposite poles that they both felt unprepared and awkward, as if they had just missed by a hair's breadth the one word which would have bridged the gap. At such times, small talk and gossip covered the silence and made them feel adequate.

The subject of Gracie was hardly small talk, but a more positive topic could scarcely be imagined. Abby and Aunt Gracie had become fast friends. From

Gracie she had learned that the sound of the screeching woman killed by pirates long ago signaled an impending disaster in the town, and from her she had also learned the old Marblehead curse words "Whip!" and "To Hell I pitch it!" This last imprecation was usually shortened to "Pitch it!" It delighted Abby to think that she could use these expressions in Boston and nobody would even know that she was swearing. In Marblehead, however, they were considered pretty strong language, something no lady would ever use, at least not in public.

Six o'clock found the entire Darcy-Curtis entourage walking in pairs down Front Street toward Crocker Park. Thomas Curtis and Maurice Darcy led the procession, carrying between them a picnic hamper of such enormous proportions that it seemed to contain enough dinner for half the town. Behind the two men were Belle and Henrietta, chatting away gaily about everything from Abigail to the latest New York fashions.

Bringing up the rear were Abigail, Tad,

and Susan. Tad was obliged to give way to the starched skirts of the girls' dresses as they made their way through the narrow harbor front street. All along the way were neatly painted eighteenth-century houses, and no matter how small each owner's property might be, each one had found a way to squeeze in a few flowers. When one considered that many a front yard consisted of graduated ledge, this was no mean feat. Tucked into crevices no wider than a woman's hand were tiny buds and blossoms. The overall effect was so perfect as to be almost artificial if one didn't know that underneath this blatant display of beauty was old-fashioned New England labor and common sense. If the hardworking people of Marblehead chose to indulge their love of hollyhocks and gardens, who had any right to criticize? After all, from the Revolution right up to the recent Spanish American War, Marbleheaders had been the first to rush to the aid of their country. It was their courage that had manned the first boats of the navy, their muscle that had carried Washington across the Delaware, their rectitude that had fought the evil of slavery, and their stoic pride which had endured the losses that had inevitably followed each new commitment.

Abigail was beginning to recognize the tough and caring nature of this town, and she hoped that she could become, perhaps, more like those people than she had previously imagined possible.

Andrew was conspicuously absent from the family party; he had gone out into his boat to prepare for the harbor procession. Abigail was curiously unhappy about his absence. Strangely enough, it seemed suddenly very important that he should see her in her white sundress with her hair up on her head and tied with a silver grosgrain ribbon generously brought from Boston by Henrietta. She was beginning to feel vaguely annoyed when he treated her in sisterly fashion. After all, she wasn't even a first cousin. He was rarely home in the evenings, and when he was, he paid her precisely the required amount of cousinly attention and not a whit more. He seemed to regard herself, Susan, and Tad as members of some childish group from which he was now removed. She knew he worked very hard, but surely he must have some fun. Once she had managed to ask Susan about his romantic life. They had been curled up in their beds, and from Josiah the talk had gone around to other young men in their twenties who might be considered good catches. Abigail had casually tossed in Andrew's name.

"Andrew? Why he's the best catch of all, of course. But he's too involved in his business to have any time for girls. Besides he thinks my friends are too frivolous. He's determined to be the best shoreman around."

"What's a shoreman exactly?"

"He's someone who arranges to market fish, from drying to shipping. He's really a fish merchant, but Andrew still goes out to sea for awhile every day just to keep an eye on that part of it, too. He's really doing too much, both catching and merchandising fish, but that's the way he's always been. You know, the man who built this house was a shoreman. His name was Joseph Homan. He started out way

back around 1740 setting up fish flakes —
that's what they called the racks they used
for drying the fish. He used to work out
of Fort Beach. In fact, they used to call
that stretch of beach on the Little Harbor
side of Fort Sewall Homan's Beach.
Anyway, he did so well that he eventually
owned three sailing boats and became a
wealthy merchant and finally built this
house somewhere between 1748 and 1764.
Gracie used to tell Andrew all the stories
about Joseph Homan and how he made
his fortune from the sea. I guess Andrew
decided right then and there that that's
what he wanted to do. It's kind of nice in
a way. It brings the house full circle, do
you understand?''

"I think so," Abigail had replied, and
then, not daring to persist in her questions
about Andrew for fear that Susan might
become suspicious, she had changed the
subject.

Now, approaching the Town Landing,
she found herself scanning the cluster of
boats for the one bright red one she
wanted to see. But amidst the decorated
masses of pleasure and commercial boats,

it was difficult to spot Andrew's.

"There he is!" cried Tad, jumping up and down in his zeal to see through the already crowded street. "Right in front of the Corinthian."

Abigail knew the town well enough to know that this meant the Corinthian Yacht Club.

"Yes, I see him now. Will he be joining us?"

Her heart gave a funny skip as Tad replied. "Just for supper. Then he's got to parade the boat, but maybe after that he'll take us out. It's terrific to see the whole show from the water."

"Perhaps he will," said Abigail, but inside she felt that he would not. Well, what did she care anyway? He was just an ordinary fisherman whose opinion of himself matched his physical size. To hell I pitch him! she thought, then giggled at her own temerity.

Crocker Park was near the southern end of Front Street overlooking the harbor. When the Franklin Street group arrived, they were greeted by the growing crowd of picnickers who had in many cases already spread out blankets and begun to feast. A bandstand had been erected near the edge of the cliff which dropped down to the ocean. Beside this was the stairway cut into the rocks which led to the floating dock below. Tied to this dock was Andrew's boat, the *Joseph Homan.* He had made good time in order to secure a spot next to the small float. Tad ran to greet him as he mounted the steps. When the two were next to the bandstand, Andrew laughed. "The band had better not drink too much town liquor tonight. One extra note of enthusiasm is going to land them in the drink."

"Can I come out with you during Susan's song?" begged Tad.

"That'd hurt her feelings, Taddie. You'd better stay up here, but I promise I'll come in right after the intermission and get you."

"Promise?"

"Promise! Now let's eat. I'm starved!"

The eight diners began to open baskets and unlid bowls while corks popped out of the champagne bottles which Thomas had brought in honor of the occasion.

Cold chicken, ham salad, homemade rolls, sweet butter, cold vegetables, and blueberry pie all vanished as glass after glass of bubbly wine circulated freely. The night was hot, but a breeze off the ocean kept the group comfortable and also banished the flies.

"Who's got the Joe Froggers?" said Andrew, the last to finish eating.

"They're here in the basket. Abigail made them, but I thought I'd save them for intermission," replied Belle.

"Not on your life!" cried Andrew. "I'll be in the boat then; can't wait. Hand 'em over." And the large molasses snaps were handed out and accepted even by those who minutes before had declared themselves unable to eat another bite.

"Delicious, darling," said Henrietta fondly, and the others joined in declaring the cookies first-rate.

"Guess there's hope for you yet." said Andrew. "Well, I'd best get back to the boat. Some jackass, excuse me, ladies, some fool wants us to crisscross in the middle of the harbor. Most of these fellows can hardly sail a straight line let alone cross over safely. There's likely to be hulls smashed all over the place, but it's no skin off my teeth. Got to give the rich folks a fine show!"

He ambled off, and Abigail stole a quick glance at her mother to see what her reaction was to this straightforward fellow. Surprisingly her mother wore an amused expression. Come to think of it, her mother had seemed different all day. It must be the town, thought Abby. Why, I'm as different as can be since I got here. My hair's a mess half the time, my good clothes just hang in the closet, and my best friends are a twelve-year-old boy, a toothless old woman, and a girl who's madly in love with a choirmaster. She laughed out loud, and when her father turned quickly to see the joke, he saw instead a contented young beauty whose tan made her look ever so slightly like a gypsy. The effect was startling but attractive.

Then her father's glance wandered to Belle, who was flushed with champagne and high spirits. Even with Henrietta beside him he felt his pulse quicken when he looked at Belle. And she was feeling it too; he was certain of that. He knew he was behaving badly to Henrietta, to Maurice, and mostly to Belle herself, but the warm nights and the cool Henrietta were a devastating combination for a middle-aged man.

At eight o'clock they were joined by Josiah Hoffman, a slight young man with fair hair and a serious expression.

"Please excuse me, Mr. and Mrs. Darcy, but I think it's time for Susan to assemble her group for the song."

"Oh, dear, I don't think I can go through with it," said Susan. Her voice trembled charmingly.

"Of course you can. Now let's go, and it will all be over in ten minutes," replied Josiah, helping Susan to her feet.

"Good luck!" cried the parents as Abigail and Susan went toward the bandstand gathering girls like daisies along their way. Abigail took her position in the front row. She felt uncomfortable standing in the front row, but her height and Susan's need for moral support required it.

The local girls had been kind to Abigail despite her city ways, perhaps because of their deep affection for Susan. Abby, in turn, had gone out of her way to be inconspicuous, even memorizing in advance the names of all their respective swains so that she might avoid the appearance of flirting with any of them. The very fact that she seemed oddly boy-shy made them trust her.

As for the young men in town, they had wasted no time in learning all they could about this new girl. Her red hair, her wonderful shape, and every detail of her manner had been common knowledge before she had been in Marblehead twenty-four hours. They had pumped Tad, a willing well, about her habits and manner of speech.

"Aw c'mon, she's a girl, that's all," he had replied. "Of course, she does have the greenest eyes I ever saw. Sometimes they look the color of sea lettuce, and then they turn as dark green as a lobster's tail. And you oughta see the clothes in her closet. Fifteen dresses if there's one. Not that she's stuck up, mind you! Why, she'd as soon go barefoot as I would."

The older boys would feign boredom, but they exchanged knowing looks; and Tad, knowing full well that he had the upper hand, would casually saunter off, calling behind him. "So long, fellas! Got to work on my costume with Abby." Many an infatuated twenty-year-old would have traded places with a twelve-year-old that summer. But like most pretty girls, Abigail frightened them. Not a one dared to call on her; in fact, they were so shy in her presence that Abigail began to wonder if she had lost her touch.

She had this sensation again as she scanned the faces in front of her. Each male would stare at her until she met his gaze, then hurriedly look away. Behind the group the band struck a chord, then fell silent, as the group was to sing the first verse a cappella. Leafing nervously through the pages of the small booklet containing the words of the song, Abigail saw that she was missing the last page. Perhaps Susan had decided to omit the last stanza. What a shame, thought Abigail. The last verse is the best one!

Susan raised her baton and started the song. The sound of seventeen young voices in the summer night was sweet music indeed, and as they recounted in song the heroism of Marbleheaders past, the crowd smiled in approbation. At the end of six stanzas the girls came to the last page of the booklet and, exchanging bewildered looks, faltered to a close. Susan, however, not realizing the omission of the final page, was just working up for a grand finale. Loudly she burst into the verse, unaware that she was singing alone until the shrill scream of her own discordant voice startled her back to reality. Horrified, she waved her baton frantically until Abigail and a few others, recognizing the mistake, joined in for a lame finish. Red with shame, Susan ran from the bandstand into the shrubbery while the group disbanded, some giggling, others abashed. Abigail followed Susan into the darkness and found her sitting on a rock sobbing, her blond head on her crossed arms.

"Don't cry, Susan. Please! Can't you hear the applause? They loved your song.

So what if you sang the end alone? They probably thought it was supposed to be that way.''

No response. Then the figure of Josiah Hoffman came into the thicket and sat down beside the tearful girl.

''Go away,'' sobbed Susan.

''No, I won't,'' said Josiah firmly. ''Now, what's the matter here?'' he asked, putting his arm around her shoulder.

''You heard! I ruined the song with my hideous voice and now you won't ever like me again and I could die!'' wailed Susan, still from under crossed arms.

''Susan! Sit up now and be still. I want to talk to you,'' said Josiah. Abigail was fascinated by the command in his voice. She knew she should leave the two alone, but she was curious to learn how this new Josiah would handle the distraught Susan.

''First of all, it's clear that you're embarrassed by finding yourself singing alone. It's also clear that you are no nightingale. Now don't start crying again. Here, take my handkerchief. Now blow your nose.'' Susan snuffled halfheartedly. ''That's better.'' Josiah paused as he put his handkerchief back into the rear pocket of his summer suit.

"Do you know why I love you? Don't look surprised. Surely you know that I've come to care for you. It's because you are so lovely and kind and sympathetic and a hundred other good things. I don't care at all if you can sing. After all, a person who can play the piano and write poetry can hardly be considered lacking in talent. Susan, people don't fall in love with talents or God-given gifts. It's the quality of the person that counts. Tell me now, does it bother you that I'm short and thin and wear glasses?"

A startled shaking of the head from Susan. "It might, you know; all the men in your family are so tall and hardy. But it never occurred to me to worry about it. I might have with another girl, but not with you, because I knew you would look deeper than the others. Do you have so low an opinion of me as to think I could ever lose affection for you over anything as unimportant as a singing voice?"

"I guess not," said Susan.

"Of course not," replied Josiah. He

tipped her face upward and looked at her. Abigail withdrew and, turning around, bumped into Andrew.

"Goodness, Abigail! We do have a way of bumping into each other. Where's Susan? Mother and Dad are looking all over for her. What happened, anyway?" said Andrew, tall in the darkness.

"Sssh! Let's get away from here and I'll tell you all about it," whispered Abigail.

"I promised Tad a turn around the harbor. Want to join us?"

"All right. I'll go tell my folks and yours."

They went back to the family group, and Abby reassured Belle and Maurice that Susan was fine — better, in fact, than ever before in her life.

"I'm sorry to be such a poor sport, but I'm exhausted," said Henrietta. "Would you all mind terribly if I went home? The train ride seems to have tired me out."

"I'll walk you back," said Thomas.

"No, no! The concert's not over yet. I'll walk Henrietta back, and you stay and enjoy the show. I've seen it all before," said Maurice. "Please, I insist."

So Tad, Abigail, and Andrew went down the stone steps and climbed aboard the *Joseph Homan,* and Henrietta and Maurice set off for home, the almost empty picnic basket between them.

CHAPTER 13

Once aboard the boat, Tad found a cozy spot amidst the life preservers in the stern and soon settled into a private ocean reverie of his own.

Abigail sat on a built-in seat next to her captain and tried to see through the darkness. From above came music from the band, which was now playing some of the popular tunes of the day.

Deftly Andrew maneuvered the boat between many others, taking his hand from the wheel long enough to wave greetings to kindred spirits in other boats. He seemed to have as many friends on the sea as Susan did on land.

Neither spoke a word. Abigail, wondering at Tad's silence, walked to the stern and found him fast asleep. His young face was surprisingly angelic in repose. Seeing him asleep and vulnerable touched a maternal chord in Abigail. So many new feelings were crowding in around her. Looking once again toward Andrew, she watched his silhouette against the mottled summer sky. As the moon came out from behind a cloud, he was thrown into sudden relief, and she could see the breadth of his shoulders and the shock of dark hair which surrounded the leonine head. If he was aware of her gaze, his body did not betray it. She went to his side. He was the first to break the silence.

"Tell me about Susan. Was her singing so very bad?"

"Do you want the truth?" asked Abigail.

"I always want the truth," replied Andrew, turning his head to look her full in the face.

"She ended up singing alone. She had forgotten to give the rest of us the last page, you see. Unfortunately she was singing loudly. I couldn't do anything to console her, but Josiah was wonderful! He just took over and made everything fine again. He talked to her about people loving each other for deeper reasons and how looks and special talents shouldn't matter at all. Susan's a very lucky girl to have him, but I don't think I thought so before tonight."

"Oh?" questioned Andrew.

"You wanted the truth. I guess I thought he was rather insignificant, unexciting; but the way he handled the situation tonight was not only kind, it was strong — and do you know something? I thought he was positively handsome there in the bushes." She smiled. "Tell me about you and the sea. Remember, you promised to tell me why you loved it."

"I remember, but it's difficult to put into words. Ever since I was small . . ." Abigail smiled and Andrew added with a broad grin of his own, "Oh, yes, I was small once."

"How good to see you smile! I was beginning to think the only time you smiled was at Tad or when you were making fun of me," said Abigail. "But go on; I'm always interrupting people."

"I've noticed. However, as a boy I always felt that I needed the sea. It was always there when I wanted fun or food, and now I need it to earn my living. Guess that's where I part company with the pleasure boaters. They use the sea for their own recreation, and then they just walk away from it. There's no continuity there. It's not part of them, so they treat it lightly. Perhaps I just wasn't meant to take things lightly. The sea deserves better than that. She doesn't forgive your mistakes. You can use her and take from her, and she'll give you beauty and pleasure enough for a lifetime, but don't think for a minute that she's soft. She'd take me under as quickly as anyone else if I started taking her for granted."

"You make the ocean sound like a woman."

"She'll have to do unless I can find a real woman as exciting and beautiful who doesn't mind if I have a jealous mistress.

"Did you know that your eyes are the color of the ocean?" he asked, turning around to face her, one hand still on the wheel.

"Are they?" she whispered. "And am I exciting and beautiful?"

Letting go of the wheel, he took her in

his arms and pulled her close to him. She raised her face to his, and for a lingering moment they forgot to hide from each other. His mouth came down on hers full and strong, and she felt his rough hands caressing her back and hair. Deafened by the pounding of her heart, she almost became lost in pleasure, but suddenly the image of herself and Burton Madison reared up before her and she panicked. Overwhelmed with guilt for her own passions, she broke away and raised her hand to strike at her fear.

Before she could slap his face, however, Andrew grasped her wrist and turned a look of astounded fury on her.

"Now just wait a minute, Abigail! You can pretend you didn't want me to kiss you if that soothes your Boston notions of conscience, but don't think I'll play your little games. And don't ever, as long as you live, try to hit me again."

He dropped her wrist as though it were unclean and, taking the wheel, headed for the dock. Abigail choked back tears of humiliation in the dark. In her own misery at her ridiculous reaction, she was unaware of the blow she had dealt to Andrew.

Andrew Darcy was not at all the sort of man who exposed his feelings easily. That he had opened up so rashly to an unknown personality both angered and mortified him. Now she would think him just another unsubtle fool who had allowed himself to be made ridiculous by a lovely face. His whole sense of dignity was outraged, and his anger was directed as much at himself as at Abigail. He steered toward the dock below the bandstand, oblivious to Abigail's consternation. Indeed, he never looked at her again, not even after he gently awakened Tad and left his brother and his cousin on the dock.

"Where is everyone? Looks like they've all gone home," said Tad, fully awake again.

"No, there's Susan over there," replied Abigail, trying to speak normally despite the hollow feeling inside her.

"Hallo, Abby. Hi, Tad!" called Susan. "They've all gone home. The older generation just can't keep up, I guess."

Goodness thought Abigail. She certainly bounced back fast. Susan was holding Josiah's arm as they approached Tad and Abigail. "You two may as well head back too. Josiah has to supervise the packing up of the bandstand, so we'll be along a little later."

Abigail could take a hint. "Come on, Tad, let's get on home. Even lobsters need rest. Nine o'clock will come pretty quickly."

The two slipped away down the incline to Front Street. The streets were almost deserted as they approached the town landing, where a few old-timers sat on benches savoring the last remnants of the parade of passersby. It was a new sensation for Abigail to be out walking in the dark, yet she felt perfectly safe. The alleys they passed held no menace. All around the old town the breeze was lovingly covering the lanes and pathways with a gentle salt mist as one by one lamps went out in windows. The petals of the flowers along the way shone luminescent in the dim moonlight. All in all it was a perfect evening, unless you were a girl who was just beginning to realize how stupidly you had behaved. Her mind could not grasp the fact that what she had almost given away in Boston had found, and lost, the chance for safe harbor in Marblehead.

As they approached the small beach just before Lovis Cove, Abigail saw two figures on the beach. She almost cried out as she recognized the forms of her father and Aunt Belle, but when she saw that they were embracing, she quickly looked away and spoke to Tad about something on the opposite side of the street. He obligingly followed her lead and, arriving home, went innocently to bed.

Not so Abigail. She tiptoed past the guest room where her mother slept unaware. She couldn't face intimate late-night talk tonight; there was too much to conceal. Numbly she went to bed, but sleep eluded her. The shock of her father's infidelity was only slightly less devastating than the sudden, sickening realization that she was in love with Andrew Darcy. There was no other explanation for the fascination she felt for him. She must have been attracted to him for a long time. Her strong reactions to his presence should have warned her. Once again she feared her own nature. After all, she was her father's daughter! She wondered what he was doing down on the beach with Belle, but she already knew the answer. What angered her was not the physical weakness; after all she had lived enough this last few months to recognize the power of sexual need. No, what distressed her was that Thomas could be making love to Belle while Henrietta slept unknowing less than four stone skips away. The insensitivity appalled her. What could she do? Probably very little, but she would try to shield Henrietta. Perhaps it would blow over before anyone was hurt, but she doubted it. Why, if Tad had turned his head at the wrong moment tonight, his young life would have come crashing down around him.

How selfish passion could make people! Had she given even a thought to her parents when she let Burt touch her in the garden?

She heard a door click and then the heavy step of Andrew as he went into his own room. A painful half-hour later she heard the door again and the whispered good-nights.

When Maurice had insisted on walking Henrietta home, Thomas had been mildly elated, but when first Abigail and then Susan had gone off with their own companions, he had been self-conscious and burningly aware of Belle looking at him across the picnic blanket. For a half-hour they sat quietly listening to the band music. At its conclusion Belle said, "I suppose we old folk had best be getting back. May as well give the young people a time alone to enjoy the night. They'll grow up soon enough!"

"Will they be all right? Abigail's not accustomed to being out alone," said Thomas.

"She's not alone. She has Tad and Andrew. Don't worry, Tom, they can look after themselves. Besides, haven't you learned yet that people can't be protected from some things? There comes a time when people just up and do what they want to do, and nobody could stop them even if they tried."

Thomas was impressed with the intimacy implied in this comment. He was also touched by her use of the nickname Tom.

"Nobody's called me Tom since I was a little boy," he said.

"Do you mind?" asked Belle, rising to her feet and brushing off her skirt.

Thomas carefully folded the blanket as he replied, "No, I like it. It makes me feel young again."

"We're not all that old, you know," chided Belle, smiling up at him as they went down to Front Street.

They were playing out some kind of mysterious scene. Thomas sensed that everything he said from this point on would be of the utmost significance. Words had meanings beyond the obvious. Belle was playing the scene with a skill he found irresistible. It was as though they were two marionettes being manipulated by a master of the craft.

"Where's this cove where the woman was killed?" he asked. "Abigail is in love with the whole notion of a screeching woman."

Had he misspoken his line? The mention of Abigail seemed to dampen Belle's spirits, but she picked up the dialogue a moment later.

"The cove is ahead on the right. There are stone steps going down to it."

How had they come so close to home without his awareness? Approaching the end of Front Street, he saw Franklin Street beckoning to the left, but the lure of the night and the necessity to finish the play drew him seaward.

"Let's go down on the beach, shall we?" he asked. Without a word Belle turned right, and in one irrevocable moment they were on the beach.

Above, the moon was almost full. Only a narrow sliver was needed to complete its circle. The waves lapped gently over phosphorescent pebbles. The periwinkle shells gave way under their feet as they automatically sought the shelter of a large rock. Belle started to sit down, but Thomas pulled her to her feet and, brushing a tangled blond curl from her brow, took her in his arms for a long embrace. Her breath was coming quickly, and he could feel her heart racing against his chest.

He had expected her to protest, but she was quiet, and he felt her body relaxing as he held her fast. The sound of footsteps came overhead on the street.

"What was that?" she whispered as voices trailed off in the distance.

"Just someone passing. They couldn't see us," he answered.

He kissed her now, many times, and she responded with tentative movements which became more yielding and yet, at the same time, demanding.

At some point Thomas moved away, and, picking up the blanket from where it had fallen, he spread it out against the seawall. Here, behind a jutting ledge, they were sheltered and unseen by all except the sea, who, without conscience abetted their sin with a soft ripple of sound and a golden reflection of moonlight on Belle's outspread hair.

CHAPTER 14

Down Pleasant Street they came. Little ones with mothers in attendance, young ones holding the hands of older brothers and sisters, and finally the small band of independent thinkers, those who had devised their own costumes and wore them defiantly as if aware that they had almost outgrown the Horribles Parade.

The Horribles Parade was always a major event; more than seventy children poured in erratic array down the street. They were dressed in every conceivable costume. Cardboard buildings marched next to bewigged statesmen while flower girls tripped daintily over their skirts and little revolutionary soldiers brandished muskets made of wood. Proud parents beamed and applauded as the entire mass approached. Occasionally one costume would catch the fancy of the crowd and then disappear into the swarm once again.

From the sidelines Abigail stood between her mother and father and searched for the spot of red that would signal Tad's arrival. Now appeared a miniature General Glover, and here swayed a dory supported by three small bodies, using arms as oars.

"There he is! See? Just behind George Washington — or is that Jefferson?" she cried. "Look, he's waving his claw!" She felt proud and happy to have contributed to Tad's obvious success. As he passed, the crowd cheered and Abby's hopes rose for a prize. The dory also got a big hand, as did Moll Pitcher, a local favorite. Moll Pitcher, not to be confused with Molly Pitcher, had been a seer and the daughter of old Wizard Dimond.

In the background could be heard wailing babies and laughing parents. Small boys darted in and out between skirts and trouser legs, and occasionally a scuffle would break out among the partisans of the entries.

Thomas seemed unruffled by last night's misbehavior. Scrutinizing his face for telltale signs of guilt, Abigail was disconcerted to find none. Perhaps this was a way of life for him, yet she was having trouble perceiving him as a villain. Henrietta looked a bit pale, but certainly she did not have the expression of a woman who had caught out a wayward husband. Well, that was a relief. At least her mother hadn't noticed anything wrong.

Abigail tried to lay plans, but something was wrong with all of them. At first she had considered pleading to go home. After all, she had been here a month; perhaps her mother would relent? But now that she had discovered her feelings for Andrew, she was reluctant to leave. Perversely she was attracted to his disdain. Then she had considered confronting her father with what she had seen. This too was rejected when she realized that it would probably spoil their own special relationship forever. She needed a father right now, not an adversary, and the role of Abigail as moralist hardly seemed appropriate under the circumstances. Also, if she told her father, he would tell Belle, and then it would be impossible for her to stay on; and if she didn't stay on, Henrietta would ask why and so on and so forth. It was a dilemma.

The lobster was getting a bit carried away with his success. Now he was snapping his claws at children on the sides of the street. They were reacting most satisfactorily with screams of delighted terror, but over there a baby howled in fright and a mother glared at the lobster with undisguised anger. This subdued Tad temporarily, but his feelers started flying again when he spotted his family grouped near the corner store by School Street.

Abigail was coming face to face with one of life's great ironies. Lips may be kissed, hearts may stray, and passion may rule the night; but come morning, breakfast must be cooked, beds must be made, and parading children must be watched and celebrated. Her spirit, steeped in romance, resisted this idea. Surely there must be a place where time is suspended, where kisses never have to stop. She began to understand how Andrew felt about the sea. He wanted it to be special, monumental; and here were hundreds of weekend sailors trivializing it for him. Her father's passion for Belle would be romantic were it not for Henrietta. Abigail knew that somewhere, in some lost corner of her mind, there would always be a speck of herself that would hate her father and perhaps all men for what she had seen on the beach. She also knew that she would continue to be in love with Andrew despite all this. It all made very little sense.

The paraders had dispersed and the judges were conferring.

"How'd I look? Great, huh?" Tad was shining with excitement.

"You were wonderful, dear!" said Belle, giving him a hug complicated by feelers and claws.

"Sssh! They're gonna make the announcement," cried Tad.

"Third prize," called the head judge, "is Miss Moll Pitcher!" Cheers from the crowd.

"Second prize goes to General Lafayette!" he cried. A boy in an elegant plumed hat skipped happily up to the judge amidst applause and more cheers.

"And, in first place," — the judge

paused — "the winner is A Marblehead Dory!" Tad's face fell with disappointment.

"And also, because there was a tie, our fine red lobster!" The judge joined in the applause as Tad was bumped on the back by congratulating friends. Abigail kissed him full on the mouth, and the lobster's face grew as red as his body.

"Oh, boy, Tad!" called one of the older boys. "I could sure get dressed up like a lobster for that!"

This sally was greeted with more laughter from those within earshot and more blushing from Tad. Abigail hoped she had not embarrassed him with her affectionate outburst, but he seemed quite recovered as he shook hands with all six oars of the dory.

Back at home, Tad passed the blue ribbon around for everyone to admire. Seated around the dining room table for the traditional Fourth of July luncheon of salmon and peas, they looked like a typically happy family. No one would have suspected the liaison between Belle and Thomas. As a matter of fact, Belle was just now patting Maurice on the arm with unfeigned affection, and Thomas was helping Henrietta to the fresh minted peas.

As for Abigail and Andrew, they were both too proud to admit to anything amiss. Andrew did, however, call Abigail "cousin" several times with an unnecessary deliberateness. Very well, if that's what he wants, so be it, thought Abigail stubbornly. But in her heart she hoped for better. Andrew was no Burt Madison. His kisses were serious, and Abigail knew he would not throw them away where there was no genuine feeling.

"You were right, Mother," she said. "The food here is wonderful. You can't imagine how much I've eaten since I came."

"Well, Belle's a fine cook. She can't stand to let anyone else run her kitchen, and we're all happy for it," said Maurice.

Where were the hidden looks, the sly glances? thought Abigail. But then, she was the only one who knew, and both Thomas and Belle were unaware of her probing looks. When her mother and father left for the train station, Thomas pecked Belle's cheek as usual, but this time Abigail saw the squeeze she gave his hand in return. In an odd way it was reassuring to catch this small interchange. She was beginning to think she had dreamed the whole night — Andrew, Belle, Thomas, all of it. She kissed her mother good-bye. Thomas would not return to Boston until tomorrow; by then perhaps she would have figured out what to do.

Once on the train, Henrietta lost her usual self-control. Fortunately she was alone in the seat next to a window so that her consternation was hidden from all except the people outside the window, people who may have glanced up long enough to catch a glimpse of the white-faced beauty who stared, unseeing, out at them.

Ever since Abigail had gone to Marblehead, Henrietta had been aware of a change in Thomas. They had both gone along in alien worlds for so long that a pattern had developed. Thomas was kind, polite, and courteous; Henrietta was remote but aware of her responsibilities. It had become a way of life, albeit an unhappy one. The appearance of this new Thomas was frightening. Up until now, Henrietta had assumed that Thomas's outside affairs were being conducted according to whatever bizarre protocol governed such matters. Now, however, he had become intense, jocular. Even a fool could tell that something had happened to reawaken his interest in life and Henrietta was no fool.

At first she attributed his gaiety to the change of scene brought about by his visit to Abigail, but lately she had been aware of something happening, something new and threatening. Once in Marblehead it had taken her exactly ten minutes to see what this something was. Belle bloomed whenever Thomas came near, a blooming all the more obvious because of the furrows in Maurice's brow whenever he followed his wife's glance to its object. How could this have happened? The train rattled on, putting miles between Thomas and Henrietta. It was all so sordid, incestuous even, although there was no blood involved. And how could Belle do this to her? She had come to expect a certain amount of discreet disloyalty from Thomas, but she couldn't believe that they would both sink so low as to conduct a liaison under the very roof which sheltered four children and Maurice. Did Maurice know? How could he help it? No. Maurice suspected, but he loved Belle, and it was his nature to do things the right way. Unless he had proof, he would not overreact. Especially he would not risk losing Belle for something she was perhaps not yet aware of herself.

Henrietta took hope for the first time. Brushing away an errant tear, she looked around her at the businessmen in the car. So stolid, all of them! But who knew what churning went on under the stiff waistcoats and collars. Surely if Maurice had taken no action it was because he felt that nothing had happened yet. That meant that there was still time. But how to get Thomas away from Marblehead? The train pulled into the Boston station, where the carriage was waiting. All the way back to Louisburg Square, Henrietta fought back the tears, but once she entered the dark, lonely hall, her courage failed and she ran up the stairs, choking back the sobs until she reached her bedroom. Once inside she sat down at her dressing table and cried until her breath came in great shuddering gasps. She was a child again, desperate for comfort and uncaring who witnessed her despair.

And in Marblehead, standing on the hill at Fort Sewall, Maurice Darcy looked out to sea and felt his pain like a stone in his heart. So much joy! So many memories of tiny hands and shared moments. A lifetime of happiness and concern all thrown away — and for what? He looked north past Baker's Island. The view became blurred. He had failed her. In some deep, unforgivable way he had let her down. What a fool he had been to believe that a home and children were enough! A woman like Belle needed attention, all the extra things that life could bring. And because he had forgotten this, she had taken a poor substitute like Thomas Curtis as her dream-bearer. It would pass, he was sure. Thomas was not the kind of man to make Belle's dreams come true. He was attractive but weak, while Belle was salt-of-the-ocean strong. But now, in the meantime, he looked out to sea and felt the dull ache of a life gone sour.

In the morning, Henrietta awakened refreshed. She had not slept better in months. The deluge had washed the cobwebs out of her musty thinking. She went to the dressing table and took stock. She was thirty-nine years old. Still young. Younger than Belle. Her figure was better, and she was at least as smart. Having been so fond of Belle all these years, she had carefully avoided comparisons, but things were different now.

She poured a deep tub of water and, shedding her dressing gown, slid first one pointed foot and then a pale calf into the steaming water. Easing herself down, she relaxed her muscles and leaned her dark head against the copper.

Later, having washed and dried her hair, she left it streaming down her back, and, putting on her pink wrapper, she went downstairs into the kitchen.

"Mr. Curtis and I will dine in the garden tonight. Please serve something light, and be sure to have a good bottle of wine set out." The cook, having never seen Mrs. Curtis in such deshabille, was speechless.

Ignoring the cook's bewilderment, Henrietta went to the telephone. Raising the receiver, she asked the operator to call her doctor. "Doctor Walters? This is Henrietta Curtis calling. No, I'm quite well, thank you, but I would like to talk with you. Privately. Yes, I'll be in all morning. Thank you."

She replaced the receiver and, elated by her nerve, did a little dance in the hall. Had Mrs. Byors been home, Henrietta would have been urged to rest immediately, but Mrs. Byors was not home, and Henrietta went up the stairs humming a snatch from one of the tunes she had heard at the band concert.

When the doctor arrived, Henrietta was dressed sedately in deep blue. She ushered Doctor Walters into the drawing room and closed the doors.

CHAPTER 15

At the very moment when Henrietta was beginning to pull her life together, Belle was feeling hers unraveling. After Thomas's early morning departure, she went about the house with a dustcloth in her hand. The three youngest children were at Little Harbor beach, and Maurice had gone to Salem at eight o'clock. Andrew had not spent the night at home. He owned a small shack down with the fishermen in Barnegat, where he often slept during the busy summer months.

Entering her formal front room, Belle felt inexplicably tired. She sat down in the gold wing chair and tried to make some sense out of her behavior. Yes, she had felt neglected, but was this really Maurice's fault? All she had to do was speak up, share her feelings. But she had chosen not to reveal her frustrations.

Instead she had let them fester into a hard knot of discontent. She imagined that her age was the culprit. When she sorted things out rationally, she knew that she would not part with one year of her life with Maurice. The children were a constant delight, each one different from the other.

Andrew, her first born, so serious and responsible. Yet his mother sensed a deep well of passion under all that stoicism. She had half-expected him to fall in love with Abigail, but that had not happened. In fact, the two had seemed like strangers. Abigail was young, but Belle had seen her intelligence and warmth from the first day she arrived. Perhaps Andrew was put off by her beauty? Some men were, but she had not imagined Andrew to be one of these. He had always been so sure of himself.

And Susan, her mother's best friend, conventional yet never stiff. She expected so little from life and had that rarest of gifts, the ability to take joy in ordinary things. No castles for Susan. A good man, children, and a home of her own. Belle knew a wedding was coming, but she also knew that Susan would stay in Marblehead with Josiah. The town was part of her, as much a part as her sunny smile.

That left Tad, the unexpected joy of her life. Already she could see him stretching a tentative toe toward manhood. He had been their rudder, the family funny bone, the one who broke up serious discussions with outrageous comments. And so unspoiled. Despite his popularity he seemed as unaware of his charm as he had been when he was a bowlegged toddler following Aunt Gracie down the street. Even then heads had turned to see the dark, curly-haired child grinning and calling out "hiya" to everyone he saw. Belle could foresee the day when he would be a town character, just like Gracie. He could do worse.

Suddenly she stood up, took the scarf from around her curls, and marched out the door. Gracie was home. Gracie was almost always home. Belle felt an additional pang of guilt at her neglect over the past weeks, although, to be fair, she had seen Gracie at the band concert tapping her heels against the footrest of her wheelchair and having a grand old time.

"Hello, dear. I was wonderin' when you'd show up," said Gracie, totally unsurprised. Gracie was sitting in a straight-back chair which Andrew had invented for her. It had little wheels on each leg, and by pushing off walls and using a cane which Andrew had fastened to the chair back, she could maneuver much more efficiently than in the large wheelchair that she used for outings. It was especially handy in the kitchen because it rolled freely over the boards and allowed her to come closer to her stove and icebox than did the other.

"Come in and set down. You look terrible. What's going on?" asked Gracie, not one to beat around the bush.

"Oh, I don't know! I guess it's just my age," said Belle, sitting on the old divan.

"What age are you talking about? They all have their quirks, y'know. Let's see, you're about forty-two." Gracie looked closely at Belle's face.

"Forty-three," replied Belle.

"Oh yes, I can surely recall my forties. My George could sure recall 'em too. He used to say that if I didn't hurry up and grow old pretty damn quick, I'd wear him out. Why, I was so randy in my forties that he hardly dared let me on the street. Course, he kept me pretty busy at home, so there wasn't any real problem, but I can remember giving 'em all the eye. Why the firemen across the street used to give such a smile. They could tell, y'see? A thing like that shows on a woman. You can spot it a mile away. It's funny, too, when you think about it. Most folks think a woman cares the most about that sort of thing when she's younger, but it just ain't so. You could have asked my George! He'd tell ya. Is that the problem honey?" she asked, her great gapped smile relaxing into a furrow of concern.

"I guess so," said Belle, suddenly feeling less wicked and more understood.

"Well, here's my advice, and listen good, because it's hard to be sensible while you're goin' through it! In the first place don't give in to it. Flirt if you want and talk a little daring, but don't go thinking you're in love with someone just because you're crazy mad to sleep with him. That's plain talk, I know, but it's true. Why, those men we poor women get all bothered about could just as well be trees or park benches, 'cause it's not in them; it's coming from ourselves, and it's just lookin' for someone to land on. Can't help it, it's nature. Trouble is, most of us get to feeling this way just when we got the most to lose — children still at home and all.

"Now, that's the first advice. Here's some more if you don't care to take that part of it. If you do get carried away, and it happens — why, there's many a last child in this town that don't look a mite like his father! — then for heaven's sake, don't go all soft about it. It's not your husband's problem; don't spoil his happiness by confessin' it. Just chalk it up to experience and keep yer mouth shut. Nothin you can do after the fact. Might as well forget it.

"Now, have I said anything useful?" she grinned, her small eyes penetrating into Belle's brown ones. Despite her scraggly appearance it was not impossible to believe that she had temporarily driven the firemen wild.

"Yes, you have. I'd tell you the whole story, but I just can't, not right now," said Belle, smiling for the first time that day.

"No need to tell me anything at all. Time was when I'd have sat you down and had it all out of you in ten minutes, but nowadays it seems more important to help out than to hear all the gory details. Must be *my* age!" She chortled good-naturedly, and Belle decided to make her a chocolate cake that very afternoon.

"You're so good, Aunt Gracie," said Belle.

"Life's been good to me child. You just try to pass it on, that's all."

At Little Harbor beach, Abigail, Susan, and Tad were undergoing a daily ritual. It had been decided among them that Abigail should learn to swim. This remarkable feat was to be achieved in the utmost secrecy, not counting Belle, and the grand accomplishment was to be unveiled at summer's end for the benefit of Henrietta and Thomas Curtis.

Since the night of the band concert, much of the fun had gone out of it for Abigail. She scarcely knew whether her parents would still be together come August. Besides, although she would never admit it aloud, she had been most anxious that Andrew should see her wonderful achievement, and now she realized that he would be uninterested in anything his Boston cousin might do. He had avoided her these last few days in such a skillful way that only she was aware of his absence whenever she entered a room.

Sometimes when the three were in the Little Harbor she would see the sails of the *Joseph Homan,* and the little dot of red on the horizon would make her head dizzy with straining to see its master.

Standing waist deep in the icy Atlantic, she would feel disoriented and apart, wondering whatever was she doing here with seaweed winding around her calves and hard stones under her city feet. Then a wave would come, and another, and she would be forced to face the moment or topple over in the current. Tad took his job seriously. First he would make her stand waist deep and make overhand motions with her hands. Then, when he felt that she was sufficiently proficient in this elementary exercise, he would stand with his back to her and, instructing her to grasp his shoulders, would make her kick her feet in flutter fashion. The problem came whenever she would try to synchronize these movements. But she was game!

"Okay, try it once more. Quick, before those swells reach us. Just sort of lie down and let the water lift you up."

She was fine until her feet left the water; then she went under, taking in a mouthful of brine as she sank. Up she came, coughing and sputtering.

"It's those dumb clothes!" cried Tad, whacking her between her shoulder blades. "How in tarnation do they expect a person to swim in a full set of clothes, anyway? Here, take off those stupid stockings." Like an obedient wardrobe mistress, Susan stretched out her arm to accept the black stockings that

Abigail peeled off.

"That's better, but those petticoats will have to go too. Oh, for heaven's sake, nobody's lookin! Do you want to swim or not?"

Abigail peeled down until she was wearing only her underwear and the dark blue cotton dress her mother had bought for her in Boston specifically for purposes of bathing.

"You've still got on enough clothes to sink a whale, but I guess that's as far as we can go," he said regretfully. "This time I'll hold you under the middle, and we'll see if you can get the rest of it."

How pleasant it was to feel the salt water on her bare legs. Surely she must be ten pounds lighter without all those wet petticoats! She did as Tad instructed. From beside her Susan called encouragement. Susan could swim like a fish from the age of four.

This time, with Tad's palm beneath her, she was able to balance in the water.

"Don't let go!" she cried as her body began to move forward with the carefully learned movements of arms and legs.

"Next time I want to try it alone," she called, wiping water from her face.

"Whaddya mean, next time? I let go of you ten feet back," cried Tad, exultant.

"Do you mean it? You mean I really swam? All by myself?" said the awestruck Abigail.

"You were wonderful!" called Susan, ploughing through the water to give her a hug.

"Oh, I was, wasn't I!" seconded the victorious girl. Standing half-concealed by the water, her red hair streaming down, her full mouth exposing white teeth in a delighted grin, she was irresistible.

"Yeah. Modest too," added Tad. "How about some credit for the teacher?" He took several bows which plunged his face into the water. Delighted by this comic touch, the girls followed suit until all three were bobbing in and out of the water like corks.

Their laughter rippled over the water until it reached the deck of a red fishing boat parked just behind Gerry Island. Andrew wiped sweat-soaked palms against the cloth which encased his sturdy thighs.

Why, he thought are they all so comfortable with her, while I always feel like a fool when she's around? Turning the boat around he headed out to sea, away from the confusion of red-haired cousins and especially away from the memory of a kiss in the night — a kiss which, try as he might, he could not forget. He wanted her, with a longing that sprang as much from his head as from his loins. But he would not play the clown to a spoiled city girl. No, the woman he loved must be deep, as deep as his own blue Atlantic, not a silly child who could kiss and strike out in almost the same instant! Ordinarily the clear sunshine of mid-July was enough to brace him against all ills, but today the sun seemed a fickle friend, shining down on the cause of his consternation.

CHAPTER 16

Thomas Curtis walked up the steps to his own home. He dreaded the meeting with Henrietta. All the way home he had rehearsed the exact tone he must take in order to assure her that nothing was amiss. Nothing must touch her. Even as he vowed to protect his wife, the thought of Belle on the beach came rushing over him and he felt his body grow warm. His business suit was stained in a dark circle in the center of his back, and the once red hair was lying in damp curls on the wide brow.

Henrietta was at the door before he could finish turning the brass handle. She was dressed in pale blue, a color which made her eyes the purest azure. Despite the heat her hair was down, and her cheeks were pink from Marblehead sunshine.

Ordinarily Thomas would have caught the obvious meaning in her deliberately chosen toilette, but tonight he was bone weary. The first tugs of guilt were taking their toll, and he felt totally exhausted and asexual.

Henrietta had set her course, however, and Thomas's evident fatigue would not deter her.

"Welcome home. Was it hot on the train? I've arranged to eat in the garden tonight; I thought it would be cooler."

"Actually I'd just as soon have a cold supper and go to bed," he returned, but then, seeing the disappointment which clouded the blue eyes, he added, "The idea of a garden supper is nice, though. Give me just a few minutes to change, and I'll join you presently."

Henrietta watched him go up the stairs. Her newly attuned eye missed nothing; not even the rumpled edges of his damp handkerchief escaped her. He looked older. Where was the youth of last week? It could be the heat, but she thought she had caught an inner fatigue, a stoop in the usually square shoulders.

In his room Thomas sat on the bed and dropped his head in his hands. What charade was he to act out in his own house? Henrietta's accessibility annoyed him, coming as it did too late. He fell flat on his back and stared up at the ceiling. He did not love Belle, but her energy and responsiveness were just what he had needed these past months. He supposed that he still loved Henrietta, but in almost the way he would cherish an art treasure, a beautiful thing left in his hands for safekeeping. What he wanted was the best of both worlds, but, as this was impossible he refused to settle for nothing. Standing, he washed his neck and face, noting the slight sag in his once firm throat and neck. How could he throw away these good years in a state of meaningless celibacy? But what of Belle? At this moment he was too enervated to think beyond supper. He went down the stairs and out into the garden.

"Do come and see the marigolds. They're perfectly beautiful this year," said Henrietta, taking his arm. Her vivacity shamed him. Graciously he followed her around the garden, commenting favorably on the miniature wonders she had accomplished in the small space.

"Do you think Abigail is happy in Marblehead?" she asked. "She seemed a bit downcast yesterday morning."

"She seems to be having a grand time whenever I see her. Certainly she has put that damned Madison out of her mind," he responded.

"Perhaps she could come home, then," suggested Henrietta, deliberately trying to keep her tone light. "After all, it wouldn't do to have her turn completely into a country girl."

"I'm beginning to wonder about that," said Thomas, sitting down at the glass-topped table which had been set with the loveliest of Henrietta's wedding china. "She's really much more in her element there."

"I don't know what you mean," said Henrietta, accepting a cold glass of wine.

"Why, just look at her, clamming and sewing lobster costumes and cooking those crazy cookies and singing at a band concert. Let's face it, she's having the time of her life! She's always been too lively for this house. At least there she can let off a little steam once in awhile. There don't seem to be any problems with young men, either," said Thomas.

"Yes, I wondered about that. Belle said that there had been several who've tried to come calling, but she doesn't want anything to do with any of them. I do hope that Madison boy hasn't turned her the other way. There's nothing so unattractive as a man-hater."

"Somehow I don't quite see our Abigail in that role. More likely she's just looking over the field. Besides, you wouldn't want her to fall in love with a Marblehead fellow anyway, would you?" he asked smiling. The wine was having its effect, and he felt agreeable and relaxed.

"No, of course not. If all the families were like the Darcys it would be different, but it's such a peculiar town. So many odd types! Why, take that strange Aunt Gracie, for example," said Henrietta.

"She's quite a character all right," agreed Thomas. "Say! What's this delicious concoction?"

"It's a French cold soup recipe. I read

about it in last week's rotogravure and asked Cook to try it." Henrietta was pleased that her supper was being appreciated.

The supper went well. At one point Thomas almost asked Henrietta why she was wearing her hair down, but he checked himself in time. It was bewitching however. He hadn't seen her this way in months. Could she be declaring a truce in their bedroom war? He rather doubted it. She was not the type to surrender. But her conversation was sparkling, and her wine glass never empty. She reminded him of Abigail when she wanted something and was making herself particularly charming to get it. But his nerves were still raw from his encounter with Belle. Things were complicated enough without another rebuff from this dark-haired enigma.

They talked of many matters both domestic and worldly, but somehow the important issue never arose. Several times Thomas tried to create an opening for whatever it was that was on Henrietta's mind, but she seemed unable to get on with it despite the fact that she had thought of little else throughout the entire evening. Eventually they fell silent, and finally, after smoking a cigar, he thanked her for a delightful evening, rose, and bade her goodnight.

Alone in the garden, Henrietta sat like one of her own stone statues. What had she expected? She had lacked the courage to come out with her feelings. Especially she had not been able to discuss her visit with Doctor Walters. Once again she felt the desolation that had come over her on the train. She went into the kitchen, where the cook was awaiting the orders to clean up and, going up the stairs, went to her own room. Once in her bed, the great sobs of yesterday again overtook her. Anger at herself, at Thomas, and at Belle overwhelmed her. No! She would not let this happen. Forgetting her wrapper and ignoring her tearstained eyes, she walked to Thomas's room and without knocking opened the door.

"Thomas? Make love to me!" she demanded.

Thomas had been awake in his bed listening to the muffled sobs coming from down the hall. When they suddenly stopped he tensed like an animal wary in the dark. When he heard Henrietta's voice, he turned and saw her there, an apparition in white. He was touched beyond words. What an effort it must have taken to bring her here! He went to her side. She was trembling as he led her to his bed.

"What about babies, you know?" he asked gently.

"I've seen the doctor. It's all right," she said in a barely audible voice.

"Oh, Henny, I've missed you so." His voice broke as he kissed the tearstained face.

"No more talk, not tonight," she whispered.

In the morning she was gone, vanished as abruptly as she had appeared. Springing from his bed, Thomas went to her room. It was empty. He went downstairs and found her in the garden, a cup of tea in her hand.

"Thank God you're here!" he said.

"Why, where else would I be?" she asked, her eyes sparkling.

"I don't know. I wasn't thinking, I guess," he replied. "I was afraid it was all a dream." He took the teacup from her hand and, laying it on the table, held her in his arms. "I do love you, Henny."

"And I love you, too. But don't call me Henny!" she replied.

"Can't help it. You'll always be Henny to me, so you'll just have to put up with it."

CHAPTER 17

In Marblehead summer had her glorious moment. With August, changes came.

Josiah Hoffman asked for Susan's hand in marriage. It was a scene of charming decorum. Maurice sat, expectant, in the gold chair. Susan had warned the entire household that this was the night. Abigail and Tad had taken a walk to Lovis Cove, and Belle hovered in the kitchen trying to behave as if nothing was unusual. Andrew was out, as was his custom these days.

"How long do ya think it'll take him?" asked Tad. He sat on a rock, his long legs bent at angles as he tossed stones into the incoming tide.

"I haven't the faintest idea. No one has ever proposed to me before, so I don't know exactly how it's done," replied Abigail.

"I don't see how it can take too long. I

mean, old Josiah walks in, says 'Can I marry your daughter?', Dad says 'Yes,' and that's that.''

"Oh, I imagine there's more to it than that. Your father will probably want to know how Josiah intends to support Susan and where they're going to live and all," said Abigail.

"Why, here of course! Susan'd never go away." He turned and looked at Abigail. "Say! Is that true?" he asked, reddening.

"Is what true?" asked Abigail.

"That nobody's ever asked you to marry them before?"

"Unfortunately it's the horrible truth, but you must remember that I haven't come out yet."

"What d'you mean, come out? You're out here now, aren't you?" Tad was baffled.

"It's a ceremony we have in Boston," she explained. "The girls my age are presented to society, and then there are dances and receptions and we're all supposed to find a nice rich husband."

"God! That's awful! Would you really let them do that to you?"

"I already have. Trouble was, I found the wrong sort of man." She was relieved to finally talk about it. "That's why I'm here. My parents wanted to get me away from him."

"So that's it! I was wondering why you came, but Mum said she'd kill us if we asked you about it. Why was he the wrong sort?" Now that the secret was out, Tad had questions he wanted answered.

"He was not a gentleman. He gambled and was after my money, or so my father said." She realized that she would never know the truth about Burt. Had it been her money all along or had desire played a part?

"He sounds like a skunk! Why did you ever fall for a man like that?" She felt his opinion of her slipping.

"I don't know. I guess it was because he told me I was pretty and made me feel grown-up whenever I was with him." She knew as she spoke that she was telling the truth. "It was stupid. I know that now, but I'm only eighteen and I hadn't been out much." It mattered very much to her that Tad understand and excuse her.

"Besides, I thought I was destined to be another Sarah Bernhardt."

"Who's she?" asked Tad.

"Just an actress. No, not just an actress, the best actress in the whole world," replied Abigail.

"And you wanted to be like her?"

"I did, but not now. I was being childish," said Abby.

"Yeah. I keep forgetting that you're just six years older than me." Tad seemed older too, now that she had confided in him.

"Tad? Please don't tell anyone else what I told you."

"You mean Andrew?" he asked, a speculative expression on the usually candid face.

Now, how did he know she meant precisely that? "I mean everyone. I'm not very proud of being such a fool."

"Course I won't tell. You never told about my secret place, did you? That's what friends are for. I wonder what is takin' Josiah so long? Mum promised to get us when it's all over. Such a dumb fuss about something we all knew was gonna happen anyway!" Tad was getting bored.

Back in the front room, Josiah was earnestly declaring his honorable intentions.

"And although my wages aren't very good at the church, I've already agreed to give private music lessons to six children in the congregation. There seems to be a good living in that. I wouldn't expect anything from Susan at all, just her loyalty. She seems willing to accept the financial limitations if you are, sir."

He was painfully sincere, his hat in his hand. Maurice saw the threadbare spots on his elbows and the nervousness in the long fingers, but fortunately his inner eye also saw the goodness. Josiah Hoffman would never be unkind to Susan. Also, he could stand up for himself. Despite his sheltered occupation, he was a strong man. Besides, Susan had made up her mind to have him, so this meeting was merely a formality. Naturally Maurice would admit that to no one, but Susan was his girl. His heart had always held a special place that was for her. Visions of a pigtailed child ran across his mind, and he knew he would never refuse her anything. At least she would be here in Marblehead.

"Well, son, I'll give you my blessing. You're a good lad, and we'll be proud to have you in the family. I expect you to take good care of my girl — she's the only one I've got — but we'll give her some trinkets now and again, too, so rest your mind on that. Her grandmother left her a small inheritance which comes to her when she marries, so no doubt you'll manage.

"Belle! Come here," he shouted. "We have some good news for you girls!"

To Josiah: "They've been talking about us in the kitchen. Somehow I don't think we scare them too much. Listen to the giggles, will you? I wish you luck, boy. If she's anything like her mother, she'll have you round her finger in no time. Just don't let her sing at the wedding!" The two men burst into laughter.

"What's so funny, you two?" said Belle. "I thought this was supposed to be a serious conversation!"

"No. It's a happy one. Looks like we've got us a new son."

Maurice went for something with which to toast the happy couple. The creaking of the back door signaled Andrew's arrival.

"What are you doing here?" asked Maurice, fetching glasses from the kitchen.

"I don't know. Sue said to come home tonight around ten, that she'd have some good news."

"The Devil you say! Why, the minx certainly has confidence. She and Josiah are engaged," said Maurice. "Run down to the cove and get Abby and Tad, would you? They've been making themselves scarce while Josiah had it out with his terrible father-in-law."

Ambling in slow strides down the street, Andrew heard the voices of his brother and Abigail — Tad's high and sharp, not yet broken, and then Abigail's throaty response. They seemed to be having a serious conversation. He approached the steps down to the beach. It had grown dark, and he was reluctant to reveal his presence. He got so little chance to study this strange Abigail creature.

He overheard just enough to realize that

he had walked in on some secret shared by the two. Not for the first time this summer he felt jealous of Tad's obvious affection for Abigail. For twelve years he had been the whole world to Tad. Now it was obvious that Abigail had usurped his position as confidant. Well, thought Andrew, what did you expect? It's your own damned fault. He had been out on his boats before daybreak each morning, and he spent the afternoons doing his shore duties. By sunset he was too tired to do more than eat and sleep. Thoughtlessly he had shut Tad out. Before he acquired the additional boats, he had spent a good part of each day with his younger brother, throwing a ball back and forth or just pleasure fishing. Those had been golden moments of precious intimacy. Why had he stopped having fun? Some days he felt older than his father. Perhaps that was why Abigail disturbed him so. She was always having such a good time. Her laughter rang throughout the house each time he ventured home. It was baffling to him that she had no fear of not being taken seriously. As a matter of fact, she seemed to care very little for anyone's opinion. Or rather his opinion! He coughed loudly and took definite pleasure in the color that flooded Abigail's face when she turned and saw him standing there.

"He's done it!" called Andrew to the two below. "You can come home now and drink champagne. I wonder if Josiah will notice that the bottle was all chilled and waiting. Guess not! He's too happy to notice anything at all tonight."

Andrew was happy for Susan. He had never been able to imagine what would become of her. She was the sort who seemed to be content with her lot — too content, Andrew had sometimes thought. He, on the other hand, wanted a great deal out of life. Not necessarily money or power, although he would refuse neither; rather he suffered from the universal delusion that his life would be unique, that his dreams and aspirations were born specifically with him and would die the same way. He was like his mother in this respect. His vision was constantly hovering somewhere just above the dark roofs of

Barnegat or soaring seaward to a remote spot where only a thin line of horizon could limit his imagination. But the anchor of his heritage laid a foundation of cold realism under his dreams, and recently he had begun to perceive himself as a fairly well-balanced fellow.

It was at this felicitous moment that Abigail had entered his life. Everything about her appealed to that part of him which he had tried so hard to contain, even eliminate. Her special scent when they passed in the hall, the angle of her pointed chin when she bent over to speak to Tad, and especially the slow smile that would start by dimpling one cheek and then spread out to reveal the white teeth; all these sent his imagination into a maelstrom of new sensations. Ever since the night when he had taken her on the boat, sleeping in the same house with her had become a torment. It was easier to go down to Barnegat on a summer's night and sit around on the dock smoking with the fishermen, or to lie on his cot wondering and trying to get himself back into the comfortable rut he had been in before she came. Even now as she climbed up to Front Street he felt once again under the charm of her presence.

Back at home the three gave kisses and congratulations. It seemed to Abigail that she only had a few swallows of champagne, yet she was suddenly very warm. Tears of sentiment sprang unbidden into her eyes as she toasted Josiah and Susan from stemmed goblets of Sandwich glass. She discovered that she was more than disconcerted to learn that the wedding would take place before summer's end. Susan married! Up until now the sight of Susan and Josiah together had been a pleasant diversion, not without its comic overtones. Looking at them now, eyes full of each other, she felt the realities for the first time. It had all been so gentle and gradual for Susan! None of this "Stop your heart" nonsense which had governed Abigail's romances to date. She wondered if she could ever make a man feel safe and beloved the way Susan did Josiah. Perhaps she was just a vain shallow creature who would always inspire lust but never tenderness. Wearily, she said good-night to everyone and went up to bed.

She was tired of waiting, tired perhaps of herself.

Fortunately it is difficult to remain unhappy when you are surrounded by bright sun and the bluest sky. Morning, plus nine hours of dreamless sleep, did much to restore her spirits. Belle and Maurice had stayed up late finishing the dregs of the champagne. At breakfast they were tired but content. Abigail was relieved to see that they were seemingly intimate again. Looking at Belle, her thoughts flew to Thomas. He had been back to Marblehead only twice since the Fourth of July and both times he had been constantly at his daughter's side. He had insisted on spending every second with her, which was very nice except that she missed her swimming lesson, an event which she was beginning to expect as the proper way to start the day.

The second time he had come, she had taken him out to Gerry Island for a picnic lunch. Tad had come with them, and when they passed over his secret spot, he and Abby had exchanged a quick conspiratorial smile.

"All right, Tad, my boy. Tell your poor landlubber uncle what that island is out there." Thomas pointed straight out from the point of the island.

"That's Baker's Island. There are summer people on it now." Tad was nut brown, and the worn-out school pants from last year were scarcely covering his knees before dissolving into shredded hems. His dark curls stirred in the light breeze, and the sun flecked the brown eyes with little jets of topaz. Under the thin gray shirt his shoulder blades made little points as he raised his arms to point out the various rocks and islands. If he had noticed Thomas's unusual interest in the outdoors, he never showed it. And if Thomas avoided Belle, she didn't seem to mind. Since her conversation with Gracie she had had time to think. Maurice had been very affectionate recently, and the memory of Thomas was beginning to go away. She was ashamed to realize that, like the child who tires quickly of a long-awaited toy, she had found the quest more exciting than the attainment.

CHAPTER 18

Maurice had decided to take a vacation and spend a concentrated period of time with Belle; consequently they were both crestfallen when, the day after Thomas's most recent departure, they awoke to find dark skies and rain like slivers of steel lancing the heavy air. And the rain settled in for a week, laying a shroud of dingy gray over all their plans. Gone were the picnics and the boat rides. In their place were long lazy days beside the fire, days full of games from the cupboard in the front room, and days full of the slothful intimacy forced on them by the incessant rain. Leaks began to appear, which in turn called for the bringing out of pans and pails to catch the drips in the attic. All the old houses on Franklin Street had their own special leaks, and like the old song, no one bothered to fix them because, as one man put it, "They don't leak 'less it's rainin!"

They were all old acquaintances of this sort of rain. In New England these spells were frequent in summer. The rain would stay on and on until even the upholstery grew damp. There was little wind; just the incessantly falling shroud of fog and creeping moisture which stubbornly hung on, waiting for the competitive sun to drive it away. It was no use hoping for a quick change. In Marblehead most sensible folks accepted the state of siege and made the best of it.

The rain brought Andrew back into the fold. The fishing was bad. Huge waves tangled nets, and sails were overpowered by the gales. He left one boat on duty close to shore and decided to share his father's vacation. Sprawled out on the floor in the library, he looked like an overgrown version of Tad as the two dark heads almost met over a hard-fought game of chess. Abigail learned a great deal about him as she sat in the big armchair sewing bits of embroidery for Susan's trousseau. She discovered that he liked very much to win but lost gracefully, and that he never lost on purpose just to please Tad. This trait stirred her respect. She had hated it when Mrs. Byors had let her win every game they played. She had found it patronizing and insulting, and she was happy that Andrew agreed. Occasionally he would tap Tad on the shoulder and say, "Are you sure you want to move that man?" but that was as far as he would go. Abigail learned that she could beat everyone but Maurice in games which required quick recall of factual knowledge but that she invariably lost those games which required planning and thinking ahead.

One dreary afternoon she sang while Susan played the piano. The piano was in the library, which was what they all called the front room across the hall from the formal living room. Susan was seated, with Abigail standing at her right shoulder singing. Suddenly her voice was joined by a rich baritone which blended perfectly with her own alto. She didn't dare to turn around, because she was afraid he would stop if she made him self-conscious, but her heart set up a rhythm of its own as the sound of the two voices filled the room and echoed into the hall. After that she and Andrew would sing together each evening while Belle and Maurice listened in contented silence. It was a good time for everyone. They became a family again, and the extremes of last month were tempered into a new unity. Only Tad chafed at the enforced imprisonment. He wandered restlessly from room to room looking for a diversion, and the phrase "Anyone wanna play a game?" became his constant query.

Susan took advantage of having the whole family together to set wedding plans. These plans had a way of changing from day to day, so that each morning Andrew would greet her with, "Well? What's it to be today? Purple organdy? Or perhaps a nice shade of fire engine red!"

"What I'd really like," she said one day, "is to be married out of doors at Fort Sewall. Do you think I could do that?" When, after several mornings of the same declaration, it became apparent that this wish was a real one, it was decided that they should ask the minister to perform the ceremony at the fort; but — and here Belle was adamant — they would also reserve the Old North Church in case of rain. Compromise reached, they went on to other matters.

Belle had given her house girl the week off. She had never enjoyed having someone about who was neither a friend nor family. A born Yankee, she always felt guilty that someone should be doing those things which she was perfectly capable of doing herself. The girl needed the wages, though, so at Maurice's insistence she had agreed to hire her on a daily basis. This vacation week, however, Abigail and Susan were doing all the dishes. It was while standing over the sink that Susan asked Abigail if she would be her maid of honor.

When Abigail accepted, Susan said, "You're just like a sister to me now! It's nice; I've never had a sister before. Do you remember your first night here? After we went to bed, I pretended to be asleep because I didn't know what to say to you.

I couldn't think of anything that didn't sound stupid."

"Isn't that funny, because I was the same way with all of you!" replied Abigail. "You all seemed too healthy and so — I don't know, so capable! I felt like an ignoramus not even knowing anything about the ocean. I guess you have to grow up with the ocean to really know all about it."

"According to Andrew, nobody ever does get to know the ocean, at least not all of it. Oh, we know our own little bit of beach or harbor, but when you think of how enormous the ocean is, why, there must be thousands of girls just like us who feel as though they own a piece of it. That's one reason I'd like to be married at Fort Sewall. It would make me feel as if it were mine, just for that one day. Fort Sewall has been our playground since we were old enough to walk. It's nice to think that some day maybe Josiah and I will take our children up there to play." Susan was wistful, standing with her elbows in the suds.

Once again, Abigail felt a pang. "I'm

afraid I'm just a little jealous." she said. "Your future looks so perfect."

"But so will yours be!" cried Susan. "Just as soon as you find the right man, it will all fall into place."

"I wonder," said Abigail.

She thought of her mother. Had it all fallen into place for Henrietta? She didn't think so. Perhaps it fell into place and then kept falling out and you had to keep putting it back in place again. She wondered if Belle had put it back in place. It seemed so, but how could she just ignore what had happened? Perhaps nothing much had happened. That, at least, was a comforting thought. Drying her hands on a linen dish towel, she went back to the library to continue work on the jigsaw puzzle she had started that afternoon.

"C'n I help?" asked Tad. Ordinarily Abigail loathed interference in her puzzle doing, but poor Tad was so restless that she acquiesced.

"I'm looking for a piece that looks like a man with a big round head and a long left arm."

"Huh! There's hundreds like that!" he replied.

For an hour she was silent, engrossed in the puzzle. Tad had given up after ten minutes, declaring that anyone who could stand to do puzzles must be partially insane. The doorbell rang. Susan rushed to open it for Josiah, who was a pitiful sight indeed. All spring he had intended to get himself a set of oilskins, but he had put it off once too often. Water poured from the brim of his ruined hat in little streams that trickled from his chin onto his chest.

"Quick, come inside. Oh, you poor thing! You're soaked!" cried Susan.

"Such devotion should not go unrewarded," said Andrew, making his way to the kitchen for a mug of ale to present to the drenched Josiah.

"Wait up a minute, will you, Andrew?" said Josiah, peeling off his wet coat and smoothing back his hair. "There's something I'd like to discuss with you."

Abigail guessed what the something was. Susan and Josiah must have decided that this was the day to ask Abigail and

Andrew to stand up for them. The idea was intriguing — she and Andrew standing together while the minister read the ageless words. Surely it would make him stop and think.

Up until now she had never even thought of Andrew in the context of marriage. He had always been so distant, just like a storybook hero who rode off on the deck of a ship rather than a white charger. Now, however, she could be with him without flying into a state of near panic. Why, there were times this past week when she had been totally relaxed in his presence. She was not exactly sure what this meant, but she did know that this feeling of comfort with Andrew was much easier on her nerves. He was very pleasant to her, so pleasant that she felt he had perhaps forgiven her for her idiotic behavior on the boat. But forgiveness was all; any sign of romantic interest had gone. He stayed home all week and wore the broken-in clothes of the other fishermen, dressing up in a jacket only when the family had dinner together in the dining room.

Abigail thought that the dining room was perhaps her favorite room in the house. The old beehive oven still opened into the fireplace, and the crane that had held the pots of generations still swung over the fire. Occasionally Belle would cook over the open fire for old time's sake, and it was these meals that Abigail enjoyed the most. Steaming crocks of baked beans and thick stews which had cooked all day were favorites. By candlelight, they could have been living back in 1750. She liked to imagine herself in wide hoopskirts raising a glass to an elegant Andrew in powdered wig and silk breeches. She was sure he would have cut a fine figure. Speaking of which, she must give some thought to her dress for the wedding. Susan had decided to have just one attendant so she had told Abigail to choose her own color. Thank heavens she was finally allowed to select her own clothes! Of course, the wedding was to be at the end of August, so in all probability Mrs. Byors would be back from New York and would accompany the Curtises to Marblehead for the wedding.

Nevertheless, it took Abigail less than a minute to say, "Pink! I'd like to have pink, if it's all right with you."

"Do redheads wear pink?" asked Susan.

"You sound just like my governess," sighed Abigail. "Let me just say that although it is possible that most redheads don't wear pink, it is a positive fact that this particular redhead does!"

"Well, of course, dear, if that's what you want," said Susan, surprised at Abigail's vehemence.

"When I am married, I shall wear pink every day," said Abigail with a determined jut to her chin.

"See? You are planning on getting married after all," teased Susan.

Ah yes, thought Abigail. She was definitely counting on marriage. Young women always got married unless they wanted to wake up one day and find themselves spinsters. The spinsters Abigail had known were like half-people, barely tolerated by society. When the dinner party became too crowded, they were the first to be crossed off the list, if indeed they had been invited in the first place.

Society, having declared the couple to be its lowest common denominator, was particularly cruel to spinsters. It was an unbeatable conspiracy. If one was plain and discreet, one never got asked to go anywhere. On the other hand, if one had charm and a sparkling wit, one became a threat to the security of the married hostesses and, consequently, was never invited out at all. It was a conspiracy designed to promote early marriage and the quick transference of a daughter's dependence on her father to her husband. The fact that the marriages it promoted were often loveless was rarely admitted because, were a wife to attempt escape from her situation, she would once again find herself among the sorority of spinsters. It was a vicious spinning wheel which spun feelings and happiness alike into an ever tighter knot.

No, there would be no spinsterhood for Abigail! But what of marriage? Many times Abigail had tried unsuccessfully to envision herself in a happy marriage. Today, the prospect seemed dimmer than ever, and, feeling depression crowding in on her, she left Susan sewing in the library and went up the winding side stairs. Passing the landing on the second floor, she continued up another flight until she came to the attic door. It creaked in haunted house fashion as she pushed it open and went inside. The first attic room contained a marvelous artifactual display of six generations of family life. Belle's people liked to throw things away, but the Darcys were collectors. In the room were broken toys, ancient lanterns, scientific books full of outdated information, and best of all, trunk after trunk of old clothes. Many a Horribles Parade had been made festive by the addition of a feathered hat or a pair of pantaloons from the Darcy attics.

Winding gingerly between the boxes so as to avoid the dust which lay over everything, Abigail slowly made her way to still another stairway. This narrow set of ten steps led from the center of the room up to a scuttle (she had early learned this Marblehead word for a skylight) which was set into the rear roof just beyond its apex. Unlike the rest of the room, these steps were free of dust, for it was here that Abigail came when she wanted to think. She went up to the top step, which was broader than the others and, pushing her skirts under her, sat down and looked out. Below her lay the roofs and chimneys of downtown Marblehead. Gambrels and the steep-pitched remnants of the seventeenth century lay beneath her view like an extraterrestrial landscape. To the north lay Little Harbor, and to her right Fort Sewall stuck out like a forthright thumb. Beyond all this were the islands surrounded by a stormy gray sea. The waves crashed against rock, sending up jets of froth against the island shores, and over Abigail's head great black clouds sent down the last drops of the storm.

Last week she had come up here and looked at the spots of red on the horizon, wondering which one was the boat which held her captain; but today she knew where Andrew was. In the back bedroom which she never entered, he sat working on his financial records. She knew this because Tad had told her; Andrew never mentioned his room or what he did in it.

But he might as well be out at sea for all the comfort his nearness gave her. Abigail put her attention back on the view. Here and there a seagull would catch the currents of wind and hang seemingly motionless in ecstatic suspension — at least Abigail imagined it must be ecstasy to float so effortlessly above the churning sea. She also felt suspended in time, but she knew it was an illusion. Susan would be married in a few short weeks, and then would come the farewells and there would be Boston and parties and Abigail's real life would begin. It seemed hateful to her now, a detestable charade. The tears came. First the tears of love lost, then the tears of vanishing childhood, and finally the silent tears of the powerless. After several moments she sensed someone at the foot of the steps and looked down into the face of Andrew Darcy. He waited for her to dry her eyes on the hem of her dress.

"The others wondered where you were. I said I'd go find you. I had a feeling you might be up here. This was my secret place when I was a kid." She didn't answer but turned around and backed down the stairs.

"I'll go first; the stairs are steep," said Andrew as they went down the next flight. She was silent as they went back down into the library, where the others looked up at her and then tactfully away when they saw the swollen eyes. She sat down and picked up her needlework.

"The view is lovely from the attic scuttle," she said in an easy conversational voice. The others relaxed, and soon they were back to normal — all but Andrew, who sat staring into the fire. He was numb with the impact of the grief-stricken eyes that had stared down at him. Framed by the storm sky in the window, she had been the portrait of desolation. Pity for her shattered his resolve, and he felt his heart stir the way it did whenever he saw a beautiful creature in pain. Confused and shaken, he remained beside the fire trying to find patterns in the embers long after the others had left the room to prepare for dinner.

CHAPTER 19

After the rain came the sun, hot sunshine which raised mirages on the roads and dried the earthworms into odd curls on the sidewalks. Beds were sticky with each night's tossing, and hair either twisted into tight ringlets or refused to curl at all. Suppers were cold and tempers were hot. Plans for the wedding were forcing Belle into constant activity when she would rather have stretched out in the backyard hammock while an occasional breeze from Little Harbor blew over her.

Tad went swimming at least six times a day. First he would pull himself out of the cool August water in Lovis Cove and head home; then, after ten minutes of sweltering heat, he would head back to the beach again and jump in. He was not alone. Even Maurice came home early every night in order to cool off with a swim before supper, and the one time that Thomas had dropped in he spent sitting on a rock waist deep in blue Atlantic. Abigail had scarcely been able to conceal her swimming accomplishments from his paternal eye, but a fierce look from Tad restrained her just as she was about to plunge into the water headfirst. So she settled for wading around waist deep and dunking down so that her head looked like a floating ball on the ocean's surface. She loved the way the ocean looked from this exact eye level. Small boats loomed like privateers and short jutting rocks resembled the mountains of the moon. It was lovely to turn a complete circle and see water all around. Later at home Susan said. "You've become a mermaid this summer, hasn't she Tad?"

The three were setting the table for another of Belle's delicious cold suppers. Tonight it was to be a cold codfish loaf with an icy dressing of cucumbers and dill weed. Last night they had gone to the Adams House Restaurant for a shore dinner. Maurice had said correctly that it was too hot to cook. No doubt the cook at the restaurant would have agreed, but nobody asked him. And the heat continued.

Abigail started spending a good part of each day at Fort Sewall. Here, sitting on the eastern bank she was able to catch the air from both the north and the east. There was a particular tree whose branches mushroomed out and provided a circular canopy of shade over the reclining girl. Wiggling her toes in the thick grass, she would lean back on her elbows and half-doze in the noonday heat. Occasionally a group of children would come to play ball or to picnic, and then she would watch distractedly until they passed on by and she would be alone again. Eventually she would feel guilty about leaving Susan and Belle at home with the wedding plans, and so she would rise reluctantly to her feet and head back toward Franklin Street.

Slowly a week passed, and then it was the last week in August and Susan's wedding was looming large ahead. An only daughter, she was to have the finest day that her parents and nature could provide. The heat had pulled back into its fiery lair, and timidly the summer wind returned. Browned grass regained its green, and the dogs got up from under porches and began lumbering around.

In the master bedroom Maurice opened his arms to Belle, and she returned to the comfort and warmth of guiltless passion. The woman who had so easily slipped from harness had just as easily fallen into step again, and if her step was lighter for the wandering, who was to say that she was not still a good woman? Belle had never told Maurice about her infidelity. She had taken Aunt Gracie's second piece of advice after listening too late to benefit from the first.

She had not, however, had any chance to clear the air with Thomas, and she knew that she would feel involved until they talked it all out. She also knew she should feel guilty, and she did, but under her guilt and perhaps over it she cherished her sin, not for itself but because it had for a few desperate moments given her some measure of control over a life which had carried her along for twenty-five years. She wondered how many other women had used another man's passion to bolster their own self-esteem. And perhaps there was just a touch of anger there — anger for the oversights and especially anger against the relentless passage of time. For one night she and Thomas had suspended time, but the clock was once again ticking, and strangely enough, she didn't mind too much anymore.

Maurice was like a sailor who had almost drowned in a storm but had woken up to find himself safe on dry land; he didn't quite know how he got there, but he was grateful. He was also determined never to get into such rough waters again. By God! Belle was one fine woman, and he supposed he'd have to forgive Thomas for being attracted to her.

Forgiveness was his limit, though; he'd never trust Thomas as far as he could throw him again. Funny, he thought, how you could go on liking a man who had tried to steal your wife! He didn't quite understand it himself, but he supposed it had something to do with the fact that

Belle had come back home in the end. And it helped that he knew nothing of that night on the beach.

"Mum," asked Susan one morning, "will four hundred sandwiches be enough?"

"Well, I certainly hope so!" interrupted Maurice. "Who are you planning to invite anyway? The whole town?"

"Now, Maurice! Susan has lots of friends, and there are all our own friends to invite too," said Belle. "Gracie says she'll make sandwiches the whole day before if Abby will help her. We've decided to let the bride rest up that day. Oh, did I tell you that Henrietta wrote to ask Sue and Josiah if they'd like to use their Boston house for a honeymoon?"

"No. Say, that's damned nice of her, isn't it?" said Maurice.

"Yes. I guess that Thomas and Henrietta will stay here for a few days so that the newlyweds can have some time alone, and then, midweek, they'll bring Abigail home. Oh, dear! It's going to be so lonely here with Susan and Abigail both gone," Belle sighed.

"Cheer up, Ma! You've still got me!" called Tad, bounding into the kitchen with a happy grin on the freckled face. His teeth were white against his brown face as he grabbed his mother in a bear hug and squeezed until she begged for mercy.

"I guess we don't have to worry about this place becoming dull as long as you're around," said Maurice.

"No, sir! Nothing dull about me. Course, if you're worried about being lonely I could always bring home a couple dozen snakes for pets or maybe a frog or two!" Laughing at his own wit, he sat down to breakfast.

Finally the wedding plans were set. Susan was to be married at ten o'clock on the next Sunday morning. Who was to direct the choir at the Old North Church that morning had not yet been decided, but it would certainly not be Josiah. The bride would wear white, and her maid of honor would be in the palest pink. Tad would be the ring bearer and Andrew the best man. Josiah's father had died eight years before, and his mother was too old to make the long trip from his native Baltimore, but she had sent Susan a sincere letter of support and affection written in a frail hand which had brought tears to the eyes of both the bride and groom. Despite his parents' absence, Josiah would not be alone; he had made good and true friends in Marblehead. Although he did not shine socially, he was the sort in whom men put their trust and whose judgment they valued.

They had invited more than two hundred guests despite Maurice's feigned horror; thus the four hundred sandwiches (which Maurice knew would go to waste, but no one listened to him).

Tad was happy about everything except his new suit. The dressmaker was in despair after an hour of trying to make him stand still while she tried to fit him. His shoulders refused to line up, probably because his weight kept shifting from foot to foot and also because he had arranged a target game to keep himself amused where he threw spools into a wastebasket which he had placed five feet in front of him. The clatter of his successes was only slightly less unnerving than his misses, which generally bounced off the sides of the basket and went skipping across the wooden floor. The dressmaker knew that she would be making good money, what with the wedding gown, the bridesmaid's dress, and the bride's mother's blue morning gown, so she bit her tongue except for once when a spool hit her square on her round behind as she was bending to adjust a trouser leg. Then she screamed but settled down quickly enough when Tad apologized with the full force of his twelve-year-old charm.

Maurice's job was to pay the bills and keep out of the way. Paying the bills was distasteful, and keeping out of the way became increasingly difficult as room after room was taken up with supplies and projects. Eventually he would head to his club, where he was given the amused sympathy of those who had already been through it. What bothered him the most was the way the women would ask his advice on a subject and then decide it among themselves before he could even get his mouth open. But Belle was happy again, and he sustained himself with that.

Abigail was feeling more than a little bit sorry for herself. As each day passed and Susan came closer to her happiness, Abigail came nearer to the end of this almost magical summer. She couldn't imagine going back to her shell in Boston, but then, she hadn't been able to imagine coming to Marblehead either. She wondered what would become of Andrew. Most likely he would meet some sensible girl and settle down to raise good sensible children. There would be many eligible girls at the wedding; surely one would catch his eye. Jealousy tore across her chest, and she closed her eyes tightly to shut out the image of Andrew with someone else. But the image remained under her lids like red rings of sunshine, and she hovered between wanting it to end quickly and wanting to savor each painful moment up to the end.

CHAPTER 20

Out of nowhere an opportunity arose which raised Abigail from the well of despondency into which she had crawled. The Darcy family decided to accept a long-standing invitation to a dance at the Corinthian Yacht Club on the Friday evening before Susan's wedding. At first Belle had declined the invitation, fearing that a dance would be too much for everyone to cope with so soon before the Sunday wedding. But the event was special; the dance honored the yachtsmen of Germany and America who were to compete in the German-American races to be held a week hence, and as Sunday approached the Darcys were all so near to overflowing with excitement that it seemed a good thing for everyone to get out and let off a little steam. The only disappointment, and it was a big one, came when Andrew announced at dinner on Thursday that although he would be happy to deliver them all to the Corinthian pier by boat, he would not be attending the dance himself.

"But Andrew! Please come! You know how much everyone loves to see you. Besides it will be your last chance to dance with me before I become a stuffy old married lady!" said Susan.

"Why I like that!" retorted Belle. "Stuffy old married lady, indeed!"

"No offense, Mama," laughed Susan. "But honestly, Andrew. You're becoming a regular recluse. Everywhere I go people ask for you, and all I can say is that you're working as usual."

"C'mon now. I don't have anything against a good time, but you know how I feel about the yachting crowd. I just don't have anything in common with them. All they can talk about is speed! How can you be comfortable with men who're so busy thinking about getting there before everybody else that they forget why boats were invented in the first place. It's all just little games to them."

"You could at least come and dance with me and Abigail; then you could go home if you want," persisted Susan unaware that Abigail was shifting uncomfortably in her chair.

"All right, all right. I'll come in for a dance or two and then get lost. And," he continued, "I can guarantee that no one will even miss me."

"Not true," said Susan. "I'll miss you, and Abigail will too. Right, Abby?"

"Of course," said Abigail, unable to say more. As it was, she had kept her head down over her dinner plate throughout this entire conversation to avoid looking at Andrew.

So the weekend came, and on Friday Maurice, Belle, Susan, and Abigail walked once again down Front Street to the public landing where Andrew was to meet them in the *Joseph Homan*. Tad was considered too young for an evening dance. Susan and Abigail had made a special trip to Webbers store for new hair ribbons to accent their white summer frocks, and now they made a pretty picture as together they passed the old-timers on their bench.

Susan, the taller, wore her blond hair straight and tied back with a blue ribbon, while Abigail, her shoulders almost bare, wore a yellow ribbon amongst her pinned-up curls. They speeded up as they spotted Andrew, who had pulled up to the float and was now waiting patiently as he stood ready to help them all in. In his white summer dress suit he made a startling picture, surrounded as he was by ropes and seines and all the other accoutrements of his profession; but such scenes were not uncommon in a Marblehead summer where society and the sea were forced into close quarters.

Abigail thought that he looked wonderful, like some debonair pirate tanned a deep mahogany during endless hours at sea. His smile was white in the dusk, and he looked not too unhappy to be escorting his good-looking cargo to its destination.

The trip across the harbor took a scant five minutes. As they approached the Corinthian float, Abigail looked around her and saw the great number of visiting yachts which had gathered to honor the

German visitors — beautiful boats with burnished teak decks, and jaunty sloops inhabited by white-coated gentlemen who waved or saluted as they cast admiring glances toward the covey of beauties aboard the *Joseph Homan*. The air was warm with a light salt flavor, and Abigail was genuinely happy for the first time in days when Andrew took her arm and smiled at her as he helped her onto the float.

"Oh, wait!" she cried. "I've left my shawl on board. You others go on up. I'll be right there."

"It's all right. Go ahead. I'll bring Abby up," said Andrew. He jumped easily back on board and retrieved the shawl.

At the exact moment when he turned his back, a lovely white forty-foot yacht pulled up to the other side of the float, and out jumped Burton Madison. For a terrible moment, Abigail thought she was going to faint. Burton, however, seemed his usual unruffled self.

"Good heavens, can it really be? Mother said you had gone to Marblehead, but I had no idea you were still here.'' He came closer and she could smell the whiskey on his breath.

''Actually that's a lie. I came here determined to find you again. Somehow I can't forget how nice you looked the last time I saw you.''

The impertinence of him! thought Abigail, red with confusion. She could see that he was nearly drunk. She had still not found her voice when Andrew turned around holding her shawl, and the two men stood face to face.

''Why, it's the cousin, right?'' said Burt an insolent edge to his voice. ''I hadn't realized that fishermen were fond of dancing.'' He wasn't smiling anymore.

''Don't be rude, Burt!'' said Abigail, regaining her poise in defense of Andrew.

''No need to defend me, Abigail. It's obvious your friend here doesn't know enough about the sea to have any idea about what fishermen like. Just look at the knot he tied, or tried to tie, if you want proof.'' Andrew was glaring at Burt with undisguised contempt.

''Now, just stop it, you two!'' said

Abigail, astonished by Andrew's sudden display of rudeness.

"Your cousin seems a little put out at me," said Burton. "Perhaps he resents our former friendship."

"I don't know what you're talking about," insisted Abigail. Her breath started coming too fast, and she fought down the color which threatened to turn her face into a beacon. "I'm sure Andrew doesn't mind any of my friends," she said.

"Speak for yourself," said Andrew sharply. "As a matter of fact, he's quite right about one thing. I find myself in no mood for dancing. We poor fishermen are too busy with our stinking work to find time for the more elegant things in life."

He bowed to Abigail with mock courtliness, and with two deft yanks at his bow and stern lines he jumped aboard the *Joseph Homan* and sailed away, never looking back to where Abigail was left alone on the float with Burt. Behind him she could see Burt's companions still sitting on the deck of the yacht, glasses in hand.

"Do come meet my friends from

Newport, Abigail, dear. Why, I've told them all about you! They'd be devastated if you didn't give them a chance to see for themselves how beautiful you are."

He tried to put his arm around her waist, and once again she smelled the odor of alcohol and that special scent she had always found so attractive. How could Andrew just leave her like this? Of course, he didn't know the whole story about herself and Burt, thank God, but he was cruel to just sail away like that. She could no longer deny to herself that she obviously meant less than nothing to Andrew Darcy.

"No. I certainly cannot meet your friends." She spoke as firmly as her shaken self-respect would allow. "My aunt and uncle are waiting for me inside."

She started up the gangplank holding tightly to the rail for support, but he grabbed at her and turned her around. She stared into the familiar blue eyes and noticed the fair hair which was disheveled with wind or whiskey. He was looking at her with unmasked desire. She felt her own body give an involuntary lurch in response.

"Don't go. We have unfinished business, you and I." His voice was husky.

"Any 'business' we have had is over!" she replied in a fierce whisper, and wrenched herself free.

"I'll see you later," said Burt as Abigail walked unsteadily up the ramp, uncertain of whether it was the movement of the ocean beneath her or her own heart that made her footsteps so unsure.

Inside the yacht club the American Watch Club Band was already playing. The band was a good one and the dancers were having a fine time whirling this way and that. She glanced around the room. Susan was dancing with Josiah, and Maurice was standing in front of the large trophy case talking with his friends. Belle came toward her and, noticing the strange expression on her face, said. "What's wrong, dear, and where is Andrew?"

"Oh, Aunt Belle. Something dreadful has happened! Do you remember that Burton Madison from Boston? The one I was sent here to get away from? Well, he's here and he's been drinking and he and Andrew have had words and Andrew has sailed off." She said all this in a single breath, and Belle quickly broke in.

"There, there, dear; nobody knows a thing about Burton Madison except me. I told Maurice there was a boy, but I never mentioned his name, and anyway Maurice would never have remembered even if I had; he's terrible with names. So let's just forget him, and if he makes any trouble I shall simply have the Commodore throw him out! So that's that." She spoke cheerfully, and Abigail was reassured.

"Oh, thank you, Aunt Belle. I never wanted to see him again." But was she being honest? She could not forget the brief flicker of response she had felt when Burt had looked at her on the float.

"And," Belle continued, "don't you worry about Andrew. He doesn't enjoy dancing much anyway. He was probably just looking for an excuse to get away. He'll be fine by morning. Don't you go blaming yourself."

The music continued, and Abigail found herself the center of much attention when one of the German captains clicked his heels and bent his lips over her hand as he requested a dance. He danced very well, holding her firmly in his arms as he waltzed her around the floor.

"Huh, Fraulein! You dance the waltz very good, I think."

"Thank you, captain," responded Abigail, beginning to enjoy herself despite the ugly encounter between Andrew and Burton. Whirling in large circles so that the skirt of her summer dress floated out behind her, she was the object of all eyes. Several gentlemen asked each other who she was, and altogether it was a very satisfying experience, rather like being Cinderella at the ball. When the waltz ended, she thanked the captain again, but he had scarcely delivered her back to Belle's side when another fellow asked her to dance.

And so it continued, until she felt as if she were in another world. The sensation of being young and attractive was balm to her wounded ego. She realized that her relationship with Andrew during the last tenuous months had battered her self-esteem. Try as she might, she couldn't see where she had gone wrong! Of course, she had bungled that whole episode on the night before Independence Day, but if you didn't count the raised hand, she had done only what any other decently reared girl should have done. Well, perhaps she shouldn't have responded to the kiss, but gracious! She was only human. Couldn't he understand her confusion? As these thoughts meandered through her brain, she knew that she was reluctantly beginning to comprehend Andrew's nature; he was not so much the mysterious stranger anymore. There was a stubborn Yankee pride there, and she couldn't quite figure a way to get around or through it. And tonight had been a disaster. Damn that Burton Madison and his blue eyes! He always seemed to spell trouble for her. Why was it that he drew out her physical side so? Because, there was no denying it, she had felt the same warmth tonight when he had held her gaze for those few moments. I hope he's gone, thought Abigail, and, turning back to more pleasant thoughts, she accepted a dance from a fine-looking gentlemen in evening dress.

As the evening wore on, the Darcys became more and more involved with their own friends, and as a consequence Abigail found herself almost completely on her own. During the band's intermission she wandered out on the veranda to cool off after all the dancing. Feeling the sudden rush of night air, she missed her shawl. In his haste to get away, Andrew had forgotten to give it to her. She took a few steps down the broad staircase that led to the beach below and, finding a sheltered spot halfway down, sat and put her arms around her knees.

From far behind her she could hear the voices of the crowd, merry with wine and good will. Before her lay the harbor dappled with a hundred boats, their lamps casting shimmering light trails across the water to where she sat. The moon was half-hidden behind a cloud, and she strained to see across the harbor to Fort Sewall. She located the point easily enough and traced the shore back to Oakum Bay, which was what most people called Lovis Cove nowadays, according to Tad, who still preferred the old name. So many quaint names. And she must try to remember them all and imprint them firmly on her memory so that they might not drift off with next week's tide. The evening was becoming cool, and she stood slowly in order to rejoin the warmth of the dance floor, but as she turned to go back up a hand came down on her shoulder. A cry rose to her lips, but before she could call out, another hand covered her mouth, and she was pulled down the steps and down under the porch. Overhead the band had started to play, and even when the hand released her and she spun around to see her captor, she knew that her voice would never be heard above the music. A very drunk Burt Madison held her firmly around the waist.

"Let me go!" she cried, genuinely frightened.

"Not this time, Abby dear!" His words were slurred and his eyes glinted steel in the latticed shadows of the porch. The entire scene was unreal, a dream evening turned into a nightmare.

"The fellows are ready to go out to the mooring, but I told 'em I had some unfinished business to attend to first."

She struggled against his grip and he staggered slightly, but not for a second did he let her go. His other hand held the curls behind her head, and he forced her mouth up to his. Gone was the sweetness of his first kiss; instead she felt his mouth grind painfully against hers. The smell of whiskey was overpowering, and she felt that she would be sick. His hand roughly pulled at her dress, and despite her one free hand struggling to cover herself, he exposed her once again and began mauling her breasts. His thigh pressed hard against her, and she knew he had no intention of letting her go. Down she fell as he pushed his body weight onto hers. The sand was coarse under her bare shoulders, and she screamed, but her voice was lost in the loud German music which thundered above.

No, she thought. No! This will not happen. With a strength that surprised her, she kicked out at him and at the same instant clawed his face. He let go, cursing for an instant as blood coursed down his face, and in that instant Abigail scrambled to her feet and ran out onto the beach. She ran up the steps as fast as she could and, finding a dark corner, tried to rearrange herself.

Her hair had fallen down, and there was sand everywhere on her back. Her dress was disheveled but fortunately not torn. She did the best she could to adjust her clothing and then tapped on a window to get the attention of a club waiter inside. He came obediently out onto the porch.

"Would you please find Mrs. Darcy and ask her come out here?"

The waiter scurried off, a perplexed expression on his face, and minutes later Belle emerged onto the porch.

"Good heavens, dear! What happened?" she asked.

"It was Burt. Oh, Aunt Belle, he attacked me. He tried to . . ." She broke into sobs.

"Oh, my poor girl, you're safe now," said Belle, embracing her. "Is he gone, do you think?"

"I think so," said Abigail.

"Shall I send Maurice after him?"

"Oh please, no! I just want to forget about it. If anyone found out, I'd die."

"All right, darling. We'll just hope he goes away forever. Now, let's put you back together." With sure fingers, Belle rearranged the dark red hair and brushed the sand away. Within minutes Abigail was set to rights, and only the bright stain on her cheeks remained to testify to her ordeal. The two women went inside, where Maurice looked questioningly across at them. Belle gave him a signal that all was well, and soon Abigail was back in the arms of the German Captain who clearly fancied her, and together they danced to the oom-pah-pah until even Abigail's flush was indistinguishable from everyone else's.

At one o'clock the band packed away their instruments and the dancers bade prolonged good-nights to each other and prepared to depart.

"Auf wiedersehen, Fraulein," said the German captain, who Abigail had learned was Captain Neumeister, and he bowed again as the Darcys departed.

At the end of the Corinthian float

Andrew waited silently in the *Joseph Homan*. As the group approached he helped them aboard, and as Abigail stepped onto the deck he said, "Your shawl, madame!" Was that a trace of good humor on his face? Well, the very idea! Here he was completely restored to good spirits while she had just undergone the worst experience of her life. She would never understand men! Wrapping her shawl tightly around her, she sat furiously quiet all the way across the harbor.

CHAPTER 21

The next day, which was the day before the wedding, Abigail and Tad took the cart down to the bakery, where they picked up the dozens of loaves of bread for the sandwiches. Driving the horse down Washington Street, Abigail recalled her first day in town. The shops were old friends now, and she waved to several people who had been strangers only a few months ago. Her hair was up on her head under a straw bonnet, and her skin was the color of the dusky roses which climbed over the fence behind Gracie's house. Her hands were still smooth but firmer, and new muscles moved under her shirtwaist as she guided the animal past the Town House. Swimming had smoothed her out, and given a firm foundation to the rounded figure. The summer had underscored her sensuality by replacing morbid curiosity with healthy desire based on strength and genuine appetite for nature.

At the bakery her small nostrils dilated to inhale the aroma of the bread which Tad was heaping into the cart. When they reentered Franklin Street, she saw Andrew unloading the chairs which they had borrowed from the church for tomorrow's reception. He was barechested, his long back tapering from broad shoulders, and a rivulet of sweat was trickling down the curve of his spine. Under the August sun his curled hair gleamed blue black. Coming upon him like this, Abigail was defenseless. All the desire in her young body rose up like a tide until she felt tears stinging in her eyes. She looked away and focused on the house across the street, a seventeenth-century classic with steep-pitched roof and high-placed windows. When she had regained her composure, she looked back. Andrew had disappeared and Gracie was beckoning at the door.

"Hurry up, child! We've got a lot to do before sundown," cried Gracie as Abigail alighted and went into the now familiar kitchen. "Your aunt brought over most of the fillings, so I guess we'll just make up the chicken salad and then put everything together." Within half an hour the two were seated across from each other at the large kitchen table. They had worked out a system where Abigail spread the filling on one piece of bread and passed it over to Gracie, who put on the top slice of bread and then cut it and packed it away on a tray which, when filled, would go tightly covered into the icebox until tomorrow.

"Well, Abby. You haven't got much time. What are you planning to do?" asked Gracie after ten minutes of absolute quiet.

"About what?" asked Abigail, avoiding the sharp eyes.

"About Andrew, of course. Maybe I can't walk, but I sure can see. What in the name of God have you two been doing to each other? Why, just now he turned and saw you and took off into the house like a jackrabbit. He's been acting queer ever since you came, and if you ask me, you're just as bad. So what's going on?" She peered intently at Abigail.

"Nothing's going on. That's just the trouble. You said it yourself. He avoids me whenever he can."

"There's got to be more to it than that. Why does he avoid you? What happened?" Gracie was determined to have it out. She had known Andrew since he was born, and she loved him like a son — better in fact than all the others, though she'd never admit it.

"I did something stupid early in the summer, and he's been like this ever since," said Abigail, sensing that Gracie's will was stronger than her own pride. Gracie waited for her to continue, and finally Abby went on. "We were out on his boat the night of the band concert before the Fourth of July and he kissed me and I tried to slap him."

"Why, you damned fool! Whatever did you do that for? Andy'd never take advantage! And don't tell me you don't think he's attractive. Huh! I've seen you look at him. Why, coming down the street you were looking at him like he was a big piece of chocolate and you were in front of the candy store."

"But don't you see? That's just it! I found him too attractive, and I hardly knew him. In Boston I let someone kiss me — and more — and he turned out to be a fortune hunter."

"Andy's no fortune hunter. Why, the very idea is ridiculous! The only fortune he's busy hunting is his own, and that too damned hard if you ask me. But just what do you mean, 'I let him kiss me — and more'?"

"Oh, not what you're thinking! But enough so that it scared me," said Abigail, spreading ham salad on a square of bread and passing it over.

"Well, that's a relief. Andrew may be a good-looking man, but I doubt if he's ever acted up much with the girls. Too much self-respect to go chasing what he didn't really plan to hold on to. But he'll be glad to know you're all in one piece, so to speak." Gracie grinned her toothless smile.

"He'll never know or care. The damage is done already, Aunt Gracie; he doesn't want me anymore."

"Oh, whip! That's foolishness, and you know it. Abigail, you listen to me! You're just exactly what he does want and just what he needs, too, though I doubt if he knows that yet. He's always been too serious and hard on himself. He needs someone who will keep him cheerful and who'll warm him up at night and keep his mind off the ocean all the time. There are lots of sailors like Andrew. They fall in love with the sea and never get over it, and it turns them strange after awhile. What they need is something real on the land to balance it and make them a whole person. It takes a mighty potent woman to manage it, but you're that, Abigail, if I ever saw one! And he knows it, too. That's why he's fighting it so hard. Help him out, Abby. He's shy in his way. You'll have to move quick! You've only got a week, and he might be stubborn enough to let you walk off without a word."

"But what can I do? If I throw myself at him, he'll just be more sure than ever that I'm no good. Besides, I've never thrown myself at any man and I don't intend to start now. If he's half the man you seem to think he is, and if he cares for me — which I don't believe for a second! — then he'll have to come his share of the distance. But Aunt Gracie! What if he doesn't? I don't think I can ever forget him.''

''There'll be no need to forget him, child; just wait and see.''

''Aunt Gracie? Promise you'll never tell anyone about our talk, please?''

''Course I won't! Besides, it'd be bad strategy.'' She chuckled. Then, ''Good heavens! Look at the time. It's past noon. What do you say we steal a few of these sandwiches?''

CHAPTER 22

Susan woke up with a start and leapt out of bed. Throwing open the muslin curtains at her window, she looked out at a haze of morning fog.

"Oh dear! I hope it's not going to rain!" she cried.

"What time is it?" mumbled Abigail with a trace of early morning grumpiness in her voice. She turned over and contemplated the blond figure at the window.

"It's overcast. Oh, Abby, it mustn't rain! Not today!"

"Oh, Susan! It's your wedding day. I almost forgot," said Abigail. She threw her sleepiness aside and tried to give her full attention to the matter at hand. Going to the window, she put a sisterly arm around Susan's waist and said, "It's not going to rain, silly. It always looks like this early in the morning. Remember how clear the sky was last night? How could it possibly rain?"

Last night they had sent Josiah home early and all gone for a last-minute walk to Fort Sewall. In the twilight the branches of Abigail's favorite tree had stretched dark fingers against the last lingering rays of light which hovered over the harbor as if reluctant to abandon such beauty to the night. The family group moved up to the point and stood together as a unit for the last time. Scanning their faces, Abigail saw the mist in Belle's eyes as she held her husband's hand. Susan was exhausted but happy, anticipating the morning; she was too busy looking ahead to be nostalgic, which was just as it should be.

All evening Andrew had been in a jovial mood, teasing Susan about her new responsibilities and taking every available opportunity to give her an affectionate squeeze, but now he became sober as evening surrounded him. Like Abigail, he realized that Susan's marriage represented an end to any attachment he might have had with his cousin. His thoughts were still confused, but he had managed to come up with one conclusion — he cared for her. Although she was the furthest thing from any of his former notions about a wife, he wanted her badly. Counterbalancing his instincts was the reasonable thought that she could probably never be content as a fisherman's wife; and despite his good income, he could imagine the face of Henrietta Curtis if she ever thought that Abigail might remain forever in Marblehead. Even deeper than these reservations was the fear that she might prove too volatile for him. He had seen her hand raised once, and the emotion that had shot from those incredible green eyes had almost knocked him down. He had no doubts whatever about his ability to stand his ground, but he had certainly never thought it would be necessary. It bothered him that he would never fully understand her.

He had imagined a comfortable life with a comfortable wife. The idea of spending the rest of his life slightly-off-balance was most unsettling. But, he thought, it's only speculation anyway. She'll be gone in two days, and that will be the end of it. There remained, however, the rapidly forming conviction that he could never allow her to go away. Some sign, some indication that she loved him, and he knew he would throw his dreams of tranquility to the summer wind.

Those had been evening thoughts; mornings were made for deeds. At seven o'clock on her wedding day Susan rushed to her mother's room only to discover that Belle had been awake since dawn running over innumerable lists in her mind, lists of guests and clothes and food. Particularly she wondered how they were ever going to fit all the guests into the house. Although the house itself was large, the rooms, in typical eighteenth-century style, were small. They had been designed so that each could be heated thoroughly by a fireplace. This gave a cozy feeling to the house, but cozy was the last thing Belle wanted at a summer wedding. Space was the one necessity, and so she too prayed for sun so that the guests could spread out into the backyard. Maurice awoke at seven-thirty wishing that it was two in the afternoon and that Susan was safely married and that he was standing, wine glass in hand, among his peers accepting their congratulations and relaxing for the first time in two weeks. Breakfast was eaten on the run while beds were hastily made.

"Do you suppose I should be getting dressed?" asked Susan at nine o'clock.

"I don't think so," replied Abigail. "I can remember getting dressed too early for my first dinner party, and by the time the guests arrived I was all droopy. It's better to jump into your clothes at the last minute. That way you look fresh!"

"I feel as if I've been up for hours. Oh, why do they have that idiotic rule about the groom not being allowed to see the bride before the wedding? Somehow I think I'd feel so much better if Josiah were here. It's ridiculous, because I know Josiah loves me, and he's really the most reliable man I've ever met, but I still have this terrible feeling that he might not show up at Fort Sewall!"

Susan was undergoing all the necessary

qualms and fears which face normal folk on momentous occasions. It was Abigail's brainstorm to take Susan next door. She was certain that Aunt Gracie could do a far better job than she of calming Susan down, and Gracie didn't disappoint her.

Sitting in her "outdoor" wheelchair, Gracie was downright overpowering. Her sparse hair was done up in a chignon, and she had pulled the knob of hair so tightly that her eyes slanted up at the corners. The resultant expression on the old face was that of an ancient enthroned mandarin holding court. The effect was heightened by the red silk dress she had chosen for the occasion. Around her neck was a necklace of white coral. Abigail and Susan were spellbound by this apparition. There was something about Gracie's expression, however, which stifled any desire the girls might have had to smile.

"What's the matter? Never seen me all dressed up before? Well, nothing's too grand for a wedding, I say. C'mon in!" she wheeled rapidly around, and they followed her inside.

"I suppose you're all worked up?" She

357

looked at Susan. "That's a good sign. The only people who don't get a little nervous about things are the ones who don't give a hoot, and it seems to me that a person ought to give a hoot on their wedding day. I'll bet your Josiah's a total wreck!" She grinned and the girls grinned back.

"Why, that's right, isn't it?" said Susan, relieved. "Of course I'm nervous. This is probably the most important day of my life. It's natural to be nervous."

"That's the way to think, honey," said Gracie proudly. "And it's true for new mothers too, which no doubt you'll find out before long. Show me a relaxed new mother and I'll show you a damned fool! Babies are serious business until you get used to them; you need some nervousness to keep you on your toes. Now, that doesn't mean you can't relax and enjoy 'em some of the time; life's supposed to be some fun, but you need to care, that's all. But why are you two over here today? You'd best run along and get ready. Mustn't keep a good man waiting!"

"We just wanted to make sure you were all set for the wedding, that's all," said Abigail.

"Andrew's coming for me soon. He's goin' to push me up the hill. It's a good thing he grew up to be so strong — otherwise I'd end up head-over-teakettle in the harbor." She looked directly at Abigail as she spoke. Fortunately Susan was in no mood to notice.

"Now give me a kiss and scoot!" she ordered.

When they went up to change, Abigail heard Andrew's voice coming from the back of the house.

"How in the name of God do you tie this damned thing?!" he bellowed. "Somebody help me before I strangle myself!"

"I'll help!" called Abigail.

Many times as a child she had tied her father's black bow tie before he went out to a formal dinner. It had been their special time together, a shared moment before she surrendered him to the outside world. But now as she went toward Andrew's room her hands were shaking. Gracie had said to grab her opportunity before it was too late, and heaven knew she was no coward!

Andrew's room was small, too small for the great lumbering male who occupied it. His bed was long and narrow. Abigail was impressed with its lovely coverlet, an Indian shawl in shades of amber and gold. She was even more impressed by the fact that the bed was so neatly made that the family cat who slept curled up in its center made scarcely a wrinkle. On the walls were framed navigational charts. The charts were the only decoration, yet the rows of books that lined one wall softened the bareness of the uncovered floor. Abigail's mind flashed back to her first meeting with Andrew when he had contradicted her assumption that he was an illiterate rustic. Glancing at the titles, Abigail was surprised to see the poems of Lord Byron and a well-worn set of Shakespearean plays among the many volumes on fishing and sailing.

"You've never been here, have you?" said Andrew, still struggling with his tie. He stood facing a maple-framed mirror which was placed over a simple chest of drawers. She realized that he had been watching her eyes as they had roamed over his private sanctuary.

"I should have remembered that you would probably have more experience with formal dress than I do." He spoke not unkindly, although Abigail had become accustomed to hearing criticism in every word he spoke.

"Goodness," she said, "you've certainly made a botch of that! Now just let go and let me do it. I've done this dozens of times."

"Oh, really?" His eyebrows rose and Abigail blushed. "For my father, of course," she stated, exasperated by her inability to retain her composure around him.

"Of course!" said Andrew. His dark eyes danced as her fingers trembled but deftly tied the bow. His head was bent so that she felt his breath stirring the wisps of auburn hair on her brow. She knew that he was staring down at her. All she would have to do was raise her eyes the slightest bit and . . .

"There you are! You'd better hurry up. Aunt Gracie's waiting at the door, and

Susan needs help with her veil." Tad was flushed with excitement, and in his new suit he was quite dashing. He was also the last person Abigail wanted to see at this particular moment.

Quickly she stepped back as if caught in an indiscretion, but as she left the room she looked back at Andrew and saw the fire in his dark eyes and the two spots of color on the angular cheekbones.

Reentering her own room, Abigail was taken aback by the sight of Susan in full wedding dress. Standing immobile, she was a frail cloud of white and gold. Her veil made a nimbus around the blond head, and against the summer glow of her skin the eyes shone brightest blue.

"You look beautiful, Susan," whispered Abigail. She remembered the barefoot girl with the muddy skirt whom she had met a few months ago in the kitchen. Strange how these sudden pictures of earlier moments kept coming into her head today. Didn't they say that a drowning person saw his entire life flashing before his eyes? But, of course, she wasn't drowning! Or was she?

"Mum says I must wait until all the guests are at Fort Sewall before I go up in the carriage. I do believe she is expecting me to make a grand entrance." Susan was remarkably calm. Abigail was sure she herself would be close to fainting in Susan's place.

"There is no possible way you could do anything but make a grand entrance, the way you look. Why, I won't be surprised if some of those old revolutionary ghosts come floating up to admire you. Tad said you were having trouble with your veil; it looks just fine to me."

"Is it really all right? Oh, Abigail, it's time almost."

The two girls went to the window and saw the last of the guests heading down Franklin Street toward the fort. Below the window Andrew was pushing a chatting Aunt Gracie along in her wheelchair. He suddenly looked up at the window and blew a quick kiss toward his sister, but Abigail caught the kiss in her heart and kept it for herself.

Downstairs Belle and Maurice were waiting for the girls, and Tad was plumping up the little cushion on which he was to bear the ring. All three were hushed as Susan descended the staircase. The train of her gown spread out behind her.

"Stop!" called Maurice. "Just stay there a minute. I want to remember you just like that, coming down the stairs."

For a lingering moment Susan and Maurice shared a look full of the special feelings understood only by fathers and daughters. It was in that moment that Maurice gave away his daughter.

Then the five of them climbed carefully into the waiting open carriage, which slowly trundled toward its destination.

At Fort Sewall, the many wedding guests were milling about under the hazy August sky. Several youngsters ran back and forth from the end of the road to the northern point where the ceremony would be performed. "Not yet," they would cry and then run back to assume their vigil.

Finally the call went out, "She's coming!", and a hush came over the assembly as they quickly took their places in a large semicircle around the stand of flowers which would serve as altar. By the time the carriage entered the park, the stillness was so complete that each squeak of the carriage wheels echoed ahead and signaled the arrival. The air was warm — Susan had chosen to be married in the late morning in anticipation of the heat which usually settled in during the midafternoon — and true to Abigail's promise, the overcast sky of morning had thinned out into a haze as fine as the veil which floated around Susan's golden hair.

While all eyes were on the wedding party, Josiah, the Reverend Hamilton, and Andrew materialized from an adjoining yard. The ceremony was to be traditional with the setting the only exception to New England taste. Abigail led the procession down the path which served as an aisle. Her eyes were dropped demurely, and her hands clasped a bouquet of roses. Her upswept hair was partially covered by a veil of pink which matched the pink of her gown. So beautiful was she that the eyes which watched her approach were reluctant to pass on to those behind her. Andrew, standing darkly attractive in formal dress, looked at the rose figure and gave up his last remnant of resistance. He knew in that moment that regardless of how much he might deny it, this girl was wedged firmly into his heart. And Abigail, raising her gaze in order to ascend the small altar mound, looked directly into those dark eyes and knew absolutely that she would never leave this place until she had found out the truth about his feelings. How clean he looked. The memory of Burton Madison came back, and shame flooded her. She felt guilty for even having compared him to Andrew.

The rest of the ceremony passed in a blur for Abigail. Not so Susan. Unlike most brides, she was clearheaded and serene. From the moment she saw her beloved Josiah, she felt tension flow out and away. Behind his head she saw the gulls and the muted coastline of Manchester and Rockport. Carefully she took her place beside Josiah and turned her full attention to the minister. The Reverend Hamilton was a man of solid stature, a man of confidence and more than a slight histrionic bent. After an exaggerated clearing of his throat, he began the service, and it became apparent why he had been the perfect choice for this particular ceremony. No Demosthenes could have projected his voice over the sound of waves below better than Reverend Hamilton. The clear voice lent majesty to the scene, though it would have been difficult to imagine a more impressive sight than the wedding party which stood apart, surrounded by the most overwhelming beauty that nature could provide. A light breeze stirred the skirts of the bride and maid of honor, and the scent of summer blossoms pervaded the senses of the already enchanted onlookers. In the clear light of day the vows were declared, and even those who had thought the wedding unorthodox were forced to admit that it was a moving experience, a wedding of nature and God as well as man and woman.

Belle held on tightly to Maurice, never giving a thought to Thomas and Henrietta Curtis who were standing as befitted family, in the front row. Beside them stood dear Mrs. Byors, who was dabbing away at her eyes as much from the joy of seeing her own Abigail again as from the emotion of the wedding.

Thomas and Henrietta repeated to themselves the same vows they had made twenty years before. Just last week they had celebrated their twentieth wedding anniversary, and Henrietta was definitely hopeful. Not complacent — no, never complacent again — but hopeful. Thomas had made his own vows with all the zeal of a reformed sinner who more than half-suspects that he may someday sin again. Nevertheless, he pledged to try and he also was hopeful.

As soon as the minister said, "You may kiss the bride," the crowd broke into happy conversation and began closing around Susan and Josiah with cheerful congratulations.

Abigail ran to her parents and, hugging Mrs. Byors, almost lifted her off the ground in her happiness to see her again.

"Mercy! You've grown as strong as a bull," cried Mrs. Byors. "But you're still my own dear girl now, aren't you?"

"Of course I am — that is, as long as

you promise not to criticize my pink dress!'' She spun around to show it off, and at least one gentlemen in the crowd stumbled and almost fell as he forgot to watch where he was going.

"Oh, you haven't changed a bit! Still acting up as much as ever!'' cried Mrs. Byors, delighted. She tactfully refrained from comment on her darling's deep complexion and on the new muscles in the exposed forearm.

"You must have missed Boston terribly, Abigail,'' she said.

"Boston? No, not at all. Of course I missed you and Mummy and Daddy, but, do you know, I've scarcely thought about Boston at all since the first day I arrived.''

"Hmm.'' Mrs. Byors clearly disapproved of this response but kept her silence — for the moment.

Henrietta embraced her daughter and then moved aside to make way for Thomas. For a few seconds she stood apart from the others. Admiring guests may have seen an elegant woman in blue standing almost motionless, a lace shawl over her shoulders, but the familiar eye of

Maurice Darcy catching sight of her across the heads of the milling group saw a repose that had not been there in July. The hand which hung gracefully at her side was relaxed, the fingers quiet, and the line of her chin was softer, less defiant. Even the arrangement of her hair was different somehow. The curls were looser so that the breeze which played with the fringes of her shawl also caused her hair to gleam onyxlike under the noonday sun.

But duty took Maurice away. He knew he must hurry home to play host to the small horde of well-wishers, so, kissing Susan on the brow, he made his way inconspicuously down the hill.

Within minutes of his arrival home, the thirstiest of the well-wishers had already found their way to the punch which was sitting in two large barrels behind the house. The ell of the house made an alcove which was perpetually in the shade. It was in the bend of this ell that Maurice had set the punch barrel. Across the yard, the refreshments had been set out on a table under a tree. Belle had decided that the party would go to the food and drink. By Belle's final decree the punch was innocent of alcohol, but inside the house Maurice had laid in a modest stock which he was prepared to clandestinely bestow on his cronies. Belle was aware of this and only hoped Susan would be well on her way to Boston before the carryings-on began. A wedding reception was no place for brides! She counted on Josiah's connection with the church to set the right tone, especially since Henrietta and Thomas were here. She loved her friends dearly and wouldn't dream of censoring them, but she couldn't help but hope that nothing too startling would happen in front of the Curtises.

By two o'clock everyone was in fine form. Hearts were mellow and tongues were loose. From the yard a gradually increasing rumble of conversation and laughter arose, but as all the neighbors were part of it, there was no one to complain. The fact that some were clandestinely drinking on a Sunday seemed to have been overlooked by all except a small cluster of temperance ladies who drank lemonade in the front room and tried successfully to ignore the behavior of their husbands in the backyard. Because it was the Sabbath, Belle and Maurice had decided against music. The punch also was a concession; Maurice had wanted good honest whiskey and rum in their own bottles, but Belle was adamant. The Reverend Hamilton had come back to the house for a few minutes but had made a hasty retreat when he saw the florid faces of the fishermen who had already made a dent in Maurice's cache of liquor. It would have been considered poor taste for him to have stuck around too long, and despite his thundering voice, Mr. Hamilton was not a man to defy convention.

Abigail mingled with the guests, managing to bridge the distance between the front room and the backyard with such dexterity that she seemed to be in two places at once. The ladies in the front room were impressed with her pretty manners, while the imbibers out back talked behind her back and said that she really was a good sort and not nearly as stuck up as her looks gave her a right to be.

The men were gathered in prides of three or four exchanging gossip and calling it news.

"Did you hear about Moss Bottom? Seems that last Thursday he went out fishing with old Scummy White just for sport, and they brought along a couple bottles of rum. (You know Moss Bottom's wife is temperance.) Well, anyhow, they were out there maybe five, six hours, and Moss Bottom's missus was gettin' a bit worried, so down she goes to the landing just in time to see Scummy comin' in alone. 'Oh, dear heavens!' she cries. 'You've drowned my husband!' No such luck!' calls back Scummy. 'The damned fool fell overboard into the net, and he's there still. You get him out if you want him!' And with that, off he goes, leaving old Moss Bottom dragged up on the wharf, drunk as a goat and sunburned red as a boiled lobster. He was all tangled up in a net; you ought to 'ave seen him! Well, missus takes one look and stomps off madder'n hell, so a few of us goes over and untangles him, and do you know what? When we got him out, damned if he didn't have a mackerel in one hand and an empty rum bottle in the other!''

The tales continued to unfold, each man trying to top the others, until finally the periodic bursts of laughter caused Belle to state that it was definitely time for the bride to cut the cake and make her farewells.

The bridal cake was dark fruitcake made by the loving hands of Aunt Gracie, who wheeled herself around to position herself directly in front of it. Susan cut the cake into as many small pieces as she could manage, saving the crest for herself, and fed a mouthful to Josiah, who seemed very much at ease. She supposed that with his church associations he had become accustomed to large gatherings; as for herself, she could hardly wait to get away and begin her new life as Mrs. Hoffman.

Turning into the house, she caught Abigail's eye. It was time to change into her traveling costume, and she wanted Abigail to help her. Gladly Abigail joined her, and they made their way upstairs past the group who had gathered in the hall, making it all but impossible for anyone to go in or out.

"Mrs. Hoffman? Are you ready?" said Abigail with a twinkle in her eye.

"Oh my, yes! I've been ready for such a long time. Honestly, Abby, last night Mum gave me a talk about married life, and I couldn't tell from the way she talked if she thought I was frightened or what! In case you couldn't tell, I'm not frightened at all. And I imagine you won't be either when it's your turn."

"I imagine you're right," said Abigail, blushing slightly. The two girls carefully hung up the lovely wedding gown and folded the veil between layers of tissue paper. Then Susan put on the lavender traveling dress and set a marvelous leghorn hat on her head.

"Susan, you look so . . . married," said Abigail weakly.

"I don't feel married — yet!" said Susan, an impish smile on the usually composed face. "Let's go down and get this over with," she cried, and off they went down the hall.

Susan paused halfway down the stairs

while Josiah came up to meet her. Below them the guests had gathered, maidens in front for the tossing of the bouquet. Abigail had decided to forego this little game; she refused to appear eager in front of Andrew. There he was now, standing a good head over the crowd, slightly flushed with heat and drink. No point in trying to find him alone tonight, although he had never looked more appealing, hair tousled and the carefully tied bow slightly askew. His coat was open, and even under the dress shirt she could see that he was as flat and hard as a plank.

Don't do this to yourself, she thought as she backed away and stood by the front door. Susan raised her arm and sent the bouquet sailing over all the heads until it landed on the small arms that involuntarily rose to catch it.

"Oh, it was planned in advance!" cried one chubby lass, who looked downcast as Abigail stood surprised with the bunch of white flowers clutched against her bosom. There was much laughter as the others caught Abigail's expression.

"Shouldn't think she'd be overmuch

surprised at the notion of finding herself next married,'' said one admiring friend of Andrew's.

''No, I should think not,'' replied Andrew.

''Well,'' continued the friend, ''you've sure let the grass grow under your feet all summer. Why, if I'd had half the chance at her that you have, I'd have fished her in by now.'' He spoke good-naturedly and was thus astonished when Andrew glared at him and stalked out the front door, where Susan was saying her good-byes. What did I say? thought the poor fellow and went to get another glass of punch.

Outside on Franklin Street the bride and groom were exchanging kisses and handshakes while Maurice sat in the carriage and urged them to hurry up or they'd miss their train.

''Now remember, dear, our man will meet you at the station, and if there's anything you need, just ask for it. I know it's just for a few days, but I want it to be a perfect beginning for you,'' said Henrietta as she kissed her niece and pressed a small box into her hand.

Belle held her daughter, then quickly let her go. The carriage trundled off amidst cries of "Good-bye!" and the last thing they heard as the carriage turned the corner was Susan's voice crying "Thank you all!" as she held up the new locket which Henrietta had just given her. They watched its gold twinkling in the sun.

"C'mon, Mother! I'm going to get you some special punch," said Andrew. He put his arm around her waist and planted a kiss on her forehead as he led her back to her guests.

Many people began to leave, and before seven o'clock had come there were less than twenty left. These few hangers-on were close friends of the family, and Belle and Maurice would have been disappointed if they had gone home too soon. In the backyard Maurice had pulled the chairs into a circle. Abigail was next to Aunt Gracie, who bent over and asked, "Where's Andrew?"

"I don't know," whispered Abby. "He was here a few minutes ago."

"Where's Andrew?" bellowed Gracie to the group at large.

"Oh, he's gone to put a friend of his to bed; he said he might as well spend the night down at Barnegat. He's got to get right back to work in the morning, and he didn't want to wake us too soon. Say, Belle," continued Maurice, "are there any more of those sandwiches left?"

"Yes, I'll get them. Now don't anybody go away!" Belle went off into the kitchen, never noticing that Abigail had turned pale and had lost all interest in the conversation.

The party broke up around ten o'clock, and everyone went to bed. Tad admitted that it had been worth missing the Sunday morning model boat races, and Thomas began to think that it might be nice to have a daughter safely married away. Belle was sad but too exhausted to lie awake. Only Abigail stayed alert in her bed counting the hours — no, the minutes — left in her Marblehead summer. Tomorrow there would be a family lobster bake on Gashouse Beach across from the islands, and then she would sleep one more time in this dear room and be gone forever. Each board in the floor was her friend, each carved molding on the ceiling. The elm tree which shaded the front room and the little warming oven next to the library fireplace — all belonged to her now. How many other souls have lived here and felt as if they owned it, she wondered? And soon she would be just another ghost, a tiny mist that might pervade a stranger's heart someday and cause him to wonder what this strange feeling was of having been here before. Had she been more herself, she might have noticed the ring around the moon or heard the faint shrill cry that came up on the breeze from Lovis Cove.

CHAPTER 23

On the morning of Abigail's last day in Marblehead, the sun pulled wearily into the sky dragging behind it a threatening haze which made the view from Abigail's window opaque. Somberly Abby dressed and began to pack her things. Mrs. Byors had wanted to stay and do this for her, but she was needed in Boston and had gone home on last night's train.

As they folded her linens, Abigail's hands felt slow and unwilling. She could not bear to think of Andrew's face last evening and her lost chance. How sure she had been that the wedding would be some sort of turning point. Now there was just this afternoon's lobster bake left, and that would provide no opportunity for privacy seeing as it had been arranged as a final family get-together before the ultimate farewells.

The two families seemed completely intertwined now in Abigail's mind. Their parting would be like the simple division of some large single-celled organism. Could it really happen that she and Thomas could be neatly sliced away from Andrew and Belle without incurring some terrible injury to them all? Sadly she went down to the kitchen, where Tad sat, morose. Ruffling his hair, she felt a lump in her throat, and when he looked up at her, the pain in his eyes reflected her own.

"Let's go get some seaweed for the bake," she said, a false gaiety in her voice.

"Nah. We can do that right on the beach later."

"Where is this bake going to be held anyway?" she asked, determined to pull them up out of this funereal mood.

"Down at Lovis. I wanted to do it on Gashouse Beach, but Mum said we had too much stuff to carry. Say! Are you gonna show your parents your swimming today?"

"I guess so. It seems rather foolish now to have kept it secret so long."

"No. It'll be a good surprise; show 'em you learned something here this summer." He looked defiant.

"Oh, Tad, I've learned so much. You've all been so good to me — especially you, teaching me about all the places and how to swim. It's me who hasn't done much of anything for you."

"That's not so! Why, who made my lobster costume? It isn't every kid who gets to win in a Horribles Parade." he gave her such a fierce loving look that the tears came, and she had to turn her head and get a grip on herself.

"Now, that's just enough of this!" she cried. "There'll be plenty of time for weepy good-byes later on. Right now I think we'd better find your mother and see what we can do to get ready for this lobster bake." She smiled and he perked up, unable to sustain his melancholy in the face of her determined cheerfulness.

"Just hope it doesn't storm," said Tad. "I saw Gracie this morning, and she said that she heard the screeching woman last night and it wasn't even the anniversary of her death. Gracie thinks something bad's about to happen. I told her that this was your last day here, and she said that maybe that's it."

"Well, I'm certainly flattered to think that my departure could warrant the attention of the screeching woman," said Abigail, amused. She had never been able to reconcile the straightforward common sense of the people of Marblehead with their love of the occult. The strange thing was that they would tell you these tales about the screeching woman or Moll Pitcher, the wizard's daughter, with such conviction and such a straight face that before you knew it you were accepting them all just as if they were as factual as the changing of the tide.

Belle came in aproned in red checks and soon put them all to work removing the silk from ears of corn and packing up for the bake. "I'll have to send someone up later for the ice cream. Which reminds me, we'd better get cranking if it's to be ready at all!"

Henrietta and Thomas finished their own packing and then enlisted Abigail to take them on a tour of downtown streets.

"Go on! Best do it now; I'm afraid we're in for some weather later on. I'll ask Maurice if we can start earlier than we planned so we can beat the storm," said Belle.

Abigail took her parents past all the shops on Washington Street, and then they turned down State Street and stayed awhile at the town landing admiring the pleasure craft which floated in and out of the harbor on the freshening breeze and watching the fishermen unloading their catch. The smell of salt was strong off the water, and looking down from the wharf's end, Abigail could see dozens of starfish clustered around the stout pilings. Leaving the landing, she took her parents back down Front Street to Fort Sewall. The view impressed her again just as it had that first day with Tad. She longed to stay on, but it was past noon, and the thickening haze required that the lobster bake get under way.

Back at the house Andrew was standing in high waterproof boots, a bushel basket of crawling lobsters grasped firmly in his hands. "Do you think there are enough to go around?'' he boasted.

"Good heavens. Do you really think we can eat all that?'' asked Henrietta.

"Oh, this family can do a fine job on lobster,'' replied Andrew, laughing. "Why, even Abigail is good for one whole plus a claw or two.''

"Sorry, Mother, but I'm afraid he's right. My appetite is undiminished. In fact, I'm ravenous all the time.'' She smiled at Andrew and he smiled back, and she was suddenly hopeful again. At least they could be friends.

Two o'clock found them all down in Lovis Cove. Belle spread out three blankets as far away as possible from the spot where she had forgotten herself with Thomas and Maurice and Andrew went to dig a pit in the sand. Once this had been accomplished, they laid in stones and built a wood fire in the pit and then sat back for awhile to wait until the fire had heated the stones into something resembling coals. Tad was busily digging up the clams which he considered essential to any lobster bake, and Abigail and Belle were preparing the corn to be steamed along with everything else.

The day was hot and sticky, and soon everyone was ready for a swim. The women, Henrietta excepted, wore bathing costumes, and after receiving a signal from Tad, Abigail realized it was time to unveil her surprise.

"Come down to the water, Mother. You too, Daddy. I've got something to show you." She felt self-conscious with this group around her. Andrew especially was watching her with fascinated eyes as she approached the pebbly shore.

The water was cold — not the ice water of June, but still no Gulf Stream. Tad dove in headfirst and called her in. "C'mon Abby. Show 'em your stuff." He stood like an expectant teacher waiting for his pupil to recite.

In she plunged. She heard her mother gasp as the water covered her shoulders. boldly she struck out in long graceful strokes, ignoring the weight of her bathing dress. Her father was the first to recover.

"Brava! Brava!" he cried in delight. This encouraged her to reverse and swim all the way back to where she had started.

"My goodness!" said Henrietta, amazed. "That's absolutely wonderful! However did you dare? But you'd better come out now before you freeze to death."

"It's lovely once you're in. Of course," said Abigail, stepping onto the beach and wringing out her sodden skirts, "it all depends on your teacher. As a matter of fact, I was privileged to have received instruction from a noted professor of swimology." At this Tad dove under the water and, coming up with a clump of seaweed on his head, bowed and accepted the homage due him.

They all went up on shore, laughing despite the thickening clouds while Maurice and Andrew layered up wet seaweed on the now hot coals. On top of this they placed the lobsters, then more seaweed, then the corn, and finally the clams. Then the whole thing was covered with more seaweed and a tarpaulin and left to steam.

Maurice squatted down to guard the entire pit, and Tad and Andrew started a game of catch with a rubber ball which

Andrew produced from his pocket. Abigail made designs with periwinkle shells and began to feel the heat.

Finally the feast was ready. First they dipped the steamed clams in melted butter and devoured four quarts this way. Abigail was by this time an old hand at clams and, instead of shying away, ate her share and watched with condescension as Henrietta declined a taste. Then came the corn and the lobsters themselves. Bright tomato red, they came up with steam issuing from every joint. Andrew came around with a large rock and quickly cracked the shells so that the succulent meat could be extracted in large chunks. When he cracked Abigail's lobster, his hand touched hers and she felt a pleasant jolt go through her. He felt it too, she was certain. Aunt Gracie was right; there was something in the air today. Abigail only hoped it was not the danger that Gracie had predicted.

When they had all finished eating, they sat back against the rocks and groaned in mock agony.

"Oh, I ate too much," said Belle. "I

think I'd better go up and get the ice-cream bucket to work some of this food off."

"I'll help you. That thing weighs a ton," said Thomas easily, and without waiting for a reply, he helped Belle to her feet and they set off for the kitchen. Henrietta looked at them as they passed, but, noting no sign of collusion, she relaxed and gazed securely out at the sails which were heading into port. In the last half-hour the wind had picked up, and where it had been hot it was now becoming cool.

All the way up Franklin Street Belle and Thomas were silent, but once inside the kitchen Thomas pulled two chairs out from the table and said, "Sit down, Belle. We really ought to talk before I go back to Boston. You know my business is over. Your Andrew has a fine enterprise going there and he doesn't need my advice anymore; this might be our last chance to settle things."

"Then you do agree with me things are settled?" asked Belle, relieved.

"Yes. I think we both knew that this

was just some sort of reaction to our lives. How are you? Is everything all right between you and Maurice? I'm very fond of him, believe it or not."

"I believe you, just as I hope you know that I'm very fond of Henrietta. But it's strange, Thomas. I don't feel as guilty as I should. In fact, it's terrible to say it, but I think the whole thing did us both a world of good!"

"I think so too, but I'm glad you can see it that way. Let's face it, I hardly behaved honorably," said Thomas.

"Oh, it wasn't your fault. I'd been restless for some time, but I'm fine now — in fact, better than ever."

How astonishing, she thought, to be sitting here discussing this as dispassionately as if it was the weather. Aloud she said. "We'd better get back or they'll begin to worry."

"Of course, but before we go I just want to say that being with you this summer has been one of the most beautiful things that's ever happened to me. I'll never forget it, Belle, even though it is over and done."

He rose and took her hands. She stood and met his lips in an affectionate kiss. Then they picked up the ice-cream bucket and went out the door, lighter hearted despite the heavy weight shared by their hands. When they reached the gate, it was open but no one was there.

"Strange," said Thomas. "I thought we had shut that."

Shortly after Belle and Thomas had left the beach, Tad suddenly remembered the blackberries that he had picked as a surprise for Abigail that morning. He had left them in a pail in the backyard, and now, as he couldn't imagine eating his ice cream without them, he jumped to his feet and ran up to the street.

"Where are you going in such a hurry?" called Andrew.

"Never mind. I'll be right back. I forgot something."

He walked up the street, realizing as the clouds gathered above his head that the storm was imminent. And that would end the day, and then Abigail would go home, and next week school would start again.

Abruptly his mood swung around to despair again. By the time he reached the backyard he was so despondent that he even forgot to slam the gate. Spying the berry pail, he heard his mother's voice talking to Uncle Thomas. Stepping up to the kitchen door to join them, he heard his uncle murmuring something about it being over and done but he would never forget her, and then Uncle Thomas was kissing his mother, and then Tad was racing through the gate and running toward Little Harbor as fast as he could, his heart pounding out a denial of what he had just witnessed.

By the time Thomas and Belle returned to the beach, the sky was darkening. In the north they could see a huge thunderhead rolling in from over Cape Ann.

"No use in sticking around here," said Andrew. "We'd better pack up and eat that ice cream back at the house. That storm won't stay away much longer, I'm afraid. Sorry you had to carry the tub down for nothing. Abby, why don't you throw some sand on the pit, and I'll gather up the rest."

Andrew was so different today, thought Abigail, so natural and friendly, the way he had been when they were singing together. Perhaps he just wanted her summer to end on a pleasant note, but even though the end was drawing near, she held on to a thread of hope. Certainly he had been charming to her today, applauding her swimming skills and helping her with her lobster — and now, the way he took charge so easily, giving commands that were so gently couched that they seemed like mild suggestions. She understood why the fishermen liked him so. Another man of his size might have taken advantage, used his strength to intimidate; but Andrew spoke to everyone with good-humored common sense which was much more effective than bullying.

She filled in the pit with sand so that the next beach wanderer might not fall in, and then, looking up, she saw the rocks turn slate blue as the rolling clouds cast their shadows over them. The ocean also had turned an unsympathetic gray, glinting suddenly cold and feral as the wind picked up the incoming tide and chopped it into angry points.

"Where's Tad?" asked Andrew, raising his voice slightly to override the rising wind.

"He went back to the house for something. Didn't you see him, Aunt Belle?" asked Abigail.

"Not a sign. Perhaps he went around the other gate just as we went out," said Thomas.

"He's probably at home now. He must have seen the storm come up and decided to wait for us there," said Andrew, but Abigail noticed a look of concern cross his face.

As they all hurried up Franklin Street, the wind blew their clothing out behind them, and when they reached the house, they all fell laughing into the kitchen, their hair in tangles.

"Tad?" called Andrew. No answer. "That's strange. I'll have a look around." The others began to catch his concern.

"I'll call out back," said Abigail.

Abigail walked against the wind all the

way to the end of the yard and called repeatedly into the boatyard. Still there was no answer. For the first time Abigail was afraid. It was not like Tad to just disappear without a word. Surely he knew the storm was coming! She made her way back to the house, where the faces told her that he had not been found.

"Now, let's be sensible," said Andrew. "Tad knows this town like the back of his hand. There's no way he could come to harm. But where the devil is he?"

"I know. Let's ask the firemen if they've seen him," said Abigail.

"Good idea," answered Andrew. "Now the rest of you stay here; Abby and I'll have him back in ten minutes. Just go ahead and have your ice cream, and we'll be along in no time. Grab an oilskin, Abby. It's going to rain any second." In her concern for Tad Abigail never noticed that Andrew had singled her out to help him find the missing boy.

They went out the front door and turned right to the firehouse. The big front door was shut against the storm but opened at their knock.

"Yep. I saw him about fifteen minutes ago, running like he was being chased. Called out to him, but he didn't seem to hear me," answered the young fireman who had opened the door.

"Where did he go?" asked Andrew.

"Went 'round the corner like he was heading for the boatyard or maybe Gashouse Beach."

"He's not in the boatyard. I called and called," said Abby. "Let's try the beach."

The two began to run down Orne Street to the shore. They turned right onto the beach, entering from the opposite direction from the boatyard.

"I'll try the other end," said Abigail, running past the gashouse toward the boatyard.

Suddenly a monstrous crack of thunder split the air, and the heavens opened up. Great drops of rain fell heavily, gathering force with numbers until it seemed as though a wall of water was coming down on their heads. Abigail had an idea. She took off at a run for Gerry Island.

"Come back, Abby!" shouted Andrew. "The tide's coming in. You can't go out there!"

"But I know where he is!"

Leaving Andrew far behind, Abigail struggled across the narrowing strip of stones that connected the shore with Gerry Island. How could she have forgotten the secret place? The rain hit her face; she felt the sting of each drop as it grazed her skin. At least she was in her bathing dress. Despite the fear of the moment, this struck her as funny.

Her foot slipped on the wet ground and she stumbled. Landing on the harsh stones, she cried out. Behind her, like a faraway shadow, she saw Andrew dragging a rowboat down off the beach. Why is he doing that? she wondered as she struggled to her feet. Then she saw her answer. Behind her the path to the shore had disappeared underwater. The tide was pouring in now, swollen by the storm. Ahead, lightning creased the sky throwing everything into sudden stark relief. Racing against the rising tide, she ploughed ahead until her foot found the old stone steps that brought her up onto the island. Her clothes were heavy, and she stopped to tear off her underskirt, which she dropped behind her, where it lay under the pounding rain like a lost doll.

She knew just where to go. Finding the bush she was seeking, she pushed it aside and called down into the crack below.

"Tad!"

"I'm here!" His voice came up from far below. "I'm stuck!" he cried, a tearful edge to his voice.

Carefully, clutching the grass for support, she lowered herself over the edge until she could see the forlorn figure in the crevice. A large sumac overhung the rock, and once under this, she found a measure of protection against the driving rain. Grasping the bush for support with her right hand, she stretched her left arm into the crevice as far as it would go. She could just grasp the cold hand that reached out for her.

"Hold tight," she cried, "and try to relax your body. I'm going to count to three and then pull."

The sea was ominously high, already insinuating tentative fingers into the crevice. In a few more minutes the water would fill the crack, but Abigail blocked this from her mind and called out, "All right, now — one, two, three!" She pulled, but still he was stuck fast.

Water was pouring in around them. The storm had made the tide run high; the full moon of last night had also had its magnetic effect on the situation. Huge waves rose up around the island, pushed into an angry wall of water by the gale winds. Within minutes it would be too late to save Tad.

For one furious moment Abigail hated the sea and its merciless power. A surge of rage rose up inside her.

"Try again!" she called, panic gaining on her. "One, two, three!"

She pulled as hard as she could, and slowly he moved forward. One more pull and he was free. The thin form fell out against her, almost knocking the two of them into the angry foam below.

"Quick, put this on!" she commanded, wrapping the oilskin jacket around him. He was pale with fright, and Abigail held him tightly against her, sharing what little warmth she had. She could see Andrew heading for the island in the rowboat. The tide was against him, and she could see that each pull on the oars was a massive effort. The swells loomed so high that they intermittently hid him from sight.

"Andrew's coming. We'll be safe soon," she said. "Why did you run away? Never mind, we'll talk later."

"No. I want to tell someone. Abby? When I went home I saw your father kissing my mother. He said he'd never forget her even though it was over and done."

Andrew had pulled the boat up onto the island, but the two didn't see him approach. Standing over them, he listened thoughtfully as Abigail spoke.

"Did he say that? That it was over and done?"

"Yes, but he kissed her! How could they do that, Abby?" Tad sounded furious and hurt.

"All right, Tad. I'm going to explain it to you, and I expect you to understand. After all, you're twelve years old now. That's almost a man, so you've got to start understanding some things.

"I think my father fell a little bit in love with your mother this summer. He was lonely, and you must admit that your mother is a very lovable person. My father can be very charming, and I am sure he said lots of pretty things to her and made her feel wonderful. That's another thing you have to understand, Tad — that even grown-up people like to feel wanted and needed. Now, the important thing for you to remember is that your mother loves your father just as my father really loves my mother. It was just a little flirtation, that's all. But you must promise not to blame your mother. She'd die if she thought she'd hurt you, and Tad, believe me, she's a good woman and she loves you all more than you'll ever know. The kiss you saw was just a special good-bye, I'm sure." She hugged him close and saw the brown eyes looking up at her, trying desperately to believe.

"Do I have your promise that you won't say anything? Remember, I kept my promise to you about this place. Why do you think I came out here all alone, you scalawag!" She laughed and planted a kiss on his wet forehead.

"Okay. It's a deal. I guess you're right about Mom. She'd never do anything really wrong."

"Of course she wouldn't!" said Abigail vehemently.

"Come on, you two! I'm drowning up here waiting for you to finish your conversation!" Andrew's voice boomed down at them, and they jumped. Carefully he pulled them up over the edge, and they made their way over the slippery grass to the rowboat.

"Did you hear?" asked Tad, looking up at Andrew with a worried frown.

"Hear you? I couldn't even hear myself think in this racket. Why, was it a secret?"

"Sort of." He trembled with cold.

Andrew put an arm around both of them and led them down into the rowboat. The rain continued unabated, but the thunder seemed to be moving further away with each roll.

"Now, hold on to each other; it's rough out there."

Abigail and Tad sat in the stern of the

little boat, and Andrew once again took the oars. He was anxious to get them home as soon as possible. Abigail was almost blue with cold, and Tad was still shaking uncontrollably. The boat tossed about like a piece of cork in the pounding surf, but the tide was with them now, and Andrew brought them safely to shore in a few dozen strokes. Waiting on the shore were Thomas and Maurice.

''Thank God, you're all right!'' said Thomas, wrapping a blanket around Abigail. Maurice did the same for Tad, rubbing the cold, thin arms as he held the shivering boy. ''Whatever made you run off like that?'' he asked.

''I dunno,'' faltered Tad.

Abigail intervened. ''He was feeling sad about my leaving tomorrow, and he went out onto the island to be alone for awhile and got stuck between some rocks.'' She knew that her explanation was weak, but, by God, it was all they were going to get! She missed the look of wonder on Andrew's face as she spoke.

''We'd best get these children home,'' said Thomas.

"Go on ahead," said Andrew. "I've got to tie up the rowboat." He ran to the little craft and began to haul it up onto the beach.

"Go ahead, Daddy. I'll come up with Andrew in a second. Tad needs attention quickly, I'm afraid. Oh, do go on, please; I'm fine, really!" said Abigail. There was a determination in her voice that stifled argument.

The two men hastened out of the boatyard, the boy between them. Abigail turned toward Andrew. He had fastened the boat and was coming toward her. Her legs were suddenly weak, her foot slipped on a wet stone, and she stumbled. In one long stride Andrew was at her side. Her last vestige of strength dissolved as he lifted her up into his arms as easily as he had that first day in his boat. She let her head fall against the powerful chest. Andrew looked down at the pale face and slowly began to kiss her forehead with a dozen small kisses. She was soaked through to her skin, and she gave herself up to the warmth of his body and the delicious sensations of his touch. She could feel his heart thudding through the thin cloth of her bathing dress. His lips persisted, and he continued to cover her face with innumerable tiny kisses until she felt she could not endure the ecstasy a single moment longer. Then his mouth found hers, and he was kissing her with a hunger and fury that rocked her very soul. She returned his passion as he held her fast against the elemental forces which surrounded them. Behind them the sea spewed up jets of frothing water, and the rain began again and fell on her upturned face. Still he held her, his mouth unwilling to relinquish its treasure, and she felt as if her heart was shattering into a thousand crystal fragments. After a long moment he reluctantly set her down, still holding her tightly against his side. His arm held her sheltered from the dying howls of the wind, and slowly, dreamlike, they made their way back to the house. The sky above framed them with dark, rolling clouds, and they were alone together, finally at peace.

The two mothers were waiting by the window, and when the last two sodden adventurers came inside, they were hurriedly embraced.

"Now, Tad and Abigail, it's straight to bed for you," said Belle.

"Wait!" said Andrew. "I want to talk to you, Abby!"

"Not now, for heaven's sake. Can't you see she's half frozen to death?" Belle looked in outrage at her oldest son, forgetting in her haste to restore Tad and Abigail to health that it was Andrew who had rescued them.

The fires were lit upstairs, and Abigail was put to bed with a hot water bottle while Tad was given identical treatment in his mother's big bed.

When Belle and Henrietta came downstairs a half-hour later, the kitchen fire was also lit and the three men were drinking hot buttered rum.

"May I see her now?" asked Andrew impatiently.

"I'd rather you waited 'til morning," said Belle.

"Damn it! This can't wait 'til morning," said Andrew, and abruptly he left the astonished group and stormed up to Abigail's room two steps at a time.

Lying warm amidst all her covers, Abigail saw Andrew's large form almost filling the door frame.

"Hello, Andrew," she said sleepily.

"Abigail, I want to talk to you." Reaching her bedside in three strides, he sat beside her, causing the mattress to sink on one side and her body to slide over against his leg.

"Abigail, I love you. I've loved you all summer, and I've been such a damned fool not to have told you. Today on the island I heard what you told Tad, and I'll be grateful to you for that for the rest of my life. What he saw today could have ruined his life, but you fixed it all up, just like that! Guess I'm not as bright as my brother; he knew he loved you the first day you came. I've made a mess of it, I know. Can you forgive me?"

"No, I guess not!" Abigail laughed at the desolate look which crossed Andrew's face. "I mean, you've been the most maddening person I ever met. Everything I did around you came out wrong, and here it's taken you right up until my last day to tell me how you feel. You know, I met Sarah Bernhardt once, and she warned me about a boy moving too fast. I wonder what she'd have said if she had met you!" She sat up in bed, and he held her tight and warm against his chest. His lips came down onto the still damp curls which shone like copper in the firelight.

"Oh, Abby." He kissed her then, long and sweetly. She laid her head against his chest and began to cry.

"Why are you crying?" he asked, the dark eyes clouding.

"I'm just relieved, I guess. We came so close to losing each other. Would you have let me go away?" The green eyes held his.

"Never. Would you have gone off without a word?"

"Never."

The door opened, and in came Tad wrapped in a blanket. "Say! Are you two in love or something?" he asked, grinning with embarrassment.

"Yeah! Wanna make something of it?" asked Andrew, smiling.

"Nope!" replied Tad. "Just wondering.

Guess you'd better tell Gracie, though. She hates to be left out of things.''

"I think she already knows," said Abigail sheepishly. Andrew met her eyes again, and they all laughed.

"Gee!" said Tad. "She must be able to keep a secret even better than you, Abby. Oh, by the way, I figured it out and you're right. I am growing up. That must be why I got stuck in the crack."

They all burst out laughing again, this time bringing Belle to the door.

"What's going on here?" she demanded.

"Oh, nothing," said Tad.

The publishers hope that this Large Print Book has brought you pleasurable reading. Each title is designed to make the text as easy to see as possible. G. K. Hall Large Print Books are available from your library and your local bookstore. Or you can receive information on upcoming and current Large Print Books by mail and order directly from the publisher. Just send your name and address to:

G. K. Hall & Co.
70 Lincoln Street
Boston, Mass. 02111